AND

# TIME'S ARROW
## BOOK 1: THE PAST

MARVEL COMICS ®

AND

# SPIDER-MAN®

# TIME'S ARROW
## BOOK 1: THE PAST

### Tom DeFalco & Jason Henderson

ILLUSTRATIONS BY
TOM GRUMMETT & DOUG HAZLEWOOD

BYRON PREISS MULTIMEDIA COMPANY, INC.

NEW YORK

BERKLEY BOULEVARD BOOKS, NEW YORK

Special thanks to Ginjer Buchanan, Steve Roman, Howard Zimmerman, Michelle LaMarca, Emily Epstein, Ursula Ward, Mike Thomas, and Steve Behling.

X-MEN & SPIDER-MAN: TIME'S ARROW Book 1: THE PAST

A Berkley Boulevard Book
A Byron Preiss Multimedia Company, Inc. Book

PRINTING HISTORY
Berkley Boulevard paperback edition/July 1998

The Penguin Putnam Inc. World Wide Web site address is
http://www.penguinputnam.com

Check out the Byron Preiss Multimedia Co., Inc. site on the
World Wide Web:
http://www.byronpreiss.com

Check out the Ace Science Fiction/Fantasy newsletter, and much more,
at Club PPI!

ISBN: 0-425-16452-7

BERKLEY BOULEVARD
Berkley Boulevard Books are published by The Berkley Publishing Group,
a member of Penguin Putnam Inc.
200 Madison Avenue, New York, New York 10016.
BERKLEY BOULEVARD and its logo
are trademarks belonging to Berkley Publishing Corporation.

PRINTED IN THE UNITED STATES OF AMERICA

10 9 8 7 6 5 4 3 2 1

This one's for Stan, Jack, and Steve. Thanks for creating the world's greatest playground and inviting the rest of us to join the fun!

—TD

For Benjamin Banchs, my godson, with love.

—JH

# PROLOGUE

There is a place called Limbo. It sways and writhes like something beyond life, misty and winding and unmeasurable. It is a place outside of time and space.

Limbo was ruled, forever outside time, by Immortus. Immortus had been the ruler and guardian and loving servant of time. In his fortress in Limbo he observed the workings of time, watching it stretch like silk through the fabric of existence, tracking it by machine and soul alike. Again and again, mortals, whose lives were measured in infinitesimal increments, found ways to move outside their own segments of the fabric and muck about with things. Again and again they ripped the fabric, and always for selfish reasons: to gain riches, to eradicate enemies, to save lost loved ones. Always they thought of their goals, never of time, of the delicate, beautiful expanse of existential fabric that time was, and which Immortus strove to protect. Immortus was the timekeeper.

Kang, now, he was a different story. Kang was a conqueror.

Born in the technological wonderland of the thirty-first century, Kang was ambitious in a world that favored apathy, an explorer amid stultification. Unable to stand his fellow humans, who allowed their technology to sap them of the will to do anything beyond simply exist, he explored his world, and stumbled across an ancient time machine built by some distant ancestor.

Thus began a career that would span centuries. First, he went to ancient Egypt and became the Pharaoh Rama-Tut, who used his advanced technology to become in flesh what had previously existed only in

3

myth and legend: a god. After that, he travelled to his own future to find the Earth of the year 4000 to be a barbarous wasteland. He conquered that era as well—but, as with the backward Egyptians, it was too easy. To properly conquer, one must have worthy enemies to vanquish. So he set his sights on the twentieth century, in the age of the super hero.

Time and time again, Kang the Conqueror, as he now called himself, disrupted the fabric of time to try to conquer that era of Earth's history. Armed with a tremendous array of weaponry, including his purple-and-green armor, he launched dozens of schemes of subjugation.

Time and time again, he failed. Whether at the hands of the Avengers or the Fantastic Four, or even individual members of those teams, he always lost.

But this latest occasion, this latest disruption, took him to Immortus's Limbo. Immortus himself was nowhere to be found.

A purple glove gestured at one of nearly fifty monitors on one wall. "This is one that particularly amuses me."

"And which one would that be?" Lireeb, Kang's personal valet, looked up from dusting a very different monitor to address his master.

Kang looked over his shoulder at his servant. "This one—monitor thirty-five." He refolded his arms over his armored chest and chuckled slightly. "Out of all the timelines I have observed, I like to look at this one particularly often."

"Everyone needs a favorite, I suppose," Lireeb murmured. The albino stood straight, adjusting his flowing, kimonolike gown, and stepped closer to Kang. Lireeb looked like a priest of a sect all his own, his face a slate of control, his emotions betrayed only by the occasional twinkle in his watery eyes or the slight turn of his taut, thin lips. He peered forward, squinting at the monitor. "That appears to be a pig, sir."

"Ha! Yes. A pig with the proportionate strength of a spider, no less." He could not contain his mirth. There, on the screen, what appeared to be a bipedal pig clung to a brick wall. Its face was covered in a red mask which only accentuated the length of its snout. The pig in the red-and-blue longjohns scrambled up the wall before shooting a web from a red-gloved cloven hoof, and soon went zinging off through the Manhattan streets, now and again oinking a humorous quip.

"How do you like that?"

"I'm glad to see you're putting the Lord of Time's machines to good use, sir," said Lireeb dryly, before turning around to shuffle toward a bookshelf.

Kang clapped his hands, raising an eyebrow at the tall albino. "This is your problem, Lireeb, you get so little joy out of life." Kang stepped to a console on the wall, keeping his eye on the gigantic set of screens. He tapped a button, and each of the monitors crackled and shifted once, bringing up another random shot of each screen's chosen timeline. Kang sat at the console as Lireeb brought him a cup of tea. "You should see the Avengers in that timeline. Amazing what results when something happens to make a different species evolve into the ruling sort."

Lireeb poured the tea, raising an eyebrow. "Imagine what Kang must look like in that universe.''

"Hm. I don't have to. Let's just say he was re-jected by the council of Kangs.'' Kang travelled through time so much that he had created alternate versions of himself—enough that they had to form a council to try to keep things from getting totally out of hand.

"Really?''

"Yes.'' Kang brought the cup to his lips. "But I like to think there's a little of him in all of us.''

Lireeb sighed. Out of all the Kangs in all the time-lines in the multiverse, he had ended up with one with a sense of humor. "Had any luck with your search?''

"Sadly, no. But I'm in a fairly good mood just the same. All these wonderful objects!'' He stretched out his arms, as if embracing the vast fortress. "Immor-tus, wherever you are, I thank you from the bottom of my heart.''

Lireeb nodded. The servant and the master were the only two beings in the entire fortress in Immor-tus's deserted realm. Kang had found Limbo before, of course: once he had found poor old Immortus's body, sitting at these very terminals, his cowl sinking over his skeletal face, his body long withered away. It had been a short stay—it had turned out that Im-mortus wasn't even dead. But this time, nothing. Nothing but all that Immortus had left behind.

Kang was searching for Princess Ravonna. The vast array of machines that Immortus had used to guard time, Kang looked on as a tremendous gift, and he had taken up his search furiously, his only amuse-ment the occasional enjoyment brought by the few singularly ridiculous timelines he could see. He had been searching for a time that could not be measured, as was always the case in Limbo.

Of course, the monitors were not the only boon he had received. . . .

The conqueror stood, putting down his cup and stepping to the monitors. He tapped a button and they switched again, and his eyes scanned them all. "I will find her."

"Of course you will, sir. The odds alone indicate that you will."

"I will find her alive," Kang continued.

"That too."

"And she will not die the moment I find her."

"The odds are . . . still good," Lireeb said, staring at his own post.

"And she will want to be with me."

"Not out of the realm of possibility."

"Of course not," Kang said. "Time is infinite. But my patience is not."

Lireeb looked up as four small lights lit up on the screen that lay out before him. As they flickered and bleeped to life, the coordinates on the time-space continuum rattled out below each one. "Well, then," Lireeb said, turning back to the conqueror. "This should please you."

"Eh?"

"The Time Arrows have been triggered."

Kang pursed his lips and held forth his purple gauntlet. "Wine." It was no time at all before Lireeb placed a sloshing goblet into the master's hand, and the conqueror held the cup aloft. "I propose a toast, Lireeb."

"Indeed," the albino said, dutifully taking up a

goblet himself. "What are we toasting?"

"To the grape and the grain," said Kang. There was a gleam in the conqueror's eye as his soft, rumbling voice echoed throughout the hall that was neither ancient nor new. "To dangerous mixtures. And the fall of the pasts that were not meant to be. And to my future!"

# CHAPTER ONE

C *lick.*

    Mary Jane Watson-Parker heard the distinctive sound of a camera and glanced past the chuck wagon to see her husband, Peter, playing paparazzo. He moved, shot, moved in on a different target, shot again. *Click.* There were fifty other cameras going off at any one time, but she knew that one.

The targets were docile, if occasionally obnoxious: the wealthy patrons of the American Museum of Natural History, some of the biggest names in New York society here to pretend they cared very deeply about an exhibit commemorating the Old West. Peter was here on freelance assignment with the *Daily Bugle,* so of course, he had to keep busy, leaving Mary Jane to peruse the exhibit and listen to the patrons gab.

A woman who seemed to have been poured into the five-thousand-dollar piece of black mesh she was wearing peered through the glass case next to which Mary Jane stood. She looked at Mary Jane, and as she turned her head her fuzzy navel nearly poured out. The woman took a sip and indicated the photographs behind the glass.

"Boy, it's a shame, isn't it?"

"What?"

"He's *cute.*"

Mary Jane tilted her head and looked at the photographs. Most of them were sepia toned, that classic brown that adorns all those pictures one sees of the Civil War, General Lee standing with the wounded and the like. These pictures were almost that old, too: mostly, they were shots of towns in Texas and Indian Territory, people standing on porches and looking tired, that sort of thing.

The woman tapped the glass. "This one."

"Oh," Mary Jane said, staring through the class at the tattered photo. "Hm. Two-Gun Kid." A precursor to the masked heroes of this century, lawyer Matt Hawk had disguised himself as the Two-Gun Kid in order to fight for law and order on the frontier in the the late nineteenth century.

The photographer had caught the gunfighter in an unusually relaxed moment. The Kid was what once would have been called a tall drink of water. He leaned against a post, hat tilted back as if he were imitating James Dean eighty years too early, the bandanna covering half his face, as always. But even with his nose half-covered, you could tell the Kid was a handsome one. "Yeah," she shrugged, "I guess he is." She squinted, taking in the details.

A man spoke from behind the two women. "You really think so?"

Mary Jane glanced to her side to see Peter standing there, hands on his camera.

The woman with the fuzzy navel looked Peter up and down. "Hello."

"Hi. Peter Parker, *Daily Bugle*." Peter flicked back a comma of brown hair that fell over his eye and extended a hand, letting the camera fall to his chest.

"This is my husband," Mary Jane said.

"Lucky you," the woman said. She extended her hand to Mary Jane after shaking Peter's. "I'm Betsy Tarrant." She now took Mary Jane in with an up-and-down sweep that felt like an appraisal. "And you're . . . I've seen you before. In a . . . coat."

Mary Jane bit her lip. "The Leather Rack."

The woman thought for a second. "Yes! The bill-board! Very *nice*."

"Thanks, I owe my agent one." Mary Jane had modeled for an entire projected set of billboards, but only two had actually been produced.

Peter was looking at the photograph of the Kid. "You know, it's funny," he said. "It's like there's a face of the West, and they all wear it."

"What do you mean?" Betsy asked.

"I mean—" the photographer's fingertips pressed gingerly against the glass "—they're all so . . . not rugged, that's a word we use now when we think somebody would fit in one of these old pictures. But there's a shape you can see, a chiseling in the jaws, a burrowing to the eyes. Look at the Kid here. He's on top of his game, but even when he leans against the post, even though he's got to be dog tired, there's this alertness to his eyes. Every one of these guys has a taut face, even the fat ones. These are people on the edge of civilization—nothing to rely on but themselves. We live in an automated age. These people aren't cavemen, but they're attached to the ground in a way we can't possibly understand. But you can see that attachment in their eyes, weighing them down."

"Peter. . . ." Mary Jane started. Peter didn't often go on tangents like this, but when he did, he was worse than the most pedantic college professor.

"Oh. Sorry."

"No, no, that's all right," Betsy said. "I'm on the board of directors—I actually *enjoy* history." She sipped her drink and giggled. "But don't tell anyone. Everyone thinks I do it to be chic."

"Your secret's safe with me," Peter said with

mock seriousness. "MJ, I'm gone again. Duty calls; I just needed to take a breather." Peter backed up ten paces or so in a breath, snapped a shot, and was gone.

"Go get 'em, Tiger." In the distance she heard a *click*.

Once, Mary Jane had read an article about a sniper in Sarajevo. The young man, cocky, handsome, standing on a rooftop, actually posed with his rifle for the magazine. He told of how sometimes at night he could hear rifle fire and recognize the guns of school chums, some on the other side of the conflict, sniping away, or whatever one would call it. Each rifle, he said, had a distinctive *crack*, a signature so clear he could listen to the sky and know, *Yes, Rajko is out there*. Maybe camera shutters weren't *that* distinctive, but Mary Jane felt sure she could hear Peter snapping his camera in a roomful of other photographers and know him by that *click*.

Mary Jane traced her finger across a glass display case, half looking at the photographs, half looking at the crowd and at Peter as the freelance photographer dodged in and out of view. The man bent on his knees and sprang around the crowd and she smiled to herself, because sometimes she was sure there was just no hiding it.

Peter was Spider-Man.

How could you miss it? Despite the tux (which was very nice, even though it positively screamed *rental*), and the sort of downright dorky smile that he wore, insisting with his face, *Hey, just a perpetual grad-student shutterbug here, folks*, Peter moved as if he could barely remember to stay planted to the floor. His body twisted and coiled with every sideways step and crouch, as though he could just as easily be climbing up and down the side of a building and doing triple flips off of flagpoles—which, of course, he could.

"So," Betsy said, leaning against the case. Mary Jane watched the crowd, all the glitter—luckily, not everyone was in black. Mary Jane had thrilled to see colors return to evening wear. Over Betsy's shoulder was a partly revealed picture upon which Mary Jane lazily focused. There was a gigantic, dour-looking black man in a battered duster, standing next to a smaller white man, whose face flickered in and out of view behind Betsy's shoulder. "A model and a photographer in one family!"

"Yes," Mary Jane said. Betsy's shoulder moved and revealed the face of the man in the picture for a moment, and moved back, and Mary Jane looked at Betsy's face. "Sometimes when things are slow we work for one another."

"Does he do weddings?" The face flickered again and Mary Jane's eye snapped on it this time without her being consciously aware of it, bringing the face into full view. *And that's* . . . The shoulder moved back. The front of Mary Jane's mind continued talking. *That's.* . . .

"Not . . . generally." Mary Jane stopped. "Excuse me."

"Leaving so soon?"

"No, I . . ." she moved in, gently causing Betsy to move back, so that she could look at the tattered photograph again.

Betsy was talking again but Mary Jane nodded politely, staring at the photograph. *That's Peter.* Mary

Jane shook her head. Well, of course it wasn't actually Peter, but there was certainly an amazing resemblance. The man in the photograph to the left of the gigantic black man was the spitting image of Peter Parker, grinning widely for the camera. Despite everything, Mary Jane even found herself annoyed that he had his left arm draped around a gorgeous little blonde.

"If I'd known you were this into all this stuff," Peter said, reappearing at her shoulder, "I would have started doing sepia a long time ago."

"Peter," Mary Jane said, looking up. Betsy had wandered off, mingling into the crowd. "Get a load of this."

Peter looped his camera around his neck and leaned forward. "What am I looking at?"

"This picture . . . these three."

Peter stared for a long moment. After a second he stood straight, frowning. "Wow."

"Yeah. Pretty good, huh?"

"It's, uh—" His finger, which in Mary Jane's mind flashed red and webby and back again, brushed against the display case, as if he wished he could touch the photo "—it's unnerving." A waiter passed by with a tray, silently offering more drinks to the pair, and both Peter and Mary Jane shook their heads. As the waiter wandered off, Mary Jane saw Peter's eyes flicker and follow the man for a second before he returned his attention to the photograph.

Mary Jane chewed her lip. "Could this be a relation . . . ?"

"Don't even go there," Peter said. "The odds would be incredible. This is an amazing resemblance . . . wow. I've never seen anyone look this much like me who hadn't been . . . ah—'' he looked around, his voice dropping ''—cloned.''

Mary Jane smiled. ''What, you see a man in a nineteenth-century photograph and you immediately suppose, *My God, I think I have a time-travelling clone!* And to think, most men would just want to know who the blonde is.''

Peter rubbed his neck, scowling. ''Actually, I'd like to know who *this* is.'' He pointed at the huge dark figure to his lookalike's right.

''Big, for one.''

''Yes, and familiar. Look at his eye.''

''I can tell he's scowling, but . . .''

''He has a marking . . . a tattoo . . .'' Peter moved in, Mary Jane's head next to his so that she could hear his breath. ''God, yes, but that's . . . that's just not . . .''

''What?'' Mary Jane peered more closely at the snapshot. ''It's an M.''

''There's a guy with the X-Men called Bishop—a black man the size of a tank. He's got that tattoo over his eye. It's like a brand. He's recent to them, I think he just showed in New York not long ago.''

''Have you ever seen this guy close up?''

''I'm a photographer, Mary Jane. I have a thousand faces zipping through my brain; there are computer programs being used out there that take hours to do what we used to have to do by skill. I've only met him once or twice, and *that's Bishop!*''

''Oh, come on . . . how likely is that?''

''Mary Jane.'' Peter looked his wife in the eye, whispering. ''Think of the world we live in. I was bitten by a radioactive *arachnid* and now I *climb walls*."

"You have a point."

"It's Bishop and a clone. I know it. I just don't know why." Peter's eyes flickered brightly again and he reached up to his temple, scanning the room.

"If you say so, Peter." Mary Jane shrugged. "Maybe when all this is over you can arrange to have it—" She stopped. Peter was squinting, in a way she had seen him do a thousand times, the neck muscles tightening as he scanned the room. It was so obvious, all the signs about him, once you'd lived with him as long as she had. He might as well have little squiggles emanating from his head. "What?"

"Um. Waiters," Peter said. "Mary Jane?"

"Hm?"

"Powder your nose."

"Right." Mary Jane moved back, turning toward the ladies' room, and, dancing like a man on a web, Peter was gone.

Peter Parker passed the rickety chuck wagon and deliberately bumped against a waiter in a white dinner coat. The tray jostled and the dark-haired man holding it stared at him as Peter moved on, and Peter felt time slow to a crawl, the sense of danger tingling up and down his spine. As Peter moved he felt the waiter's eyes follow him briefly, glaring, then flit away as fast as they had fallen upon him.

Peter moved to a corner next to a window and took the party in, breathing, feeling the strange tingle travelling up and down the back of his head. The party was taking place on the second-level mezzanine of the museum, where a number of pieces of the exhibit had been temporarily set up before they were to be moved to their more scattered places tomorrow morning. This had been done so that the partygoers could see the best of the exhibit without having to leave the confines of the mezzanine—about ninety yards long and thirty yards wide. The effect was to minimize the area in which to concentrate support staff. Peter lifted his camera and clicked it. There were two available exits from the mezzanine, both on the south side: twin staircases leading to the first floor, and to the outside exit. Three more exits from the party—hallways leading back to the exhibits—were roped off.

*Click.*

There were seven waiters, all wearing white coats, all carrying trays. There were also about sixty guests, all of them well dressed. Probably a lot of cash and, as Peter had already noticed a thousand times over, a lot of jewelry. At that moment, a waiter set his tray on the railing next to one staircase, at the exact same instant as another took a position on the other staircase, thus placing a man on each exit.

The spider-sense warning buzzed again in Peter's head as one of the waiters walked by, handing out drinks. The tray was getting low on drinks, and Peter felt certain that the waiter wouldn't be running back to the kitchen for another refill.

There was no doubt—the tingle was the spider-sense reacting to a concealed weapon. Peter was looking at the scene of an armed robbery, closing fast.

Peter turned around a corner and into the men's room. A man in a tux looked up from washing his hands and smiled. Peter moved past him, mumbling something in response to the nicety. Shortly the man finished washing his hands and Peter looked under the stalls to make sure he was alone before jumping into one.

There wouldn't be much time, but Peter had done this before so often it was like changing shoes—it took less than ten seconds to slide out of the tux and lift the mask over his head and the gloves on his hands, another two seconds to web his clothing and shoes to the ceiling.

It was Peter Parker who had jumped into the stall. The figure that jumped out, clinging to the ceiling and scurrying along it back out of the men's room, was Spider-Man.

He scuttled along the high marble ceiling and stopped, scanning the room from his high vantage point, unseen. His head bobbed like that of an insect as he counted ten white coats, the waiters in position. Two in front of each exit, one in the center, the other seven evenly scattered across the mezzanine, all the trays now emptied. The wall-crawler felt his senses begin to sing, the sounds of the room rustling in the far distance, his ears pulling from the white noise the important sounds and amplifying them. Something soft rustled, over and over again, as coats opened and every waiter on the mezzanine turned to face away from as many surrounding people as possible. *Here we go.*

There was a rustle of a coat and Spider-Man saw the waiter in the center pulling a semiautomatic weapon from underneath the white cloth as his tray flipped away from his hands. He watched it happen in slow motion: people were still talking and laughing and clinking ice when the tray hit the floor and the man fired once into the air.

*Blam!*

The ringleader, who had put on a stocking mask, held his gun aloft and spun around. Spider-Man watched the entire party shrink back as one body, a huge cringing piece of flesh.

Now began the litany, and it didn't matter what it was he was going to say. Spider-Man scuttled across the ceiling, scoping, waiting for the right moment. . . .

*Do-this-right-and-nobody-gets-hurt-all-we-want-is-your-money-hand-over-your-wallets-hand-over-your-jewelry-these-men-have-guns-and-they-have-sacks-put-the-money-in-the-sacks-and-get-on-the-ground-get-on-the-ground-and-shut-up-and-this-will-all-be-over—*

The four men by the exits stood their ground, waving their weapons as the others worked the room. The weapons were the only hard part about this whole thing.

The woman Mary Jane had been talking to, Betsy whatever, shrieked as a masked waiter tapped her shoulder. She immediately pulled off her rings and necklace and emptied her purse into the sack held before her. Then the waiter pointed at the ground and she got down. It was as smooth as a faith-healing.

Spider-Man crawled over to rest directly above the ringleader, who had just turned his attention to a tall, lawyeresque gray-haired man. The ringleader held forward his sack with one hand. "Trick or treat. What have you got for me?"

"I . . . here . . ." The man reached into his pocket and pulled out a clip of money, which he dutifully dropped into the sack. The man began to faint.

"Hey! Hey!" the waiter growled. "I spy a watch, there. A big watch. Let's have it; you're nearly through here."

"Excuse me." Webbing unrolled as Spider-Man zipped down, hanging behind the waiter's head. He tapped the leader on the shoulder and the stocking-covered head turned.

"Huh?" Spider-Man was watching the waiter's hand, the gun barrel now moving away from the lawyer's body as the head turned around. In the wall-crawler's mind, there were tumblers ratcheting into place. This was the moment before the storm, the moment he had felt so many times it was like getting up in the morning, the moment before everything in the room gets really, really dangerous.

"Does anybody really know what time it is?"

'What the . . .'' Watch the eyes. Watch the stocking-masked man try to orient to talking to someone crouched upside down and hanging from the ceiling by a line of gray webbing, someone red and blue and looking like some mutant human-insect, and as the eyes try to grasp it all, get the gun.

"I'll take that." Spider-Man triggered the web-shooter in his right palm and heard the familiar wet *thwip*. He could control this stuff like Zorro controlled his whip, keep his eye on the waiter's confused face and follow the webbing with his mind for the split second that it travelled through the air and wrapped around the gun. A flick of the wrist and the web stopped extending. Spider-Man gave a slight tug and the gun came from the man's hand, the waiter letting go before he even knew what he was doing. Another flick and the gun went flying across the room, the webbing coming loose from the wall-crawler's wrist and wrapping around the weapon, so that when the gun hit the marble wall, it stuck there.

Another shot of webbing and the waiter found his own feet stuck to the floor with the quick-drying gray mass, and Spider-Man flipped over on his line and leapt back to the ceiling.

The red-masked head darted back and forth, taking in the confusion. Mary Jane had not yet reappeared from the ladies' room. There was a button on the wall below one of the northern windows. Spider-Man shot a quick strand of webbing at it and heard a dull *splat* as the chemical wad hit the panic button. Immediately the sound of a clanging alarm bell filled the mezzanine and Spider-Man felt the tension in the room rise. A moment ago the ringleader had fired into the air and taken charge of the room. In a few shots of webbing, Spider-Man had taken that power from him.

What he had replaced it with was chaos. But chaos could be controlled.

*Guns.* Spider-Man saw plaster exploding from the ceiling, little craters growing and travelling toward him, and he danced out of the way.

*That's right. Everybody shoot at me. Just keep aiming up here.*

"You'll have to do better than that," Spider-Man shouted. He danced across the ceiling, almost bouncing to the rhythm of the alarm that now harangued through the museum. He heard someone cock a gun and looked down to see one of the waiters taking aim again.

"I'll show ya better, you tights-wearin sack o'—" and that was all *he* managed to say because the piece of webbing that caught his gun also managed to end up frothing over and wrapping around his head.

"Watch your language, son." Spider-Man sprang down and landed next to the gunman as he yanked on the webbing that was attached to the waiter's hand and the man went flying until he stopped, hanging from the ceiling, twisting and trying to yell. "There are ladies present. Or so they claim."

Spider-sense tingling like a hot wire, Spider-Man jumped up and hit the wall as a spray of bullets came hailing at him. He turned, found his target, and laid into the man, swinging through the crowd and webbing the gun and feet as he passed. *All right. Let's get this over with.*

"Only so much time, gentlemen," the wall-crawler called out, as he jumped into the air and landed in the high north corner of the mezzanine. "I can hear those sirens a-comin' now."

It was true. Far in the distance, through stained-glass windows and out on the street, beyond the obnoxious clanging of the alarm system, Spider-Man could hear the sounds of police sirens. The spider's bite had not adorned him with super-hearing—he was just very sensitive to sirens. Cops generally didn't like him very much.

There was one rule Spider-Man kept in mind when dealing with a roomful of would-be robbers and a whole nest of innocent bystanders: Keep them aiming at you. You don't want anyone getting hit. Give them a target away from the people.

Oh, and there was another one, sort of a subrule: *Just don't forget you're not bulletproof, either.*

Spider-Man scoped the mezzanine in a split second

and laid out his targets. There were three men down, leaving, what—eight, eight white coats with guns left scattered throughout, and they were getting panicky, looking around, aiming at him.

Spider-Man leapt from the wall for what he hoped would be the last time and began to swing, looking down the expanse of the crowded mezzanine and firing constantly at the ceiling to keep a line of webbing going for him to swing back up at all times.

Mary Jane Watson-Parker was coming out of the ladies' room when she heard the alarm go off. She looked up to see music in motion.

Spider-Man was just leaping off the wall, and now he swooped down, moving left, kicking one gun hand while webbing the target to the ground and then moving right, flipping into the air and over the heads of the patrons, down again, left, then right. She saw him bob and dive through the crowd as if he could fly, but she knew he couldn't. It was a ballet of sweat and muscle and years of practice and nerve, those kicks and punches and shots of that amazing concoction he called webbing flying so fast no one could get a bead on him. Spider-Man moved through the room with such speed that she barely had time to count how many times he stuck back to the ceiling and then disappeared, how many gunmen he left in his wake, webbed to the floor or hanging from the ceiling as if he were saving them for dinner.

She should be hiding, she suddenly realized. But she wasn't afraid, this was too much of a show. Every night he went out and did this, and every night she feared for him, for the one moment he would move left when he should have moved right and one of those flying pieces of lead would find its mark. But now Mary Jane found herself standing against the wall next to the photographs and watching her husband fly by and she just had to take in the marvel that Spider-Man was. She had to. Because everyone else in the room was terrified of him.

Yes, terrified. The patrons were screaming, now, men and women screaming, and Mary Jane knew the strafing run would have that effect, that much fury and that much dead-on aim just made him seem so alien, so animalistic, and she watched him and told herself, *I will tell the world that he was good, if it comes to that. I will tell them.*

She noticed a sea of bodies screaming and moving out of the way, and now Spider-Man had turned and was bearing down toward her, and as one of the glittering evening dresses moved to the side she caught sight of a white coat, and a waiter, staring ahead, right through her, making for the door to the ladies' room. A piece of webbing shot past Mary Jane and webbed the door shut, and Mary Jane began to move out of the way.

"No!" The waiter screamed. Mary Jane felt a set of fingernails dig into her arm as the running gunman grabbed her. *Shouldn't have been standing still—* "No!" The gunman was shouting at Spider-Man, not at her, but now she felt herself being thrust around in front of him and the cold gun metal pressed into her ribs. "Stay right there!"

Spider-Man had been swinging in toward the waiter, but now turned in midair and fired webbing far back on the ceiling, halting his forward movement with a jerk. Even Mary Jane heard the deep grunt that came with the stopping force. The human arachnid hung there, turning his head quizzically.

The gunman spoke again. "No closer or she dies." Mary Jane looked over her shoulder at her captor—he was about twenty-three, just a kid, really, except his hair was beginning to recede, which wasn't all that uncommon. "What—what are you doing?" she asked, nervously but calmly. This had happened before. She could handle this. No sudden moves.

"I'm takin' a walk," the kid said. He was scared, she could tell, the sweat beading over the kid's brow and dripping from his brown hair. His eyes flew from her back to the statue-still Spider-Man. "You hear that? We're takin' a walk! Me and her! Okay?" The kid jabbed Mary Jane and moved his head toward the staircase. "This way. Listen, it wasn't supposed to be like this. This was supposed to be an in-and-out deal, here—this is *way* not what I expected."

"Sometimes," said Spider-Man, as he loosed the back line and swung forward, slowly, just a few feet, so that he hung a bit closer to the pair, "things don't work out as well as you plan."

"No-no-no-no!" the kid screamed, and now Mary Jane shrieked because it felt like he was going to fire that thing, "No! Don't come any closer! Just—just just let me walk on outta here . . ." *He might fire. He might fire.*

"I can't let you do that. You know I can't let you do that. You let that woman go, fella." There was just the slightest quiver in Peter's voice, Mary Jane could hear it, just the tiniest bit more nervousness than he would normally have. She had botched it for him. She'd been admiring his performance and had allowed herself to become part of the show.

And then Mary Jane remembered something, as the gunman began to walk, the gun fiercely prodded in her ribs, and they edged their way toward the stairs.

*Screw this. This joker thinks because he has a gun he can get us to do whatever he wants? I'm feeling sorry for him because this thing is getting out of control?*

Spider-Man or no Spider-Man, this much was true: The gunman was trying to take charge now. He was expecting her to play a part, the part of the person with a gun to her, the hostage, who would do what he said, or else he'd shoot her.

And maybe that was true. And so when people had a gun to their head or their ribs they went ahead and did what the man said, they got in the car, or they walked downstairs and went away with the man. *And you know what happens? They end up dead. Because in a situation like this, if he's gonna kill you, he's gonna kill you.* Spider-Man or no Spider-Man.

So Mary Jane Watson-Parker did what every cop will tell you to do when someone puts a gun to you.

Get it the hell off of you.

"No!" Mary Jane screamed, reaching down and grabbing the barrel of the weapon. No fancy footwork, no super-powers, just grab it, the guy doesn't expect you to move, so *move! Take the power away!*

The gunman looked confused for a moment and he sucked in air as she yanked on the gun and jabbed him in the ribs with her elbow.

She saw him flinch and the gun went off, and she

felt a tuft of hair fly as the bullet whizzed past her neck and embed itself in the ceiling.

"No!" Spider-Man shrieked, sending a spray of webbing so fierce that it drove the gunman staggering back as it jammed in his collar and chin, and the wall-crawler gave the line a fierce yank and the gunman lifted off the ground.

Mary Jane was just beginning to shake now, just beginning to realize what she'd done, when she saw the kid flying through the air, screaming, the force of Spider-Man's pull sending him crashing into the side of the chuck wagon that stood in the center of the mezzanine.

"Are you—" she heard her husband scream.

"I'm okay." She was shaking. She was alive. "I'm okay."

The chuck wagon staggered with the force of the man crashing into it, the few glass panels left on the hundred-year-old vehicle busting and glass tinkling out on the marble floor as the whole thing tipped over and the man lay on top of it, half in and half out. The wheels on one side spun, chunks of wood scattering.

Spider-Man dropped down and reached out, touching her face.

"Are you sure?"

"That's . . . I'm sure . . . oh, God, that's a lot of damage." She shivered, trying to stay calm, the anger ebbing away and being replaced by shock and almost drunken exhilaration.

"Damage . . ." Spider-Man looked over at the wagon, and at the gunman, injured and squirming, writhing inside. A large drawer, hidden underneath the chuck wagon, presumably for either smuggling or

29

hiding goods from raiders, had sprung loose and dumped a clattering pile of contents on the floor— papers, tin plates, cups, more photos. The sirens were growing louder now, and Mary Jane could see police lights flashing through the windows. "I have to go," Spider-Man said. "See you soon."

Half an hour later, Peter Parker lingered in the background on the near-deserted mezzanine as Mary Jane finished making her statement. She looked composed now, and he watched her, nodding and smiling as the cops finished their questioning.

Finally she was done, and she came over to him. He thrust his hands in his pockets. "I can't believe you did that," he said. "Why did you . . . where did you . . . ?"

"A book I've been reading—*Strong on Defense*."

"He could have killed you."

"Maybe. The important thing is that he wanted me to do what he said, and he didn't know what to do when I didn't. We can't always wait for the heroes, Peter."

"But he fired."

"Then he would have fired anyway."

"Huh." Peter shook his head. They began to walk and he put his arm around her. "I'd like to tell you not to scare me like that. . . ."

"But I'm sure that you won't," she said hopefully. They stopped by the chuck wagon. "The whole exhibit is a mess."

"Yeah," Peter said, kneeling by the pile of junk under the chuck wagon and his eye caught something familiar. The robber had long since been extracted, but the rest of the waiters were still stuck to the floor, silently waiting with armed police escort until the long-gone Spider-Man's webbing wore off—which could take at least another half hour. "But look at what we found when we wrecked the wagon."

"More junk."

"Yeah, but—" Peter rummaged through the pile, moving ancient, delicate papers out of the way before finally finding what had he had seen: a flash of red. He hefted the plate the red object was attached to, and stood up.

Mary Jane stared at it. "A plate?" It was an old tin plate, the kind that one used while sitting around a campfire. Nothing special at all. There were sparkles of light where years of meals had left knife-and-fork scrapes in the bottom.

The photographer nodded. "Yeah, but something else." Peter turned the plate over and showed the bottom to Mary Jane. There on the bottom was a tiny piece of plastic and metal. Some of the red paint had flaked away, but he knew it the moment it had caught his eye moments before. He had built it with his own hands. There, the size of a matchbox, was a magnetic homing device. "It's a spider-tracer," Peter whispered, looking around to make sure no one was listening.

"Are you sure?" Mary Jane asked, and then she saw Peter's face. "Lemme see that." Mary Jane took the plate and gave the tracer a slight tug, and it came off, just as it should, with a slight click. She tilted the plate in the light and noticed there were scratchings on the back as well. "Hey—hey, Peter, there's writing on here."

31

"My God, you're right." Peter peered at the plate and adjusted his eyes, and now the faint, timeworn scratchings became clearer. *Of all the ... first the clone-and-Bishop picture, and now this?*

There, on the back of a plate that had just fallen out of a hidden compartment in the bottom of a chuck wagon in the middle of the American Museum of Natural History, in block lettering that was all too familiar from a thousand greeting cards, were the following words:

CABLE!
IT'S JUNE 26, 1867, AND WE'RE STUCK HERE! SEND HELP TO THE PLACE WHERE IT ALL BEGAN! HOPE TO SEE YOU SOON!
YOUR PAL,
WEBS

Mary Jane stared blankly. The muffled sound of webbed-down gunmen echoed in the distance. "Webs? So in the picture ... the clone ..."

"It's not a clone. It's me." Peter looked up, sliding the plate quickly into his jacket. "And I'm stuck there."

# CHAPTER TWO

# CHAPTER TWO

"How far?" Aliya shouted. She was two or three steps ahead of Cable, her legs pumping as they moved through the forest. Cable felt his boots sticking in the mud, the ground belching each time he raised his foot out again, quickly, slogging on.

"Uh . . ." Cable popped open a small screen on his wrist and waited the half second before the light representing the Time Displacement Core shimmered into view. He looked around as he ran, jumping over a tall root and hitting the ground as he made the meatball calculations. "Quarter mile, Aliya. Tops."

"We can do this," she said. Aliya's hair was pulled back and tied with a green band that matched the green jumpsuit that covered her body. She nearly disappeared in the foliage, her movement betrayed only by the sparkling of the gold wristbands and the stitched leather that covered her legs and shoulders. "Where do you want to go, Askani'son?"

"Anywhere but here," Cable said. The forest was quiet except for the sound of their running, and the lack of activity bothered him.

The Time Displacement Core rested in a hidden cave in the middle of the forest, waiting to get them out of here and to a safer time. It would be a short trip.

Cable listened to the mud and the trees and felt the aching in his legs. Aliya had taken a nasty hit to the shoulder in the last battle, but as he looked at her now, the gun in her arms pumping fast, he knew she was choking all the pain down and running off it.

The last two days had been catastrophic. Nathan Dayspring, aka Cable, had led the clan against Apocalypse and Stryfe for years, often battling them to a standstill from which both sides would slink away, licking their wounds and vowing to fight another day. The dictator would be taken down, one way or another. That was Cable's destiny. Blaquesmith had seen it.

But two days ago they had met Apocalypse and Stryfe in battle and fought with valor and grim determination and sucked-up courage and they had gotten their holy Askani behinds handed to them. This was the end. There were too many dead. The war could not continue like this. There had to be another way.

The Time Displacement Core was that way. Although Blaquesmith's invention was primitive by any true time-master's standards—it would never hold a candle to the Time Displacement Core employed by an eternal guardian such as, say, Immortus—it would allow them to make a time jump. So Aliya and Cable were going to use the experimental core to make a strategic time jump out of here and to somewhere else—anywhere else—before coming back to a better position from which to attack Stryfe and his horde. Maybe. Or maybe it wouldn't work like that at all.

Maybe they were just retreating.

"We're not retreating," Aliya had said. "We're changing the rules of the game."

And part of Nathan Dayspring didn't care *what* they were doing. He was the promised leader of the clan, this great warrior who would save their culture and their religion and lead them all into a new dawn, and what had happened? He had failed. Aliya had followed him to the ends of the earth and they had seen friends and family, God, even a son, die, and when it came to Nathan's cue to do his dance he had gotten on the stage and blown it.

Cable saw Aliya flip over a high root and come to a stop on the other side, leaves flying. Cable jumped and landed beside her, sliding to a halt. They had reached the edge of a ravine, a twenty-five-foot drop. Cable looked down as Aliya said, "Listen."

At first, the only sound was Aliya's smooth, deep breathing, her chest heaving under the golden plates that covered the front of her jumpsuit. Then he heard the rushing of the waterfall.

Down the rocky, muddy ledge, through the sun-dappled leaves from the trees that stretched over either side of the river, there was water pouring from an underground spring into the ravine. Cable peered through the foliage and finally saw the sparkling of water.

"You said this is where Blaquesmith hid it?" she said.

"In a cave," Cable said, bending down, hands on his quads. "It's hidden by the waterfall."

"All right," she said. "How's your wound?"

Cable touched his rib gingerly, the pressure sending shots of pain through his side. He had been slashed pretty nastily, but the blade had merely torn a bit of flesh off his rib. "Holding up. Only hurts when I breathe."

"I know the feeling," Aliya said, jumping over the side. In a moment Cable was sliding down the ravine next to her, mud and rocks falling and making plunking sounds in the river below. "It's not very deep," she said. "We can wade to the waterfall."

Cable hit the water and felt the coldness seep through his padded suit. "I hate this . . . running."

"Let's just do it," she said, slogging on. "You've got to get it together, husband. You sound whipped and you're not going to do us any good if you think you're whipped."

Cable nodded, now cringing that his own wife was telling him he was acting immature. It was true, he felt useless. He felt like a liability. Maybe Blaquesmith was wrong, maybe someone stronger was needed, someone like Aliya . . .

In a minute they reached the pool at the end of the river where the waterfall splashed in. It was beautiful, the water cascading out of a hole in the ground in the side of the ravine, sending brilliant sparkles of light everywhere Cable's bionic left eye could see.

There was something obscene about the beauty of this place, about being alive to see it when so many were dead. The beauty of the pool and the forest mocked the tragedy in the air. No, it wasn't that—the beauty of the pool and the forest didn't care.

And then something happened in Cable's mind. He was holding his gun up over the water, the still surface lapping at his stomach as he moved through, his wife doing the same, a few feet ahead of him, and she looked back. She was thinking the same thing. Time had slowed to a crawl. It was so beautiful, this escape. Through the waterfall up ahead he could see the shadow of the cave, and for just a moment, as he looked at her smile and the cave and the waterfall over her shoulder, he jumped forward a few seconds in time.

They were in the cave next to the Time Displacement Core, and they were sitting still, listening to the water. They were about to set off the Core, but they were waiting because the water was making beautiful sounds and there was so much beauty in the world, and there was mist coming in and Nathan Dayspring felt alive again. They embraced, and the world was gone, for just a moment.

Cable saw all of that, a few seconds, a few minutes, into their future, as he slogged through the water. And for the first time in days he smiled. The water was getting deeper, and with about ten yards to go, Cable and Aliya began to swim, holding up their guns as they did so.

*Snap.* Cable spun around in the water, flailing with his gun. He peered through the dappling sunlight up onto the edge.

Aliya spun, too, spraying water in Cable's hair. "What was that?"

There was a flutter at the top of the ravine and a flock of crows erupted and flew high into the trees.

"Birds." They treaded water there for a moment; Cable looked back in Aliya's eyes. There was water glistening on her face, and she smiled slightly, but he could see the fear beginning to grow. "Let's get to the cave," he said.

They moved a few inches, and then Cable heard a new sound, above the distant chattering of crows and the sound of the waterfall. It was a faint, energetic hum.

"Plasma." Someone had just switched on a plasma rifle and powered it up. The sound echoed through the ravine, and Cable and Aliya began to swim faster, spinning around, and Cable scanned frantically along the top of the ridges, one after the other, seeing the trees and rocks and looking for the rifle.

There was an audible but echoing and impossible-to-place *kachunk*, somewhere, maybe above, maybe ahead. The sound of someone loading a cartridge into a magazine. Aliya whispered, "The same rifle?"

"No," Cable whispered back, "I don't think so. That's a different make, but— Hell, I can't tell, come on . . ."

They reached the end of the pool and Cable found that the water was more shallow, and he could stand on the muck below. The both of them moved toward the waterfall, slowly, scanning everywhere with their guns at the ready.

"Aliya . . ."

"I know," she said.

There was a sucking sound of mud separating from the wall, and Cable spun around, water sloshing as he did so. Then came the first shot.

The plasma bolt slammed into the water next to Cable and he moved to the side, staring. "Where the hell?" He almost slipped on the bottom and looked at the muddy wall of the ravine to see a figure emerging from it, the separating roots. One of Stryfe's men. "There!" The assassin cocked his rifle with a ratcheting *chunk* and was raising it to fire again.

Cable shot once, his rifle barely jumping, the stock pounding back against his body. The plasma bolt flew six feet and hit the surface, pounding under the water. Cable watched the plasma bolt move, glowing under the water, the extra foot or two before slamming into the body of the assassin. "Stryfe's onto us!"

Pebbles falling off the edge of the ravine. "Yes, he is," came a voice from up above.

Cable spun around, firing at the sound, not even having to look to see who was standing there, surrounded by soldiers—Stryfe had found them. There he stood with that glowing eye of his, just like Cable's own. "Take them," he heard Stryfe say.

Plasma bolts began to rain from both sides of the ravine—*how long were they following us, how do they know?*

There was no way out except forward. "Let's go!" Cable looked at Aliya and the two plunged forward through the waterfall, and time slowed to a crawl again.

Cable watched Aliya's face, her mouth pulled back in an expression of rage and fear, as she plunged through the waterfall to the other side. He watched the line of water swallow her as he moved under himself, and when they were under, there was calm for a second, the army outside, the two of them in, the cave before them.

And there one of Stryfe's men crouched on the edge of the cave, and Cable shot him.

Go back: Cable shot him, but the stranger shot first.

Wallow, let's not forget, record it in your mind and play it over and over when you can't sleep and you wish you were faster on the draw and none of this were necessary because you won the war back there instead of turning out to be the failure that you are, let's watch, as she's standing there, barely getting up her rifle, just like you aren't fast enough, the cave where you're supposed to kiss and hug and forget the world, except there's a soldier there and you're not fast enough and now there's a plasma bolt slamming into Aliya's chest and punching a hole through it the size of a baseball.

Cable shot him, and shot him, and shot him.

And he held Aliya and watched her die and wished she would say something, anything, that might explain why she was leaving him now and might tell him whether or not he was as much a failure as he felt. Why he was going to be alone.

And there was no time. She was dead and the men were sloshing toward him and there was no time, and he dropped her body and watched it float there like a spent shell, and he climbed over the dead assassin and found the Time Displacement Core.

He triggered it, and there was no time.

In another place, in another time, Cable tapped the monitor and grimly turned away, his face a mask of rigidity. Only the white bristles on the back of his neck showed any agitation at all, and for all the world, he was a moving statue—gigantic and carved and white haired, his left eye shining like a star.

"I can't believe you can watch that," came a voice from the stair. Slowly and with labored steps, the creature known as Blaquesmith stepped down into the dim light of the laboratory. They were in a basement underneath the basement of a winery, tucked away in the quiet bosom of Rosendale, New York. Blaquesmith stepped onto the floor, always in steps of three, his movement punctuated by the use of his cane.

Cable turned to his mentor. "I'll look until I find one where it's different."

Blaquesmith was old—even in his own past. The wizard who had dedicated his life to seeing Nathan Dayspring become the savior of the Askani people, far in what this time would call the future, had followed Cable to the past. And now he watched as his charge spent every free moment at the Time Displacement Core, scanning the alternate timelines. Searching.

"How many today?" the creature said. Blaquesmith's eyes swiveled in their protruded sockets, and he craned his elongated neck forward. Sometimes Blaquesmith resembled nothing so much as a wizened old bipedal tortoise.

Cable ran his metallic hand over the back of his neck, feeling the tension ebb away, the hairs laying flat. "I don't know. Hundreds, I guess. Sometimes I look briefly, see the images of her, dead, and look away. Sometimes I catch it early, and I watch for a long time. The differences interest me."

"Differences?"

Cable nodded. "Yes." He sat down in a chair next to the monitor on the Time Displacement Core. "This last one was . . . poetic, like I was seeing myself as a character. Details were different, so that it was beautiful for a while. This last one was a better memory than I have."

"This is not healthy." Blaquesmith shook his head. "This is morbid."

"For a second there I thought they were going to make it."

"You must stop."

"Why?" Cable stared. "Tell me why."

"You're like a child, watching fantasies, only the fantasies all feature yourself. And every one ends the way your own experience did. Aliya's death is so completely ingrained into the timeline—the time-lines—that I don't think you'll find one where she doesn't die."

"You know that's not true," Cable said. "The possibilities are limitless . . ."

"And your time here is not. I'm talking about your mental health, Cable. A man watches a story and he becomes a part of it in some way. Part of storytelling itself is the displacement of the mind into another realm. Watching the monitor is like that—you're watching stories, even though they're real to the people in them. And you feel it when you watch."

"And each time I relive her death," Cable agreed. "But there's a purpose here. I'm looking for a time-line where she lives. If I could just find it . . ."

"What?" Blaquesmith shook his head again, the long neck quavering, the high voice agitated. "You'll pluck her out of that timeline and bring her here? You'll go to that timeline and kill yourself so you can take that Nathan's place?" He clicked his tongue, pointing a quivering claw. "No, no. Nathan, you're punishing yourself. No one should have to go through what you went through. And you put yourself through it hundreds, thousands, of times. And I think you should stop." Blaquesmith nearly tripped over his robe with his cane, and he cursed softly as he pushed it aside and stepped over to a nearby chair, where he slowly deposited himself, the heavy head falling forward on his neck. "Here," said the creature, indicating a teapot and two mugs left on the table. "As long as you're going to be invading my laboratory all of the time I think you should at least partake of the other resources. This one," he said as he poured the green liquid into the mugs, "is decidedly less . . . morbid."

Cable smiled, reaching for one of the mugs. "All right, old friend. If the price of your using your equipment is drinking your tea, I'm more than happy to . . ."

The Time Displacement Core screamed out a high-pitched, rapid succession of beeps. Cable looked up from the mug and saw a light below one of the monitors on the TDC blinking on and off. "It's never done that before."

Blaquesmith hopped up from his seat, displaying a surprising spryness for one so ancient, and spoke rapidly as he danced over to the monitor. "Nor should it, Nathan. This is highly irregular." Cable moved to look over Blaquesmith's shoulder as the old creature worked.

The monitor that was blaring in alarm was the central timestream grid. The grid displayed, on one screen, the status of the entire timestream—the flowing collection of all the timelines, any of which could be viewed on the monitor. Blaquesmith busied himself excitedly tapping keys, and Cable watched as the stream enlarged, the grid display zooming down, revealing more and more rivulets making up the stream—the timelines underneath.

"What a mess." Blaquesmith shook his head. "Amazing. Once upon a . . . once, the timestream was smooth, but with all the time travel in and out of the past few centuries, it's come to look like *this*." The timelines closest to where Cable and Blaquesmith actually existed were a jumbled mess, like badly designed wiring.

"That's what's setting off the alarm? Time travel has created too many alternate timelines?"

"No, no, I don't think there actually could be too many, the overabundance is simply not very elegant. The alarm is because of . . . *this*."

The grid display swooped down farther until it revealed four throbbing green lights, alarm markings, lying on four lines like drops of water. Each now divided, sending a droplet of light across the stream, landing on four points along one particular line. "There are four . . . *four* . . . major disruptions in the timestream. All at once, someone . . . who could do this? . . . someone has sent four . . . packages into . . . our past."

"The past of this timeline? The one we're in?"

"Yes."

"Where are these packages coming from?"

Blaquesmith shook his head. "That's what's bothering the Time Displacement Core. The four packages are coming from what appear to be four different points in alternate futures."

"Four different sources from different future timelines . . . four different destinations in this past. Four different culprits?"

"I don't know. Maybe," said Blaquesmith, "or maybe they're just trying to confuse us. But who could do that?"

"Blaquesmith, people go into the past and future

all the time, even if it's *not* a good idea. What's so important about . . ."

"These packages are . . ." Blaquesmith tilted his head, watching the grid, "unique."

There was a sharp electrical *crack* and Blaquesmith and Cable both looked over at the monitor Cable had been sitting at earlier. The screen danced and jangled, the picture becoming fuzzy, until finally it melted into a screen of snow. Cable moved to the monitor and began tapping in coordinates. "What on Earth?"

"What?"

"The timeline I was looking at earlier—the one with me and Aliya in the water . . . this is impossible . . ."

"What?" Blaquesmith demanded.

Cable looked back at his mentor. "It's gone."

Blaquesmith pushed away from the grid as he watched a line on the grid go fuzzy and then fade from . . . existence.

Cable shook his head in disbelief. In his mind he was seeing houses and farms and cities and lakes, all blinking out, faces melting into nothingness, children dancing into the void.

"Murder," Blaquesmith whispered. "Murder like never before. Someone has erased an entire reality."

Cable looked back at the grid, the green droplets glowing on the screen where the "packages" had been sent off. The room was dancing with the pulsing light of the static-drenched monitor, the white light making odd shadows on the hardwood floors and the shiny metal of the TDC.

"I think someone," said Cable, "is going to do it again."

# CHAPTER THREE

CHAPTER THREE

P eter Parker had been staring at the photograph and plate for an hour. He had busied himself with work all morning, sold a few photos to the *Bugle*, even stopped by Empire State University to pick up a book or two on Old West gunfighters. But now he was home, in the house he and Mary Jane had inherited from his late aunt May, and to his consternation, the photograph and plate were still waiting for him, right where he had laid them after borrowing them from the museum. Peter heard the sound of exercise equipment powering down.

"Ever thought of being a professional thief?" Mary Jane asked, as she wandered into the den from the guest room, where she kept her Stairmaster. Peter's wife was dabbing her neck with a gray towel, and she asked the question without looking at him. Mary Jane pulled a drenched headband off her brow and immediately attacked the refrigerator. When she emerged she was carrying what appeared to be a bushel of carrots, and she plopped down on the sofa next to Peter.

"Carrot stick?"

"Nah."

The vegetables crunched as she talked. "Can you imagine what would have happened if you had been bitten by a radioactive rabbit?"

"I try not to think about things like that," said Peter. "And I borrowed this stuff, I didn't 'steal' anything."

"Absolutely, sticky-fingers," she said.

"Although I suppose the spider-tracer *was* mine. Anyway, that's not the point. I'm trying to figure out how this got in there."

"Ever been to 1867?"

"Funny you should say it that way," he mused, scratching his head. "I mean, colloquially we talk about years as if they're places once they're far enough away from us in time. It turns out that we're right to, too, because time and space are more connected than we thought when we first made words for them."

"Ever been to 1867?"

"No." He laughed. "Sorry. But I have a feeling I'm going."

"Peter, this doesn't strike me as any sort of emergency, it's just one of those super hero life oddities. You can't rush these things."

Peter sighed. "I know, I know. I've seen evidence that I'm going to the past, it doesn't mean I need to hurry up and go." He paused, his chin on his hand.

Mary Jane crunched her carrot again. "I sense a *but* here somewhere."

"But what if it is an emergency? I mean, this note—stuck here by a spider-tracer of all things? *Hurry*, it says. *We're stuck here*, it says." Peter stood up and walked briskly toward the bedroom.

Mary Jane followed close behind. "Where do you think you're going?"

"Salem Center."

"What?"

"I just need—I think I should show this to the X-Men, just—just to be on the safe side." As he talked he rummaged through a pile of spider-suits in the walk-in closet. Aunt May had kept enough material here to sew a wedding party's dresses at a moment's notice—what would she think now that Peter was using it to keep a mountain of sweaty long underwear?

"Excuse me, but aren't the X-Men, if you'll pardon the expression, a band of outlaws?"

"About as much as I am," he said, flipping over a red-and-blue outfit. "Jeez, MJ, these are getting so beat up. I hate to go out in the day in costume, it's so easy to see the . . ."

"Runs?"

"Yeah. But this'll do—heck, it'll be dark by the time I get there." Peter tore off his T-shirt and blue jeans and was in the spider outfit in the blink of an eye.

Mary Jane shook her head. "I can't believe you can change in the closet."

"It's a tough industry. I know a guy who can change in a phone booth. Man." Peter pulled the mask down over his head and he was a different person entirely. The odd lightness of his movements suddenly made sense; even his head seemed to bob around in a more insectlike fashion. Spider-Man pushed past his wife and headed toward the door.

"Peter, aren't you supposed to do a round or two tonight?"

Spider-Man looked back as he reached the foyer. "I know. I know." He and MJ had a sort of deal where he tried to keep the number of trips out in costume to a minimum, per day. Marriage had meant making a few compromises, rigid as they sounded. But this super-heroing sometimes required a certain flexibility. "And I will, but I promise it'll be a short one tonight. Promise." He flipped up the bottom of his mask, exposing his mouth. Peter glided forward and kissed his wife on the lips, briefly. "I'll be back by dinner."

Mary Jane shrugged. "Better."

Through the door and up onto a telephone pole, flipping along at a rate no car could match, the spider was gone.

In a meeting room that would not have been out of place in the remotest bowels of the Pentagon, save for all the Victorian bric-a-brac, Cable was meeting with a few of his colleagues. The tall man with the shining metallic arm was talking, gesturing at a display that echoed the one back at Blaquesmith's lab.

"What are they?" asked a man in a wheelchair. A bald-headed man peered from the display to Cable, moving the chair's joystick with his hand to roll back a few feet for a better view. This was Professor Charles Xavier, benefactor of the Xavier Institute and the owner of the mansion in Salem Center, New York. Here the Professor had gathered those who he'd discovered early on would need his help the most: *Homo sapiens superior*, those humans born with extraordinary abilities and differences both mental and physiological, which afforded them both the unique opportunity to do enormous good for the outside world—and equal opportunity to suffer at the hands of it. The vulgar expression for them—used even by the members of that genus themselves—was *mutant*. Xavier started using the word in innocence, not having watched enough science fiction as a child to know the public was already predisposed to hear the word itself with a tinge of foreboding. But the moniker had stuck. Still, Xavier was proud of the label used by him and his team of mutants, the X-Men, and had every right to be—for he was one of, if not the, most powerful telepathic mutants on the planet. And, though feared and hated by much of the outside world, the X-Men had been a powerful force for good on the planet. Which was why Cable came to Xavier and his team for help when this latest problem came up. Cable had never joined the team, but they had become valued allies in recent times.

"They're . . ." Cable paused. "We don't know what they are. We're calling them packages."

An African woman spoke up from where she stood next to the Professor's chair. Her voice was melodic and sweet, like aural nectar. She was called Storm, because the weather bowed to her whims. "Let me see if I understand this. These . . . packages . . . are travelling across time and landing in other timelines, and then—collapsing them?"

"Like some sort of virus?" This last man to speak up was Scott Summers. He looked like a tennis pro, with his short brown hair and slim but muscular frame and white cardigan. Over his eyes lay a pair of ruby-quartz glasses, some variation of which he wore constantly to shield the enormous power that poured constantly from his mutant eyes. His active name was Cyclops.

Cable knew a thing or two about viruses. The metal that covered a great portion of his body was a side effect of a techno-organic virus that had nearly killed him as a child. He fought against it constantly, sometimes losing to it and seeing it nearly consume him entirely. Cable struggled with his virus so continuously it was almost like breathing—labored breathing. Someone who thought Cable seemed sort of uptight might have done well to remember that even standing still, the man was doing a lot of work. "That might be an accurate estimation, Scott. See here." He pointed at the glowing embers representing the packages, and tapped a key, bringing up a full view of the timestream.

"The timestream," Cable continued, "is like a tree trunk, of infinite length. We don't know why, but by and large everything in existence across the timelines is pretty much like it is in its sister timelines. Now, the TDC displays branching-off points where time-lines diverge from one another. As you can see, all along the timestream there's really only marginal variation, but sometimes you run into areas where the branches get really, uh . . . weedy." The display homed in on a section of the timestream that appeared tremendously jumbled, lines branching out and back again, dividing over and over again.

"What are we looking at there?" the Professor said.

"Well," Cable said, "this is where we live. We've, uh, made a mess of the timeline. By *we* I mean people living in this galaxy in what amounts to a several-thousand-year radius. Home."

Storm smiled grimly. "We even pollute the time-stream?"

Cable looked back. "Yes. And basically it's all in this time neighborhood because most people who travel in time have something to prove. The stream tends to move back to where it was supposed to be after it's diverged, like a creek rejoining a river—so there's no sense in going too far into the past or future—besides, too far, and everything's unfamiliar.''

Cyclops nodded. ''Sure, Dr. Doom makes a time machine, and travels to the future. Kang comes back from the future to conquer the past.''

''Not just what we loosely call our favorite villains,'' the Professor said, putting a finger to his lips. He adjusted the blanket over his legs with his other hand. ''We've done some time travelling ourselves.''

''Right,'' Cable said. ''Don't I know it. And the fundamental rule of time travel—well, the rule of thumb, anyway—is that *this*—'' and here he pointed at the jumbled mess that was the time neighborhood in which he lived ''—is the only result. Point to prove or no, if you change your own past, you create an alternate timeline.''

''No going back and killing Hitler, or whatever,'' Cyclops said with a nod.

''Right. Which works out fairly nicely, when you think of it, otherwise, you'd have one chaotic timeline, constantly changing. Boggles the mind. You might even say free will is only possible if you can't change your own timeline.''

''Why would that be?'' Storm asked.

Cyclops spoke. ''Because acts of will would be meaningless. You could go back and change the past and then—bang—there was no reason for you to go back in the first place. Multiply that out and see what you get.''

''Look,'' Cable said, ''I don't want to get that deep, okay? Think of the whole theory about not being able to change the past as . . . just a means of perception. It *appears* that this is how time works. The TDC seems to confirm that time works this way. It *appears* that the truck is bearing down upon me, my senses say so, and the fact that I *appear* to be flattened by it if I don't get out of the way seems to confirm that my theory is holding. So maybe all this perception is *wrong*, fine, but it doesn't matter now so let's not get into it.''

"All right," the Professor said in the tone he'd honed over the years while dealing with teenagers who went off on tangents. "Continue, Cable."

Cable looked back at the TDC monitor. "The packages are landing in identifiable points in *our* past, the past of *this* timeline. But once they stick there—'' now the monitor displayed an animation, showing the glowing embers that represented the packages on the timeline; little tentacles of light were sprawling out from the embers ''—they send out these . . . energy tentacles. Some form of temporal energy is released and the degradation begins. A number of alternate realities have already been destroyed. It just tears them apart. I have no idea how this works,'' Cable said. "But as you can see, with all these timelines disappearing, you're talking about a cost in human lives that is . . . very high." He turned around. "Inestimably high."

Cyclops rubbed his neck. "But . . ."

"I know what you're thinking," Cable said. "And don't feel guilty; I was tempted toward it too. These are alternate timelines being wiped out, it's very much as if these people aren't even real to us. Just try to think of yourself as being an alternate to someone else and you'll realize this is real death we're talking about, as abstract as it seems."

"It's not abstract at all," Cyclops said. "You came

from an alternate timeline. You're real. No, I see it."
Cyclops didn't have to speak the rest, the whole con-
voluted story of how it came to be that Cable was,
although he appeared older than Scott Summers, actually Summers's own son, having been sent to the
future to fight his own technovirus, growing up there,
and coming back to meet his own, younger, father.
All of that was another story entirely.

"Nathan," said Storm, very smoothly, "what is it
you would like us to do?"

Cable looked at each of the gathered X-Men and
breathed. "We need to send teams back into the
past—there's four packages, that's four teams. The
teams will be charged with finding and destroying the
packages, and finding whatever we can about who's
sending the packages to begin with."

"I don't know," Cyclops said. "There's a real
danger of making things worse. You just said that
we'd only create another alternate timeline. And our
other trips through time have not always been . . . as
pleasant as we intended them to be."

The Professor scratched his chin. "How do you
propose to do this?"

Cable was saying, "We can use the TDC to—"
when he was interrupted by a sound that clanged
through the mansion and made the monitor shimmer
slightly with the vibration.

Cyclops said, "We have an intruder on the
grounds."

In an upstairs room laden with silk, lotuses, and the
occasional beer can, two X-Men were deep in a game
of poker.

A tall Cajun with a drawl as thick as Louisiana swamp scum looked up from his cards. His Lucky Strike filterless bobbed in his mouth as he eyed his opponent. "Any day, now, *mon ami*."

A thick stream of cigar smoke issued from the mouth of the man across the card table from him. "Watch yer tongue, boy," said the mutant named Logan but better known as Wolverine. "As long as yer gonna be smokin' up my room, I'm gonna take my sweet time." Logan's face was hard and wizened, but the few wrinkles there, underneath the bushy brows and wolfish-black hair that wildly flared from his temples, gave no indication that the man had been in action since before World War II. "I was taking chips when—"

Remy LeBeau finished the sentence with him: "—when you were just a gleam in yer papa's eye," he said, imitating Logan's overly macho manner of speech—which sounded odd, coming from him. " 'Sides, it's your room or mine. No one else'll let us light up and I'm sick of playing on de lawn." The Cajun looked around and regarded a silk tapestry of a tiger and a pig on a bridge. "What's the story wit' dat?"

Logan was rearranging his cards. "It's a very old Japanese story," he said, when the alarm went off, making the ash on the end of his cigar shake loose and fall over his cards. "And I'll tell it to you another time."

Remy, or Gambit, as the X-Men called him on the field, nodded. "We got a guest." He threw on his trench coat and palmed a deck of cards as Logan shot out the door.

An observer floating outside Charles Xavier's mansion would have been treated to a sight that would have made J. Jonah Jameson spontaneously combust. Storm came bursting from a window and immediately swooped down over the grounds, hanging over the orchard. A moment later she was followed by Hank McCoy, the furry blue creature known as the Beast, who sprang from his upstairs bedroom and grabbed a tree, swinging around and landing on the soft earth.

The klaxons rang throughout the mansion and at once the hallways and staircases came alive with mutants as the X-Men responded to the intruder alarm.

Logan hit the grounds and found Bobby Drake—Iceman—in the trees next to Jean Grey—Phoenix. "Who we got?"

Phoenix was turning around, scanning the trees and the walls of the mansion with her mind. The moon had come out, and Logan watched the limbs in the orchard move, casting strange, silver-fingered shadows. "I don't know," Jean said. Jean was Scott Summers's wife and, like Bobby, one of the original X-Men, Professor Xavier's first students. She had been a teenager when she had been brought to Xavier's, gawky, with a talent for telekinesis—Marvel Girl she was called then. She had grown into this—the tall, red-haired, almost monstrously powerful telepath known as Phoenix. "It's not a mutant."

Iceman said, "Wolverine! There!" Pointing at a shadow as it dashed from a tree to a nook in the wall of the mansion, he raised his voice over the sound of the alarm. "Hey, stranger! Where ya going?" Bobby

Drake's body was transformed from flesh and blood to ice; now he fired a bolt of that ice from his hand. Logan watched the white matter burst forth from Bobby's palms, splattering next to a tall window on the second floor of the mansion.

Something in the shadows sprang, and Logan watched the spindly shape burst from the shadow and dance across the window, disappearing under a gigantic storm drain. "Wait a minute. . . ."

"He's closing his mind," Jean said.

" 'Course he is," Wolverine muttered. "Think someone's gonna call on the X-Men and don't know we got telepaths about?"

Bobby lifted off the ground with a thought, shooting a platform of ice from his hand, which continuously pooled and froze under his feet, pushing him up and forward. He could ride this ice bridge for miles. "Can you push him a little?"

Phoenix shook her head. That could be dangerous. Someone deliberately trying to block his mind from a telepath's probes could suffer great damage if she tried to intrude. "I could, but I'd prefer we just bring him down."

Cable came around from the front. "You got him over here?" He was followed close behind by Cyclops and Bishop, the gigantic black mutant from the future.

"He's on the wall," Logan chuckled. "He's sticking to the shadows."

"How about we shed," said Cable, as he raised a large gun, "a little light on the subject."

"I agree," called Storm, flying around from the north side of the mansion. "On three?"

"On three." Cable nodded back. The shadow danced from one corner of the wall to a tree, flipped between a pair of high limbs, and disappeared once more. "One . . ." He cocked his gun, loading a magnesium flare into the chamber.

Storm rode high, and the wind began to whip around her, and Logan looked up to see the clouds rumbling and splitting in half at her command. "Two!"

On two, Cable's gun rocked in his arm and yellow fire spit from the barrel as a bolt of lightning crashed from the sky, striking the ground nearby. Cable felt a minor jolt run through his feet and watched the shadows dance in the light that blazed for a second only.

The shadow had not believed their ploy, and Cable distinctly saw it move after the light had died again.

But the wind brought something to Wolverine's nose, and he sniffed, and finally smiled. Walking over to a pear tree, he slowly pulled a pear from its branch, sniffed it, and took a bite. "I knew it," he said, and laughed out loud.

"What?" Iceman called, as he spat more icicles from his fingers, trying to bring the visitor out.

Logan took another bite and tossed the fruit to the ground, and stepped into a clearing, where he could look around at the shadows. "Okay, bub," he called. "What's this all about?"

Gambit came flipping around from the side of the mansion Storm had been on and landed next to Logan. "Who you talkin' to?"

Logan raised an eyebrow, tapping his nostril. "The

nose knows. I'm talkin' to Spider-Man. Hey, Spidey! C'mon and quit horsin' around!''

A shape dropped from a tree not ten feet from where Gambit and Wolverine stood. It hung upside down from a makeshift harness of chemical webbing, the dark red head moving jerkily as it scanned the area. Wolverine gave a long, high whistle.

Bishop came running up from the darkness and sprang, catching the hanging figure in midair. As the red-and-blue-clad intruder cried out, the two tumbled on the ground, flipping over once to land in the grass. Bishop straddled Spider-Man and pinned him to the ground, a gigantic brown fist pulled back as he stared at the strange mask.

"Hold on, hold on!" Spider-Man cried, and his voice was a mixture of tension and a goofy laugh. "Don't hit me, fella, you'll crush my friendly neighborhood Spider-skull. I'm here to ask the X-Men a favor!" Sensing a relaxation in Bishop's muscles, Spider-Man rocked back and brought his legs in under Bishop and gave a hard shove, sending the gigantic man sprawling back. Then he sprang into the air and lit on a tree. "You and I need to talk. But I couldn't resist having a little fun. You guys have no sense of humor, you realize that?"

"Don't push us, bug-boy," Logan said. "You could have gotten yourself killed."

"For that matter," Storm said, "you could have just rung the doorbell."

"Yeah," Spider-Man shrugged, "but where's the drama in that?"

The Beast bounded over to the wall where Spider-Man hung, and smiled. "Auspicious entrance, Spider-

Man. You're a little far from home, wouldn't you say?"

Spider-Man stayed stuck to the wall and spoke very slowly. "Like I said, I came to ask you folks a favor. Couldja put the guns down, now?"

Cable scowled, lowering his weapon. "I could have shot you, mister. What kind of favor do you think that makes me want to do?"

"Can we go inside? It's a little complicated," the super hero asked. "It's about time travel."

Cable threw a glance at Storm and Cyclops. "Let's talk."

"No doubt about it," Bishop said as he tilted the photograph in his hand and laid it on the winding dark spiral staircase next to him. "That's me." They were gathered in the large den where guests were received at the Xavier Institute. The Beast sat hunched on the stair, Iceman standing over him, his frosty arms crossed.

Cable was more interested in the metal plate. "June 26, 1867," he muttered. "It just so happens, Spider-Man, that one of these packages we told you about landed in 1867. This is all very unusual, that you would find out about this at the same time we did."

Spider-Man nodded. "Yeah. You're sending how many teams?"

"Four. I think we should keep them small—maybe just duos."

"Then it looks like Bishop and I are your 1867 team," Spider-Man observed.

"Maybe," Cable said. "Or maybe not. After all,

you're stuck there. I don't intend to let that happen to my teams.''

"Do you really want to go down this road?" Spider-Man asked. "It's an X-Men operation. Bishop is there. Why else would he be there but that you sent him?"

"Maybe he's there because he thought he should be there because he saw that photo."

"Oh, for heaven's sake," Bishop rolled his eyes. The gigantic man slumped against a wall. "There are people dying. I'm for going."

"Wait, wait, hold on." Cyclops waved his hand. "There's something I'm not getting. You just lectured us on how there's no point in going back in time to fix a mistake."

Cable looked at Cyclops and shrugged. "All right. Spider-Man, if you're on board, that's the way it'll be. We should adjourn to the Time Displacement Core." He looked at the Professor. "Agreed?"

Xavier nodded. "I believe that would be the best course of action."

"But," Iceman asked as Cable headed to the door, "what about what Cyclops asked?"

Cable's hand was on the door and he turned back to say, "About the rule that you can't change time? Let's just say that we have a wild card in the TDC. But there are rules, and I'd rather explain it to you there than here."

A quarter hour later, Blaquesmith hunched over the TDC while he spoke. "In order for Cable's idea to work," Blaquesmith said, "we must use the TDC to break the rules it exists to enforce. The TDC can, in fact, send you back in time. Normally this would create an alternate timeline, as Cable explained, but the TDC can be adjusted to force your movement to remain in the same timeline.''

''Force it?'' the Beast said. ''That doesn't sound very safe.''

Blaquesmith chuckled. ''This from a scientist who tested an experimental serum by drinking it.''

The Beast smiled, adjusting the round glasses on the end of his furry nose. He showed his teeth, which were sharp and jagged, and stroked the blue fur that covered his body. ''We all defy the scientific method from time to time.''

''But the answer is that it is not safe, Dr. McCoy, and you would all do well to remember that. There will be some hard-and-fast rules to your travel.''

''Okay, people,'' Cable said, as he laid four objects on the table. ''These are your recall devices.'' He held one up, a shiny metal disc slightly smaller than a Frisbee. From the disc hung a set of bright yellow-green straps. ''One of you per team will have to wear this.'' He tossed one to Spider-Man, one to Wolverine, one to Iceman, and kept one for himself. ''This thing is your life. Hang on to it.''

Spider-Man regarded the disc. It appeared to be brushed chrome and reminded him of a roulette wheel. All told, the thing weighed about three pounds, and had a closed cap in the center. He flipped the cap open and saw one button, and one button only. To his amusement it even said RECALL. ''I take it this is the way back.''

''Yes,'' Cable said. ''Now, if we're going to travel in our own timeline, then we have to observe three rules.'' He held up his hand, in all seriousness, and met every person's eyes. Spider-Man suppressed a laugh. This was a level of military behavior he generally didn't associate with the X-Men—but then, Cable's relationship with the X-Men had always been peripheral. Still, he knew time travel better than the rest of them, so his take-charge attitude made a certain amount of sense.

Cable continued: ''Rule Number One—and you've all seen your science fiction movies, so you can probably guess this one—do not, repeat, *do not* interfere with history. You have a mission—get the package and destroy it. That's *it*. If you come into contact with *anyone*, be careful. Don't go getting someone's grandmother killed. Don't even step on a butterfly if you can help it. Understand?''

Gambit raised his hand as the rest of the X-Men nodded solemnly. ''Dis mean no gettin' to know de tavern girls?''

''This means don't even look,'' Cable said.

''Spider-Man took a picture wit' a nice piece o' . . .''

''Gambit,'' Cyclops snapped, throwing him a nasty glance.

''Got it, boss.''

Continuing as if Gambit hadn't spoken, Cable said, ''Number Two: this is a big one, folks, so listen carefully. Blaquesmith is going to hold the TDC in place and he's going to force this timeline to keep from splitting, but this is like brain surgery. He has to keep the timeline 'awake.' It will keep moving. You will be moving across it. Your time is limited—literally. You can only return to the present an equal amount of time after you've left.'' Cable let this sink in. ''What this means is, if you spend an hour in the past, you'll come back an hour later than you left. If you stay for three hours, you will come back three hours later than you left. If you—''

''And if we stay two weeks,'' Spider-Man said, ''we don't come back for two weeks, we get it.''

''No!'' Cable stared. ''You don't come back, *ever*. That, Spider-Man, is Rule Number Three: the power the TDC will be using to do this, with all of Blaquesmith's talents, is tremendous, and will be continuously consumed. And it will run out, we estimate, after six hours.''

Blaquesmith nodded. ''Don't count on it, Nathan. I'm *hoping* for six before this device overheats.''

Iceman muttered, ''Oh, boy.''

''Six hours, people,'' Cable repeated. ''We can send you pretty close to the packages, and you'll all be equipped with trackers that Blaquesmith has fixed up for you, but you have to find the packages in the time you're allotted. If you don't find them, get back here. Got it? Bishop and Spider-Man, are you listening?''

''We're listening,'' Bishop said.

''Run out of time and the recall device will not work. You'll be pushing it and pushing it and you won't go anywhere.''

''Stuck there,'' Spider-Man said gravely. ''Well, I promised someone I'd be home for dinner.''

''Then let's do this right.'' Cable nodded, looking at Bishop and the wall-crawler. ''You two got stuck once already, it looks like, so watch out. And now that I have everyone's attention," he breathed, "here are your assignments."

"Master Kang?" Lireeb turned away from the time scanner and peered across the laboratory. Kang sat at the gigantic wall of monitors, studying them. The purple-robed conqueror scanned and rejected time-lines more quickly, now, his eyes intense behind the dark metallic mask.

"What?"

"We appear to have been met with some resistance."

"Eh?" Kang turned only slightly, using one hand to continue shifting the displays.

Lireeb stood, and he walked up behind Kang, hovering over his master's shoulder. The albino stood a good head and a half taller. "There are a number of people from 1998 in the target timeline who have just set out on separate . . . journeys."

"And where are they going?" Kang asked, idly, as if this did not concern him, but he was curious.

"They *appear* to be going, indeed to have gone, to the Time Arrows' landing points."

"Hm," Kang said.

Lireeb tilted his head. "If I'm not mistaken, Master Kang, the whole point of sending Immortus's Time Arrows to those points was to test their ability to destroy a few timelines."

"Yes."

Lireeb continued, "And don't you imagine these people might be planning to interfere?"

"Hm." Kang tapped a button and all the screens flickered and switched, and he began viewing this one as cursorily as he had the last, his eyes travelling from left to right, top to bottom. "Hm, yes, Lireeb."

"Doesn't that merit even a grunt of megalomaniacal tension?"

"I'll pretend I didn't hear that, Lireeb."

"But the time travellers are headed for the—"

Kang sighed, turning around. "Let them," he said, patting the tall man on the shoulder.

Lireeb stared forward, eyebrows raised in mystification, as Kang chuckled and turned back to the wall of screens. "Oh, look, Lireeb."

"Yes?"

"Twenty across and sixty-five down."

"You've found them?"

"No, I just thought I'd point out this world I've found where a multibillionaire industrialist was bitten by a radioactive bat. Isn't that delightful? What do you suppose is the proportionate strength of a bat, hm?"

"I shall be sure to look it up, sir," Lireeb said, shaking his head, his eyes closing with the headache he felt coming on.

"Interference," Kang repeated softly. "Excellent. Most excellent."

# CHAPTER FOUR

On a hill in Arizona, two men walked, one white, one black, and from far away they would have stood out harshly against the lightly tan earth and the rolling sage that dotted the baking landscape. It was June 26, 1867. One was of medium height with brown hair, and wore a long, faded duster over battered brown clothing. Over the bottom half of his face was a red bandanna that blew in the wind like a beard, and the wide-brimmed hat on his head buried his eyes in shadow. He moved over the sand like a man on the tendrils of a web.

The white man's companion stood a head taller and appeared to outweigh him by a couple hundred pounds. His long coat swayed in the wind, the dirty white shirt underneath opening at the top to reveal a massive chest. In his right arm he carried what appeared to be a decrepit, probably unreliable, shotgun. He, too, wore a hat, and the tattooed M over his eye sank into the shadowed dark skin. In this country, in this time, he would be branded enough.

Spider-Man regarded the battered metal compass in his hand. An extra, red needle had been added. The red needle pointed north-northwest, and he adjusted his course slightly as Bishop did the same, and watched the arrow line up with the compass. He watched the color of the metal brighten as they moved, growing lighter with every yard they grew nearer. "Okay, Li'l Joe, I think it's close."

"Fine, Cartwright." Bishop scowled. Spider-Man had insisted that if he were going to have to go without his mask, he would use the name Ben Cartwright, which he had explained might—or might not—be his real name. "But I don't understand why you insist on calling me that."

Spider-Man shrugged. "It's, ah, more friendly. We might be moving among people."

"What's the matter with Bishop?"

"Bishop is too—" Spider-Man smiled underneath his mask "—too modern. Too cynical. Besides, I like Li'l Joe."

Bishop grunted his resignation. Spider-Man had to admit to enjoying the big man's discomfort. It was obvious that Bishop knew Spider-Man was having some sort of fun at his expense, but it was equally obvious that the mutant couldn't put his finger on what, exactly, the fun was—which just made it better.

"Whatever," Bishop said. "Just pay attention to the Tracker. I don't want to get stuck here with you."

"I don't know," Spider-Man said. "We could start a ranch. What do people in Tombstone, Arizona, raise, anyway?"

"This wilderness is not here in my home time, Cartwright," Bishop said. "There are no ranches."

"The Ponderosa will be missed."

"The what?"

"Nothing."

"How far now?" Bishop asked impatiently.

" 'Are we there yet?' he asks. The needle is pretty pink, I'd estimate halfway to white. I don't know. Another mile or two?" Spider-Man moved his arms uncomfortably under all his clothing. The layers were to shield one from the sun and encourage sweat, but he had an extra layer to contend with: his Spider-Man costume was sticking to his body like a diving suit, the recall device strapped to his chest, baking against his sternum. He felt like a piece of soggy toast. Spider-Man looked ahead to see they were coming to the top of another ridge, one that looked exactly like the one at which they had appeared after being zapped by the TDC. "Boy, variety is the spice of the desert, huh?"

Bishop grunted a nonanswer.

"You're not much of a talker, are you, Li'l Joe?"

Bishop stopped and turned to look at Spider-Man, who turned as well. The effect was like watching a truck do a forty-five-degree turn on ice. His whole body was so huge and yet moved so smoothly. This was a dangerous man. "Talking, where I come from, can get you killed. Talking means you're moving your mouth and not listening. Talking means you're probably wasting resources."

"Are you always like this?" Spider-Man asked, the cloth over his lips flapping as he spoke.

"Are you?"

"Okay, okay," Spider-Man said. "Sheesh. And to think I could have come here with Wolverine."

"Five minutes with you and he'd slice you to ribbons."

"Yeah, but at least he'd say something memorable. He is the best there is at what he does, after all."

They began to walk again, Bishop shaking his head. "We live in different worlds, bug-man."

"Cartwright."

"Cartwright. Whatever." Bishop walked like an automaton, the battered shotgun slinging back and forth like a scythe in his right hand. "Are you still wearing those web-shooting devices?"

"Yes," Spider-Man said. "Under my cuffs." They

were uncomfortable, to say the least. Beads of moisture were gathering between his wrists and the web-shooters, causing them to slide around more than he'd like. Periodically he tried to adjust the bands, to little effect. "I've had worse costumes, I guess."

"I don't find these trappings particularly uncomfortable," Bishop observed. The special Old West garments had been whipped up by Professor Xavier, using a clothes-generating device given to him by Lilandra, empress of a distant alien people called the Shi'ar.

"I never trust alien clothing anymore."

"You've had problems with alien costuming?"

"Yes," Spider-Man said. "Well, sort of. One time I went to another planet and got my hands on a costume maker that built me the perfect spider-suit. Best outfit I ever owned. Didn't have to put it on or take it off; it could adapt to look like anything. Even responded to my thoughts. It was intelligent."

Bishop looked sideways. "What happened?"

"It turned out to be a symbiote that wanted to permanently bond with me. You could say we had a falling out."

"What happened to it after that?"

"It hooked up with a psychotic journalist and now they terrorize New York together," Spider-Man mused. He was watching the red needle brighten in color. "And it never calls, and it never writes. Hey," he looked up, "just went white. I think we've found it." The two men were reaching the top of the ridge and as they did so they stopped, looking at the land sprawling out before them. The terrain changed slightly below. There was a dusty yellow road a quarter mile down, and more rock formations jutted up here than before, dark splotches of rock contrasting harshly against the relentless bleached beige of the frontier. And there was a small, shallow river, not an eighth of a mile wide, winding beside the road and heading north over the next hill, presumably to Tombstone.

Bishop swept his hand across the vista. "Makes sense that there'd be a river next to the town. Water's got to come from somewhere."

"Yeah."

"Wait—" Bishop held up a hand as he turned around. "You hear that?"

"M-hm." In the distance came the sound of hooves and wheels pounding against hard earth. "Horses. And the needle's growing brighter. They're coming over the hill."

From the ridge on which they stood Bishop and Spider-Man looked down to see a pair of hatted heads appear over the next hill, on the road. "There! It's a wagon!"

"And he's in a hurry," Bishop said, as he began to walk down the hill, watching the wagon emerge, fully in view and over the ridge and in the open as soon as the heads had come into view. The driver whipped the reins, the horses galloping, and Bishop could see the wagon bouncing with the rough ride.

"There's another," Spider-Man said, and by the time he had gotten the words out, yet a third wagon appeared, all of them moving at the same breakneck pace. "And the Tracker's goin' crazy—the package is on that wagon train!"

Bishop loaded a pair of cartridges into his disguised plasma rifle and slammed back the hammers. "Then we must overtake that wagon train—now."

"Wait." Spider-Man stepped forward, touching Bishop on the shoulder. The new sound of voices filled the air from the hill, another set of horses. "Something tells me," he said, "that someone's beat us to it."

No sooner had the words escaped his mouth than Bishop and Spider-Man got the first view of what the wagon train was running from so fast—six horses came over the hill, galloping under wiry dark riders, guns waving in the air. The front man on horseback, the leader, waved his pistol and fired in the air, and Spider-Man heard the words, "Now! Stop them wagons!"

"Great," Bishop spat.

"At least we have a perfect view." The whole scene was playing out not half a mile down. Spider-Man watched in something like admiration as three of the men picked up their pace and rode past the back two wagons to get alongside and just ahead of the first. "Gonna drive 'em into the river," he said.

The three riders were alongside the horses pulling the front wagon and fired into the air, shouting, "Hyah!" The horses spooked and reared away from the riders, and the wagon jerked wildly to the left. Meanwhile, the other three riders broke off and plowed straight into the river themselves, headed in the direction the wagon was going.

"These men are smooth," Bishop said.

"Bishop," Spider-Man said, recognizing them

from his recent reading, "you're looking at the Clem Carter gang."

And that must have been Carter himself, up there in front, riding hard and driving the lead horses into the river, the wagon careening into the slick river bottom, the other wagons following at the behest of the other riders, until the first wagon overturned in the water and the driver was thrown. The driver scrambled to his feet, surrounded by the Carter gang, as the other two wagons ground to a halt in the middle of the river.

"Now they just clean up," Spider-Man said. "We should be stopping this, shouldn't—"

"Don't even think about it," Bishop said.

On the river, the Carters were surrounding the wagons and Spider-Man saw the hands of the members of the wagon train going into the air. Each wagon had one driver up front, and now he could see the heads poking out of the wagons themselves. From the overturned wagon scrambled two men who quickly climbed from the flooded interior onto the exposed side, soaking.

Spider-Man saw Carter point at the wagons, obviously demanding that whatever booty was held there be handed over. One of the men on top of the first wagon nodded, tipped his wide hat nervously, and then *pulled out a plasma rifle and blew a crater in the water the size of a pool table*.

The shock from the weapon cracked through the air and reverberated in Spider-Man's ears.

"Oh, my God," Spider-Man whispered, stepping closer, as the river erupted with plasma fire. All of the seemingly helpless, embarrassed, and cornered occupants of the wagon train had suddenly whipped plasma rifles from their dusters. Water flew and steam hissed as bolts of plasma struck the river, narrowly missing Carter himself. Spider-Man saw the man fly backward, stunned. Carter rolled back and Spider-Man distinctly heard what the man yelled:

"Let's get the hell out of here!"

Spider-Man and Bishop began to run down toward the river, and all along the way the heavy rifles ripped through the air, tearing at the ground, as the members of the wagon train fired upon and scared the living bejeezus out of the poor workaday coach robbers.

Bishop pumped his arms, running. "Do you know what this means? The packages are guarded! That's probably not even a—"

Now, even as the Carter gang whipped around on horseback and began to fly, reins whipping and hooves sending water splashing as the six headed for the hills, Bishop and Spider-Man watched the fallen first wagon right itself: the whole unit began to hum, and lifted itself from the water. The driver watched the Carter gang flee and tucked his rifle into his coat, and resumed his place.

Bishop and Spider-Man stopped at a rock and crouched, watching. The leader of the wagon train looked back at his comrades, showing no emotion whatsoever, and nodded. Spider-Man heard the man say something like, "All clear. Situation resolved." *Oh, yeah,* he thought, *then why is my spider-sense still buzzing a blue streak?*

Then the driver turned in his seat and whipped the rains, and the horses began to pull the train out of the river, as if that thing even needed horses.

"Oh, man," Spider-Man said. "That's gonna be hard to hit."

Bishop nodded. "Well, at least we know they're—"

"At least *I* know where you two are gonna be spending the night," came a third voice. The words were punctuated by the distinctive ratcheting click of a pair of six-guns being cocked. "Get 'em up, boys. Big fella, you just drop that shotgun there."

Spider-Man winced, looking at Bishop. That answered his unspoken question about his spider-sense. He hadn't even heard the horse come up behind them, so intent had he been on watching the wagon train in action. He brought his arms up and clasped them behind his hat. "I know this looks a little odd," he heard himself say.

"Just turn around slowly; I know what it looks like." They turned around to see a handsome blond man with a handkerchief over the lower half of his face. Spider-Man recognized him instantly, almost said, *Y'know, my wife thinks you're cute.*

"And *odd* is not the word for it," the cowboy continued. "You boys are under arrest."

"Great," Spider-Man muttered. One hour in the Old West, and they had already managed to get arrested by the Two-Gun Kid.

# CHAPTER FIVE

Wolverine leaned against a rubbery, greenish-blue tree, peering up at the clouded sky. The valley in which he and the Beast had landed after walking through the TDC was lush and green, now covered in the mist of dusk, so that a bluish-green haze seemed to fill the landscape. He watched the Beast pop open the cover of the tracker and said, "Hank, you recognize any of this?"

The fur-covered scientist looked up, adjusted his spectacles, and pivoted once, crushing mysterious flowers beneath his gigantic feet. Finally the Beast shook his head. "Not at all. We could be anywhere. I don't even recognize any of this foliage. I recognize *that*, though," he said, pointing at the smoking, very live volcano that brooded at the edge of the valley, among the line of mountains that closed in the blue-green valley.

Wolverine nodded. "She's alive, all right. Any chance of an eruption?"

"Right now?" the Beast asked. "I don't see why not, but I'm just going to assume that we're here to retrieve this mysterious package and not to stay for the fireworks, if any."

"What's the tracker say?"

Beast looked down at the disk, and the myriad of lights shone on his blue face, projecting spots of light there in an effect Logan remembered seeing in old pirate movies, when the pirates opened up the treasure chest. The Tracker that the Beast carried was not disguised in the way that the others' had to be—by all accounts there would be no humans in this prehistoric era. "Looks like we have a mile or two to cover. Nothing that'll earn us merit badges, I should think," the Beast sighed, clapping the Tracker closed and slipping its cord over his shoulder.

There was a faint rumble in the ground from the heavily treed section of the valley just to the north. Logan sniffed the air. "Hm."

The Beast eyed the mountain range warily. "Maybe I'll revise my statement. This is an extremely volatile period, Logan. We should hurry." He began to walk through the plants and greenish mud. "We'll be sitting ducks for a lava flow here, I'm afraid."

The rumble continued as Wolverine followed the Beast, but Logan knelt closer to the ground. Just as he stepped over a tree trunk he felt the rumble grow larger. Suddenly he stood straight and looked around. Logan saw a tall, columnar rock, maybe six feet high and smooth, and he leapt onto it to get a better view. He looked around, feeling the animal in him guide his eyes and ears as he scanned the area. The sun was going down and it was getting hard to see. "I don't think you should worry about lava," he said, nostrils flaring.

The Beast had stopped to watch his teammate climb the rock in this manner and now he folded his arms. "What do you mean?"

"I been in Montana and Oklahoma and Texas, and it's all the same. Don't matter what for, might be the water, might be the wind. But forget the lava and the volcanoes," Logan whispered, peering through the darkness, pressed against the rock like an animal scoping out its prey. "Ain't no volcano."

The rumble grew louder and the Beast had to adjust his glasses as they fell forward a bit on his nose.

He stepped up to the jutting rock on which Logan was perched. "What . . ."

And now the sun disappeared behind the mountains, and the only light was that of the bright stars piercing the inky black sky and lighting up the hazy blue-green valley. The rumbling sound grew louder, like a thousand drums pounding in the distance, drums now reaching the edge of the forest, the trees shaking in alarm. Logan looked and finally saw it, countless shapes pushing through the trees and beginning to pour out. "Stampede!"

Logan and the Beast both leapt for higher ground as a huge variety of creatures, none of which Logan recognized—dinosaur lore was not his specialty—thundered past.

As the wave poured out, Logan's eyes focused on the half-dozen or so creatures that were egging the stampede on, bringing up the rear.

From several feet away on a boulder, the Beast hissed, "Velociraptors," as the first of the creatures bounded past, its bony tail protruding behind.

The velociraptor, weighing just over two hundred pounds, was built for quick hunting. Its muscular legs carried a slim frame and a large, heavy, snapping head, the weight of which was balanced by a four-foot tail. They poured through the trees, sending mud and green moss flying, slashing and snapping at anything in the way.

The Beast looked around, flipping as two raptors brushed against him on his boulder, tearing at his fur with steely foreclaws. The ground was shaking with them and Wolverine watched his teammate dance, looking for a tree. The Beast got to a trunk and nearly lost a foot as he sprang for a branch and kicked a velociraptor in the eye. The blue X-Man grabbed on and scrambled up. The raptor stopped for a moment, its neck whipping up at him as he scrambled yet higher.

Wolverine sighed and looked around. "I think we should—" he shouted, just as a sturdy raptor tail shot past, slammed hard into the rock on which he was perched and Logan felt the whole column begin to loosen. "Oh, great." The slightest thought tensed the muscles in his arms as he let go of the rock, tiny mechanisms springing, sending long, shiny metal claws jutting from the backs of his hands with a pneumatic *snikt*.

Another velociraptor sped past, its tail slapping against the rock, then another on the other side, and Logan felt the whole perch begin to topple. As the rock fell forward, mud flying out from underneath, he jumped, claws out, legs moving in midair. He felt his boots hit the top of a raptor's head and the head whipped up angrily, eyes narrowing in, but Logan ran, springing off the flipping head and landing behind the creature. He heard the rock slam loudly against the mucky earth behind him as the raptor kept running, but now he found himself in the middle of them.

The stampeding animals began to take notice of the human that had fallen in among them, and Logan actually watched each creature as it ran past, trying to decide whether to keep with the running or stop to tear him to pieces.

Wolverine jumped again, pushing toward the trees, hit the ground, sprang, and this time felt a claw catch him in the ankle, sending him flipping over and sprawling out in the mud, and leaving his ankle a bloody mess. "Hank!" he yelled, rolling over, feeling claws tripping over him, a sharp hiss coming from nearby, "I think I got one's attention!"

He turned over and sat up, scrambling, and felt a blast of breath in his face as a long, tapered head zoomed in and stopped, nose to nose. For a tiny moment that felt like a year, he locked in on the creature's eyes. *Oh, I know you. You're a hunter. You and me got lots in common.*

As if in agreement, the gigantic mouth opened as the head whipped back, razor-sharp teeth bared, and flew forward again. Wolverine brought his claws up and slashed it across the neck, feeling the tug as his claws sliced through dense dinosaur flesh, and lunged forward with the blow. The creature writhed and screeched, snapping while still impaled on Wolverine's claws. Its own clawed feet impaled Logan's shoulder and drew blood—but were impeded by the unbreakable metal bones they hit. Wolverine slashed again, tearing through its slender throat, feeling the thick flesh rip and cold blood pour out on his arms, and he slammed it to the ground.

Wolverine hissed, feeling his chest rise and fall as his heart beat madly, blood filling his eyes. The ruckus had brought more combatants. Even as the tide of raptors kept moving around them, Logan saw, no, *felt*, two more of them lock on to him and slowly, sidestepping, claws flexing, sizing him up. Wolverine's eyes flew to the Beast's tree and saw that Hank had abandoned his perch and was now flying through the air, landing on the back of one of the raptors as the other charged.

The raptor slammed forward, butting Wolverine's chest, sending him flying back, and as he fell, Logan felt the back of his head crashing into the fallen rock. A surge of pain shot through him, the red tinge in his eyes grew wild, and he heard himself snarl.

The Beast was perched on the other attacking raptor, his legs wrapped around its body, claws wrenching at the slender neck as the creature tried to double back and bite him. The raptor bucked and spun with the Beast, its heavy tail slapping against him, and the Beast held on more fiercely as he spun. The Beast brought both arms down hard on the ridge just between the creature's eyes, and the raptor staggered, stunned, still trying to throw him. Hank brought his fists down again and the sound of bone crunching underneath heavy flesh filled the air. The raptor fell forward, crashing into the earth.

Wolverine roared and leapt forward, tearing into the raptor without even seeing it, feeling its teeth ripping the flesh of his forearms, its claws slicing through his legs. His own adamantium claws flashed and did some tearing of their own, cold blood flying, and he tore and slung until he was standing there howling, the blood rushing so loud he heard nothing else, and the creature was dead.

They stood there, for a moment, the Beast and Wolverine, blood matting them both in the prehistoric wilderness. "I can't believe," Wolverine panted, "you boosted a dinosaur."

"All in a day's—" the Beast managed to get out before he cut himself off, busy dodging a sharp raptor claw that just missed his shoulder. Wolverine watched as this new raptor reared back its head, determined to bite Hank McCoy in half.

Logan tensed and sprang, and even as he did so he saw a pair of raptors coming up fast behind, locking in, no longer interested in stampeding. He saw the Beast kicking at his own attacker's head as the two behind it jumped over him and fell on Wolverine, meeting him in midair. Suddenly he was ensnared, and there were claws reaching for him, fetid breath slicing at him. *We're going down. No way out. But I'm gonna take a few with me.*

Suddenly something roared and the valley shook, and to the left of Wolverine's head one of the passing raptors was crushed under the weight of a gigantic, leathery red foot. Something grabbed the raptors on top of him, one in each hand, and he felt them pulled away. *What the—?*

The roar continued and Logan watched the two raptors, each held in a mighty clawlike hand, moving up on gigantic red arms, squirming and snapping at the dense flesh. It was another dinosaur, a *huge* one.

The red dinosaur reared back, standing on its gigantic hind legs, holding the raptors in the smaller clawed arms, its boxish gigantic red head towering nearly forty feet in the sky. The red creature bit one of the raptors in half as it threw the other to the ground in a crumpled heap. Then it roared again, cold breath shooting past like a storm, and snatched the raptor off of the Beast, sending it flying across the valley, screeching. The stampede had reached its end and the rumbling tapered off, the last few raptors picking up speed now that the new arrival had made his appearance.

Suddenly it was quiet. Wolverine lay on the ground, looking over at the Beast, who was struggling to get up, nursing a nasty wound to his shoulder and chest, his blue fur matted and soaking. The only sound was the breathing of the forty-foot-tall red monster that had just, inexplicably, saved them. "Hank!" Wolverine whispered. "What is it?"

The Beast looked up as the creature moved slightly, tilting its massive head, actually studying them. "Iguanodon, maybe?" he whispered slowly, scratching his head. He had lost his glasses. "Lambeosaurus? It's got articulated arms, so it can't be a T. rex . . . and this color . . ."

"Hryangh!" came a shout from ten feet away. Wolverine and Beast looked up and saw a man step out from behind the legs of the red dinosaur. No, not a man, more like a boy—and a very furry boy at that. The biped seemed just this side of human, with a thick, wide, bald forecrown. His face was devoid of hair, but the rest of his body was covered in dense, dark fur.

"My God," Beast spoke, amazed. "Humans. Or close. This contradicts everything we've ever known or said." In the moonlight, the boy glistened with a bluish sheen, as he seemed to study Wolverine and Beast carefully. For a time he looked down the valley, then back at the two X-Men. He rested his moonlight-glistening eyes for a long time on Wolverine, scowling.

"I think I spook him," Wolverine said.

"He's worried about your lack of fur, I should think," answered Beast.

The creature repeated the word he had shouted and the dinosaur turned, looking down at him. Then he pointed at the two X-Men and shouted something else, and the dinosaur nodded, groaning, and lunged forward at Beast and Wolverine.

"He's siccin' his dinosaur on us," Wolverine said, but the claw that came forward simply snatched the Canadian up and clutched him close to his dense red chest, high off the ground. Another lunge and the dinosaur had plucked up the Beast, as well, who only stared wide-eyed in helplessness and shrugged at Wolverine.

Wolverine looked at his partner, cradled as he was in the arms of the red dinosaur, which began to walk under the boy's command. The ground shook as the body moved forward, the creature breathing loudly, bloodstained teeth glistening about twelve feet above the two captives' heads.

"Excuse me," the Beast said plaintively, "but do you suppose this dinosaur stops anywhere near where we need to be?"

"Something tells me," Wolverine said, grunting as the dinosaur adjusted his arm and cradled him closer to the massive body, "wherever he stops, it's up to the little guy." The dinosaur settled into a steady pace, now, the twelve-foot-tall legs swinging, the earth shaking with every step. The young, furry man rode on the red dinosaur's shoulders, arms hugging the scaly red neck. In this fashion they rode on by the light of the moon.

Wolverine was watching the alien trees swaying as

the monster passed by. There were countless unnamable creatures that skittered out of sight as they drew near, strange reptilian things no fossil remembered in his own time, shimmering in the moonlight. There were a million unfamiliar smells here, and Logan felt drenched in the strange aromas. Layer by layer he accepted the smells and pushed them to the periphery, so that he could pay attention.

The Beast pointed down at the ground from across the belly of the dinosaur. "Look at that!"

"What?" Wolverine scanned the earth.

"See those dead creatures?" Here and there, where the raptor stampede had run, lay dead bipeds, some of them rent to shreds, some simply broken and killed beneath the running beasts.

"Yeah, I'd noticed those."

"There's one lying on his back. Those aren't the same biped as our friend here. For one thing, they're all light brown—and bigger. I'd say our boy is fully grown, more or less, and all of the dead we're seeing are at least a foot taller and stockier, to boot. And," the Beast added, wrinkling his nose, "their faces seem less defined by human standards. I mean, our tour guide here might as well be a fur-covered human. Those dead fellows down there are a different race."

Wolverine adjusted himself in the red dinosaur's arm, looking up at the boy, who eyed them with a look of fairly confident wariness. "You think we came across some kinda prehistoric race war?"

"I cannot theorize that far at this time," the Beast said. "But look how well our captor has tamed this savage beast—he's actually taken a dinosaur as a pet. Now, mind you, this is a smart dinosaur—he responds to vocal commands; his brain has got to be different from all those we've always assumed that the larger dinosaurs were given. But this is a smart human, or whatever you choose to call him. Smaller than those dead we see below, almost certainly weaker, but I would be willing to wager that he is faster and smarter. I don't think we came across a race war exactly, so much as a chapter in an ongoing struggle with a different race.''

Wolverine looked at the Beast. ''You mean you think they set off the stampede to run these brown guys out?''

''I think so. If he can train an iguanodon, he can probably set off a flock of lizards running in the right direction. These two were obviously keeping track of it, and they certainly seem to have left a lot of these large, hairy bipeds to die. Yet *us* they pluck out of the fray when we've had enough. I can only deduce that the browns fell victim to a planned death and that we were not a part of the plan.''

They were reaching the edge of the valley, coming to another section of alien trees, which grew against a rock face that tapered upward for what must have been a thousand feet. The wind rushed past them and Wolverine felt the particles on the wind passing around the strange-smelling devil dinosaur and through the trees, hitting the rock wall and doubling back through. He breathed deeply, almost comfortable in the red beast's giant arm. ''One thing's for sure,'' Wolverine said. ''He ain't alone.''

''That is most likely true,'' the Beast agreed. ''It would be highly unlikely for us to run across the *sole* member of a previously unknown race of prehistoric human ancestry. That would make him a mutant, and a lone one at that, and it's highly unlikely he'd survive if he were born to the browns, who—''

"No, fur-brain," Wolverine frowned. "I mean he ain't alone, because if I ain't mistaken, that's cookin' I smell." Now the creature moved into the trees, its head remaining above the treeline as the X-Men were plunged into the foliage, brushed about by vines and small limbs.

The Beast wrinkled his nose and sniffed. "What do you know?" There was a distinct aroma of meat being cooked on a fire, and something fruity boiling. The dinosaur began to slow, moving through the high, rubbery trees, topping a small crest. The trees parted and suddenly the world erupted in flickering light.

They had found a camp. All at once the Beast and Wolverine both gasped audibly as the dinosaur brought them into a clearing that stretched on about sixty yards to the rock face, which was no face at all, but a gigantic opening to a communal cave that stretched forty yards across at the mouth. Back in the flickering shadows of the front cave opening were mouth after mouth of hewn-out caves. And in front of it all, moving in the moonlight and firelight, were what looked to be a hundred or more protohumans. Some of them were preparing food, here and there small ones wrestled, as older males sat on rocks and gesticulated with great animation, occasionally expectorating onto the rock wall to make a point.

"My God," the Beast said, his voice a whisper that betrayed the sense of wonder he was trying to contain. "Do you know what this means? Logan, *look at this!* Fire! They've brought fire from the volcano and they're *cooking* with it! This is a society!''

Already the people milling about had turned to see the boy and his dinosaur, and Wolverine watched the whole group break loose from whatever it was doing and gather excitedly around the dinosaur as it stepped onto the edge of the clearing. They were shouting something, some of the females jumping and making excited motions with their hands.

Suddenly the boy shouted something and the dinosaur bent forward, letting the young male spring from the creature's shoulders. The two X-Men remained cradled in the arms of the dinosaur.

"Well," the Beast said, as the X-Men watched the small bluish-black folk fall upon the boy, cheering, many of them touching his fur and saying what must have been his actual name, over and over. "The prince returns.''

"Somethin' like that," Wolverine said. Now a grayer male, slightly hunched but powerfully built for the smallish protohumans, came through the crowd, and shouted what Logan took to be a question. The boy nodded excitedly and leapt into a narration, swinging his arms and speaking as excitedly as those who had greeted him, jumping, punching, kicking, then, all of a sudden, turning to point directly at Wolverine and the Beast. The boy grinned wildly and shouted something at the dinosaur and the red claws relaxed, dropping the two X-Men unceremoniously to the ground.

The boy shouted something else, a phrase, which was repeated throughout the camp, and now the strange folk attacked the X-Men with touches and praise as they had done their returned hero. The boy grabbed Wolverine by the wrist and Logan shouted, "Watch it, bub!"

"Just play along, Logan," the Beast said quickly.

Wolverine found himself dragged out to the center of the beaten-down plaza, and the boy spoke on, gesturing in a way that imitated Wolverine slashing at the raptors with his claws. The boy examined the Canadian's costumed arms, searching for the claws, then beat his forehead and turned to the tall gray one, the one whom he seemed most interested in impressing. Now he looked back at Wolverine and pointed, shouting a guttural sound that seemed to be a demand.

The Beast was standing there, still being touched and patted by the tribe, who seemed far more at ease with his blue coat than with the uniform-covered Wolverine. "He wants to see your claws," he said. As if to illustrate the point the boy pantomimed the fight with the raptor again and made the sound, *snikt*.

Logan sighed, stepping back to give room. He raised his arms and triggered the mechanism that moved like rolling your tongue, easy if you can, and the six adamantium claws slid out over Logan's hands, locking into place. The crowd went wild.

"You're a hit," the Beast exclaimed, who wasn't doing so badly himself, "a very palpable hit."

"They didn't even see the fight," said Logan, who felt like an idiot for standing there popping his claws out and showing off. There were young males running up to study the claws more closely, although he was relieved to see that everyone kept a fairly healthy distance from them.

"They trust their hero. Our boy told a story and they believe, and now they see your claws. And make no mistake, these people are far more impressed with a close-up weapon than they would be, with, say, a plasma rifle, which would serve no more purpose in their minds than as something heavy to be thrown. Those claws make you a powerful ally with a fierce weapon in his body.''

After half an hour of lavish praise and adulation, a female shouted something that caught everyone's attention all over again. The whole group, males rolling around and slapping one another and pretending to use Wolverine's claws, turned at once and moved toward the woman. "Soup's on," said Logan.

Logan and Hank were given places to sit near the boy, who himself managed to have a place near the old gray. Despite the novelty of the newcomers, the true reverence of the people radiated toward the boy, who spoke on and on, now apparently discussing the whole scheme of the stampede.

The Beast looked around as he and Logan sat cross-legged in the dirt. "Look at this. They eat together too. God, there's so much detail, and I have to remember all of it. Can you imagine what all of this means?" The celebratory feast itself was a simple but tasty affair. Wolverine and the Beast each looked up as a girl, who seemed to be a daughter of the woman who had rung supper, stepped through the center of the crowd that now sat talking around a series of fires.

Finally she reached the two X-Men and knelt down, handing Logan a large clay cup and a plate of roasted meat Logan could not identify. The Beast looked at Logan's meal as the girl went back for another set. "What kind of meat is that?"

"I don't know." Logan sniffed. "Smells kinda like beef."

"Should we eat?"

"Be rude not to," Logan said, picking up the hunk of meet and tearing into it with his teeth. He savored the morsel for a long moment before swallowing. "And a mistake not to. Whatever it is, it's great."

"Probably two days' allowance of fat and protein."

"I'd guarantee it." Logan picked up the cup next to his knee and brought it to his face as the girl returned. "Huh."

"What?" The Beast took his own serving from the smiling girl and smiled back at her, twinkling his eyes beneath his furry brow and nodding politely before looking back at Logan. "What's in the drink?"

"It's like cider," Logan said approvingly. "It's boiled and a little fermented, and there's a bunch of different fruits here." He took a sip and gave a short laugh. "I *like* these people."

The Beast picked up his cup, ignoring the meat on his plate. He stopped then he realized that the girl was still kneeling there, smiling, waiting for him to drink, he assumed. He drank, and grinned. She grinned back.

Logan watched all this and added, "And the people like you, I see."

"Thank you!" the Beast said to the girl, nodding, making a little *cheers* gesture. "Mmm-mm. Thanks! Um, run along, now."

The girl looked over at the boy and remembered that the hero had not yet eaten, and so now she stood up and headed for more food, looking back at least twice at Hank McCoy.

"What was it you said?" Logan asked. "Oh, yeah. A hit—a very palpable hit."

"Well," the Beast said, grimacing, "I think we have more important matters to which to attend. For one thing," he said, sliding the Tracker and its strap off his neck and shoulders and holding it in front of him, "we've not much time left." He clicked a button and the Tracker chirped open, the central disk popping up and shimmering with light.

"How far are we from the package?"

"Well, it turns out the dinosaur did us a favor."

Logan looked across the plaza to see the red iguanodon—if it was an iguanodon—feasting on the carcass of what seemed to be some form of mammoth bull. "These people have a pretty powerful pet."

"Yes," Hank replied. "I wish I knew what the story was with our boy and that devilish dinosaur over there. And," he said, chewing his lip, "I can't tell you how pleased I am to learn that there really was color variation among the thunder lizards. How sad that there are no records of this beast. There aren't even records of these people. It's stunning what the earth forgets," he said. "But, yes, Devil Dinosaur over there brought us closer to our target. I'd say we find the opportunity to slip away, and we'll have about a mile to cover."

The girl had brought supper to the boy, who was busy talking with the old gray. She continued staring at the Beast and smiling brazenly even as she served the boy.

"Your fan is back."

"Yes," the Beast smiled politely. "Hello. Yes, hello again."

"How much time we got?"

Hank looked down and tapped a button. The Tracker disc chirped melodically and the lights changed to reveal a time display. "Another three hours."

"Oooh!" the girl exclaimed, and Logan actually found himself amused that teenage girls said *ooh* even in prehistoric times. She bent down, bringing her head close to Hank's and twisting around to look at the Tracker.

"Yes," Hank said, trying to sound civil. "It's a device for—it's—" She was reaching out her hand, looking plaintively at the Beast, attracted by the shimmering lights and polished gold. "Yes, I suppose you can touch it." The Beast threw a look at Wolverine that said, *Well, what can one do?* The girl giggled as she touched the Tracker, saying several excited things to Hank and apparently expecting no response.

Wolverine said, "One can get your attention by stealin' your toy."

"Hey!" the Beast exclaimed, as the giggling, fur-covered girl snatched the Tracker device and jumped back, waving it and laughing. Hank stood up and gestured harshly. "Give that back, young lady!" The girl put her fists on her hips in a mockery of the Beast's scolding.

"Oh, *real* good," Logan said. "That'll teach her."

"Give that here!" the Beast said again. Now the whole tribe, or at least those nearby, had noticed this display and seemed greatly amused by the whole scene. They were even more amused when the girl smiled once more and, giggling, turned and ran into the forest.

"You do have a way with women, fur-ball," said Logan.

Lireeb the albino stepped through the corridors of limbo and glided across time with every inch. Every corner of the winding corridors brought a different feel, from the strange far-off palace halls of Barsoom, to the sterile bleached linoleum of St. Elizabeths in Washington. There were hallways of times and places, all strung together, every corridor existing in a different place on the stream, every portion bleeding into Limbo and leaving a mark. It was a wonder they could find anything. But then, Lireeb knew his way around by now.

The manservant turned a final corner and stepped through a Roman arch and into a Victorian foyer, which in turn spilled into the brightly shining, surgical-steel clean and colorful technological wonder that was Kang the Conqueror's lab. Kang was in front of his screens as usual. Lireeb looked over at the terminal he had been working at before choosing to move his workstation to a different part of Immortus's fortress. Working back to back with the master in eternity was not exactly impossible, but he had found it easier to simply walk the distance when the master called or if for some reason he had something to report. By now, the moments since that change had been made had taken their toll in eternal limbo, and his old workstation had shriveled and died, a melting metal shadow of its former self. With every second encompassing an essentially infinite amount of time, so much of Limbo thrived on intention and will.

Lireeb cleared his throat. "Master Kang?"

"Eh?" Kang turned. "How good to see you. How long has it been? Years?"

"Centuries, but who is counting?"

"It's all meaningless here, anyway," Kang said with a sigh.

"Yes, well, as you instructed, I've discovered the departure point of most of the enemies going off in search of the Time Arrows."

"And?"

"They have left from Earth, 1998, New York."

Kang nodded, satisfied. "Which timeline?"

"The first of that neighborhood, your first one to approach."

"Excellent. Thank you."

"Just water under the bridge?"

"My dear Lireeb, what use is conquering with no one to conquer? It's good to have someone to *defeat*. Wouldn't you agree?"

Lireeb sighed. He had timelines to study. "If you insist, sir."

"I do insist," said Kang. "I have fought those twentieth-century altered humans more times than there are times, and I have never been satisfied in my wish to see them crushed. Oh, I've slaughtered a few sets of the Avengers here and there, here conquered one alternate timeline, there another. But that period on the timeline is a mess."

"I'm certain your own time travel was influential in that, sir, if I may say so."

Kang tilted his head. "I'll allow it. You're very right. I myself have fathered numerous bastard time-lines. But now, now, here they come, those heroes, to try to stop me. If it's my mess, then I'll see that it is cleaned. Do you know what the Time Arrows are for?"

"Please enlighten me," said Lireeb. So far, he had spent all of his time *tracking* them.

Kang wagged his finger, touching his lip. "They're really quite impressive. Easily the most stunning find of all the treasures left behind by Immortus. The Time Arrows are devices the Lord of Time used to *weed* the timestream. We found the Time Displacement Core, which he used to keep track of all the timelines. And he had these tools so that, when he wished, he could simply send out an arrow, and where it stuck, the timeline itself would unwind and degrade. Brilliant, isn't it?"

"On a whim?"

"Well, he was the Lord of Time, after all."

"I have no desire to cross you, my master, but why would Immortus seek to destroy timelines, even if he had the tools?"

"Because so many of them are being irresponsibly started by people like me—before I got in the timeline-destroying business, that is."

"What fault is that of the timelines that were created?"

"Oh, good gods!" Kang spat at the albino. "What in the name of eternity are you talking about? If he didn't plan to destroy timelines he wouldn't have had the tools to do it in the first place." Kang looked up at the video screens and back at the tall albino. "And at any rate, he's not here now, and the tools are *mine*, and I will use them as I please. I don't have to justify myself to my own servant."

Lireeb nodded so softly that he seemed to have not noticed the touchiness of the whole argument. "Of course not."

Kang seemed satisfied by this and turned back to his video displays. "So the Time Arrows go where I want them. I can use the temporal field generator developed by the ersatz Lord of Time—self-aggrandizing peace-lover though you hold him to have been—to isolate a large selection of timelines. Once it is isolated, I can spread the effects of the arrows across that whole section. All I need find is the one I want to remain. Seventy-eight across, twenty-five down—right now, anyway."

Lireeb scanned the wall until he found the screen. Displayed there was what appeared to be a midtown Manhattan department store. "You want to rule Tiffany's."

"You try me, Lireeb, you really do. But if you were paying attention, you would notice the address of that department store. You know what's missing from there? The Baxter Building. *This* timeline," he said, pointing in triumph. "All the odds rolling out correctly, this is the one I want to remain. No Fantastic Four, no Avengers, and I've checked—no super heroes at *all*. It just didn't happen. A completely mundane earth. This is the one I will rule. With Ravonna at my side, of course."

"Yet another thing not yet done," Lireeb said.

"This is a challenge," Kang agreed. "But I will find her. Then all I must do is pluck her out and deposit her safely to the one Earth I will protect from the destruction caused by the Time Arrows."

"I don't really understand why you search for

this . . . woman," Lireeb said. All he knew was that it was on the list of tasks; who knew the reasonings of Kang?

Kang sat in a chair and poured himself a glass of wine from a flask on the table next to him. The flask had been brought from a section of the Fortress that resembled pioneer-settlements in colonial Western Pennsylvania. It was stitched leather, darkly stained and treated. It looked utterly wrong in the metallic purple gauntlets Kang insisted upon wearing at all times, but Lireeb let it pass.

Kang sipped his wine for a moment before he said, "I loved her. Princess of a kingdom that I conquered ruthlessly and then allowed to shake away. I did so because I was moved by Princess Ravonna's insistence upon never, ever accepting defeat, not from me, nor anyone. And I grew to love her, even as she spat upon me and my conquering troops. And then when I saw her defending her own kingdom from yet more invaders, I aided her, and she pledged her love to me. And then, in my arms, she was killed."

Lireeb stared ahead, feeling awkward. This was uncharacteristically open for Kang.

"And so I searched for her," Kang said. "Across the timelines I have searched and searched, for a Ravonna who survives. And who loves me. And what have I found?" He gestured with his goblet at the video monitor. "I have found Ravonna. Many Ravonnas. Ravonnas who love me but die. Ravonnas who live, but hate me and try to kill me."

Lireeb looked from his master to the monitors. "And yet you continue your search."

"Somewhere," said Kang, "somewhere in the

twisting groves of time is the Ravonna who will love me and not betray me, and who will survive. And I will find her.''

Lireeb chewed his lip a bit. "Is it possible, master Kang, that perhaps it is not fated to happen?"

"There is no fate. There is only will and accident. There has to be a timeline where will and accident line up correctly."

"And if you're wrong?"

"What are you asking me?" whispered Kang, harshly, the wine gurgling in his throat. "Are you asking me to consider that there is but one love for me and we will never be together because *eternity* wishes it not to be so? That I will wander, alone, because of *fate*? I will not accept that," he said, shaking his head gravely. "I cannot accept that."

Kang's head sank for a moment while he studied his glass. Then he looked up, and with renewed energy stood and turned to the monitors once again. "I am wasting time. I must find her before the Time Arrows complete their work."

"And the enemies?"

"Let them come," said Kang.

Then, after a long moment, he looked back at Lireeb warily. "Lireeb?"

"Yes?"

"Did I hear you say you knew the departure points of *most* of the time travellers?"

# CHAPTER SIX

S torm floated over the land, hovering near the crumbled remains of what appeared to have been a wall. Slowly, her white hair glowing in the moonlight, she descended onto the wall, feeling her weight come to her ankles, as the winds that kept her aloft blew themselves out. Cable stood up straight—he had been crouched on the wall, unpacking plasma cartridges, and as he stood, the gigantic moon framed his shoulders and chest. Storm watched him turn, following the blue silhouette of Cable's jawline as he tried to appear relaxed. Just below his temples, a little muscle on either side of Cable's face was pulsing away, so fast and furious that Storm could see the muscle popping up at a rate of three times per second. He was probably clenching his teeth without even knowing it. No doubt: he could look composed, but this was a tightly wound man.

"What is this wall?" Cable asked, looking down at the square bricks on which they stood. Storm surveyed the wall herself. It stretched for miles, running east and west across Britain, apparently, cutting the island effectively in two. On one side, to the north, she could see the start of the Cheviot Hills. To the south lay fields and farms, hay meadows stretching on forever. The peacefulness of a pastoral setting could fool you, of course. Sixth-century Britain was no paradise.

"It was built by the Romans," she said, "some eighty years after they invaded England."

Cable turned around, frowning. "This is such ancient history to me."

"It's hardly recent where I'm from either," she

said with a small smile. "But I did study Rome when I got the chance."

"Were you a student when you joined the X-Men?"

"Actually, I was an African goddess," she said. "In any case, this wall was put up after the Romans invaded southern England and had moved northward. The northern parts were teeming with Scots and Picts who painted themselves blue and generally made imperialism more work than the Romans preferred to put into this theater."

"So rather than fight," Cable said, "they went as far up as they wanted, then put up a wall across the island?"

"Twice," Storm said.

"Interesting strategy."

Storm shrugged. "Not everything has to be accomplished directly, Nathan."

"Well," he said, looking down at the Tracker as he popped it open, "all of this is wonderfully educational, but we have a package to intercept. And it looks like we need to head south—only a few miles, in fact."

By the time the road Storm and Cable followed had stretched into a scrubby wood, the Tracker began to brighten. Cable stopped for a moment and listened to the wind. "Do you hear that?" As the wind shifted, Cable turned, pricking his ears in the direction the Tracker pointed. He heard shouting, a few words here and there, and a sharp, slapping, metallic sound. "Battle."

Storm nodded. "Yes."

Cable looked at the Tracker again. "And if I'm reading this correctly, the package is right there among them."

"How far?"

"Quarter mile," he said, beginning to jog. Storm summoned a wind and flew alongside him, moving along the dusty, cart-carved road, trees flying by on either side, following the Tracker, and the sounds that began to grow. "What are the odds," Cable said, "that our package has something to do with—" suddenly the road turned and sloped downhill to reveal a crossing; Cable stopped "—that?"

Cable drew his rifle and crouched as Storm got down beside him. They had not been noticed. There, in the middle of the crossroads, a man was fighting for his life. Storm whispered, "Oh, my. . . . Nathan, I believe that is the Black Knight. The original."

"Are you sure?"

She nodded.

The Knight in question was dressed head to toe in black armor, with the silver silhouette of a falcon emblazoned on his chest. His arms were wrapped in heavy black leather studded with metal bosses, the closest to mail that his time period had to offer. In his arms he held a long black sword that weighed fifty pounds if it weighed an ounce, and the way he used it, swinging it and moving like lightning, was like the magic that was said to course though the ebony blade itself. His face was hidden by a tall black helmet which barely moved on his shoulders as he slashed and parried. Cable watched this warrior bring that gigantic sword up and crashing down against the sword of one of his opponents, and no sooner did blade meet blade and sparks fly but he spun around to regard yet another.

The Black Knight was surrounded by no fewer than ten adversaries, all wearing heavy-duty studded leather and even bits of mail. Their faces were helmeted, too, in a strange, purplish metal. They were playing with him, wearing him out, and Cable and Storm could hear the Black Knight shouting.

"My familiar Merlin has warned me that there be magic hidden here, dark and sinister," came the growling voice that echoed from beneath the helmet. "And what do I find when I go to look for it, but ten men ready to attack a servant of His Majesty!" With every word he swung, and now on the word *majesty* the Black Knight spun around to see two of the attackers moving in against him. The Knight crouched and kicked out as the one on the left began to swing, and caught the man's knee with his right boot, slashing up with his sword to slam into the man's leather tunic. Pieces of studded leather erupted from the man's chest as he staggered back and the Knight slashed again, lunging in, swinging hard across, catching the lower part of the attacker's helmet, sending the man spinning back and crashing to the earth. The Knight spun around to regard his newest attackers even as the one he had just felled refused to lie still and sprang up again.

"You mock me!" he shouted, slashing and spinning, laboring to keep his eye on ten swords at once. The attackers seemed to be in a dance routine, moving in and then back, attacking fiercely and then feinting, keeping the Knight on the move. "You fall not when you should, you fight not like men but like spirits!

But I have a truth for you, gentlemen." Now the Knight hit the ground and rolled, flying under one of his attacker's legs, knocking him over, rolling back up. All ten turned toward him and moved in, as if of one mind, surrounding him immediately and renewing their strange attack. "I am Sir Percy of Scandia, the Black Knight," he cried, as he spun and hacked and spun and hacked, "and I will not fall to the minions of evil!"

"He's staggering," said Cable. "There's no way he can—" Cable began to stand, now, moving forward, and Storm touched him on the shoulder.

"Nathan, we're not supposed to interfere. You yourself said—"

"You heard what the Knight said," Cable said, his bionic eye burning hot and fiery, sending out its odd glow. His metal arm glistened in the moonlight, reaching forward to chamber a round. "He's looking for the same thing we are. These guys shouldn't even be here. And they certainly shouldn't be able to get up and keep fighting after being stabbed in the head."

"Who are they?" Storm asked.

"That's the question, isn't it?" Cable answered. The Knight was beginning to falter, his body riding a little lower on bent knees, but the sword stayed up. One of the attackers managed to work in close and hit the Knight's helmet from beneath, hard, just missing the Knight's neck as the Knight dodged, and Cable watched the black helmet fly up and off the Knight's head.

Now Cable got a good look at the cornered man. There in the circle, Sir Percy of Scandia staggered, staring through the cloth mask that covered his face.

It had been pulled out of place by the removal of his helmet and the Knight reached up and tore it away to reveal the gaunt features of the man underneath, black hair flying with sweat, eyes betraying anger and more than a little fear. He knew he was losing, but his mouth erupted in a great cry as he ripped his sword around and caught the shoulder of one of his attackers. The ebony blade sank in and leather and studs went flying. The attacker fell back for a moment, and now Cable saw the distinct spark of wiring.

Cable raised his plasma rifle and fired, yelling, "Androids!"

The blast flew through the air and caught the wounded attacker in the upper chest, right between the shoulders. The Black Knight was momentarily stunned as the android began to shake and the blast tore a chunk out of its collar, sending its mechanical, helmeted head flying back to dangle from a few wires. The attacker staggered for a moment, as if confused by its sudden realignment, before reaching down to find the sword it had dropped and renewing its attack.

Cable was already running into the fray when he felt the wind begin to swirl and looked up to see Storm in the air, her arms outstretched, clouds beginning to spin in the air around him. Cable jumped and landed behind Sir Percy and slapped his back up against the Knight's as he fired his rifle again, tearing off the sword arm of another android. This one merely reached down and picked up his sword with his remaining arm.

"Magic user," the Black Knight said, panting, "I have no idea why you have come, but your aid is most welcome."

"These are artificial men," Cable said quickly.

"*And?*" the Knight said over his shoulder, giving a slight laugh. The Knight grunted as he slashed again at the android Cable had torn asunder and ripped away the leather on its chest, the black tip yanking out a cord. Something large and probably important erupted from the android's shoulders and the android jumped, swinging madly. The Black Knight kicked the android and it fell back, spinning until it hit a tree. The android stopped for a second, confused, then proceeded to attack the tree. "That's one down, I think," said the Knight.

"And we have nine more to go," Cable said, blasting one of them with his rifle and chambering another round. As he did so one of the androids slashed at him with its sword and the blade glanced off Cable's metal arm. Cable threw the android a nasty look as he grabbed the blade and ripped it away from the android's hand, sending it flying into the woods, then punched at the mechanical attacker, feeling metal fingers digging into the armor and wiring. He grabbed a few wires and wrenched his hand back out, tearing away the whole studded leather breastplate and leaving the android with a gaping, sparking hole in the center of its chest. He aimed for the hole, fired the rifle, and watched the blast disappear into the circuitry, before a twisting nest of sparks danced across the android's innards and exploded.

Cable looked up to see a sword coming right for his distinctly unhelmeted head and felt himself already too late, even as he aimed the rifle. Suddenly the very air ripped wide and a bolt of lightning slammed into the android's purple helmet, the sword arm freezing, the metal legs stuck to the ground. Cable felt the charge jagging through the very earth as the lightning bolt fried the android, causing it to erupt in flame. Cable kicked this one over and looked up at Storm, who moved higher, looking a bit weak. "How many of those you got?" he yelled.

Storm shook her head. "Another soon." She was yelling over the wind she had created to keep her aloft, and Cable could see in her eyes just how much energy it had taken to create a bolt big enough to short out such a powerful machine.

"This isn't right," Cable yelled. "This is technology far beyond that of our time."

"It is indeed," the Knight said. "Whatever you might mean by 'your time.' But they seem to be protecting—" he grunted as he deflected another blow from a faceless, inhuman attacker "—that casket." The Knight pointed quickly to the edge of the crossroads, where lay a black, oak box about three feet long. Cable had not noticed it. "I followed Merlin's advice and it led me here. I found this casket, and a number of knights, idly standing by. But when I tried to inspect the casket in the name of Arthur, I was attacked. I think there is great magic there."

"Something like that." Cable kicked an android head off and shot his plasma rifle down into the android's chest and kicked it away before it erupted, sending sharp metal bits flying, leather smoking and falling to the ground.

They were down to five attackers, and even Cable was beginning to get tired. He looked up at Storm and saw her struggle on the air, reaching up her fists and digging her nails into her palms as she reached out. The wind began to spin, her hair was flying, and he watched, mesmerized, as the air crackled above her and erupted, another bolt flying out and down, destroying another attacker. "Four left," Cable said. Storm had had it, and now she floated downward, the wind dying.

The Black Knight was hit across the chest and cried out in furious pain and anger, his leather tunic ripping across to reveal a thin line of blood. He swung his sword, bringing all fifty pounds up and over and down again in a mighty arc, and the great ebony blade sliced through the android's shoulder into its chest. The Knight, pulling on his sword, found it stuck there; he had to kick against the android to extract it. He stepped aside and shouted to Cable, "Yours," as Cable fired off another round at the android in front of him, just clipping the android's sword arm, and then swung to fire at the ripped-open target the Black Knight had just provided for him. This one received the plasma fire with fiery zeal, exploding in great gobs of melted wiring.

"Storm! See if you can get the casket to safety. That's the package!" Cable shouted.

Storm nodded and sprang for the casket. Immediately one of the remaining three androids saw her movement and went running after her. Storm dived for the casket and Cable saw the android grab her foot, pulling the wind-rider to the ground. Storm flipped over and kicked at the android. Ignoring her, it instead crawled, fighting Storm every inch of the way, until it finally reached the casket. As if considering, it picked up the casket and cradled it for a second. Storm hit the air and began to try to summon another bolt when suddenly the android spun around several times, holding the box like a discus.

"No!" shouted Cable, and at that very moment he heard another voice shout, "No!"

Cable turned to look over his shoulder to see a slim, brown-haired figure barely make it out of the trees in time to raise a plasma rifle and fire. The plasma bolt slammed across the crossroads and caught the spinning android in the chest, just as the android sent the casket flying into the air. The android was thrown back against a tree. The casket sailed high and into the night.

The other two androids watched the casket fly and immediately broke off their attack and headed for the thrown object, as if to go and guard it somewhere else. Then, in the blink of an eye, they sped up and rocketed through the trees, leaving only the Knight, the wind-rider, and Cable. And the mysterious person in the treeline.

Cable was watching the newcomer, looking for a face, but only making out long brunette hair and the padded fatigues that she wore as she turned and disappeared into the woods, chasing in the direction of the fleeing androids.

"No!" he had heard her cry. *No*, the voice played again, over the wind and plasma fire, *no*, Cable echoed in his mind, and took off running after her.

Cable ran through the forest, panting, jumping over trunks and under branches, until he saw the back of the newcomer's head, bobbing through the trees, the slender body moving as only a warrior's could, instantly comfortable in any terrain. He was about thirty yards behind her. *No, it can't be.* And now the figure stopped and removed from a pouch a large metal box, and seemed to consult it for a moment. Cable saw her put the box away, her back still turned, and begin to run again. But by now the distance had been closed.

He sprang, already knowing, even as he tackled this mysterious fleeing figure, shoulder slamming against her back and bringing her expertly and without injury rolling onto the ground. Grass flying past his face and she was cursing at him and trying for her gun, cursing in Askani—*in Askani*. Then they stopped rolling and he heard a familiar gasp. He knew, already. But he had to know for sure.

Cable, Nathan Dayspring, straddled the fleeing warrior and looked down into the stunned face of Aliya.

After a long, silent moment she said, "Askani'son."

# CHAPTER SEVEN

**M**y brother, war is hell on the homefront, too. Has to be.

Remy LeBeau patiently shook a small mound of tobacco into his rolling paper and leaned against the New York City bar. He slid his pouch of tobacco back into his coat, looking past the pool tables at the foggy windows. A police car passed by, rounded and smooth the way cars were in the 1940s, and the tall wheels sent a sheet of water up splashing against the walk and the window glass. He watched the reflections of the pool players in the window, listening to the sound of the rain slapping time. He let the cigarette lie on his lips for a while, and turned to face the bar, raising two fingers to get the attention of the bartender. The bartender, who busied himself with alternately polishing the bar and sizing up his patrons, finally made eye contact, staring up from beneath a liver-spotted brow beset by a few stubborn strands of gray hair. "Got a light?" Remy let the cigarette jump a bit as he talked through his teeth.

All around the room, the tables were adorned by women with big shoulders and sturdy hands, and curls that limped over their eyes, which were watching Bobby Drake and Remy LeBeau in much the way that a hawk watches a mouse. Bobby was playing pool and throwing the occasional smile to the girls at the table. Nearby, a couple of older gentlemen, too old for the front line, were sweet-talking a couple of what Remy took to be the factory girls. "A light?"

Someone spoke from behind Remy, silky and thick. "I do." Gambit's eyes shot forward at the reflection in the long, dull mirror behind the bar, and he saw the flick of a lighter in a cream-colored hand.

The flicker of the flame bounced in the mirror and in the tiny black eyes of a woman in a red dress. Her hair was blonde and pulled back in a 'do Remy remembered seeing on girl-reporter types in old movie serials. He smiled, turning back, as the flicker on the end of the slender arm lit his cigarette. He took a drag and sent a long, billowing stream of smoke into the air as she clapped the lighter shut, flicking her wrist, and slid into the seat next to him.

"Hey, stranger," she said.

"Hello, *p'tite.*" Gambit flicked back the long lock of auburn hair that had fallen over his eyes to get a better look at this creature. Well, he did need information, after all.

"What brings you two in here on a rainy night?" she asked, as she popped open a small purse and drew out a battered gunmetal cigarette case. From this she extracted a tailormade and tapped it on the bar a couple of times before lighting it.

"We two?" Gambit asked.

"You and your friend, there," the woman answered, gesturing with her lighter at Bobby Drake. Gambit looked back at Iceman to see his friend standing there like a wounded puppy, scratching his head and staring at the pool table. An old man with a hawk nose was lining up a shot, and Remy noticed that the old man was down to two balls on the table, to Bobby's six.

The old man chalked up his cue and sized up the table and said aloud, "Combo-five-six-eight, there," he nodded at his target corners, "five and six in the side, and eight-ball in the corner pocket." Gambit watched as the man took his shot, sending the cue into his first target, the balls clacking and spinning until all three were in motion, five and six bouncing off the far end and depositing neatly in the side, the eight ball missing the side by an inch and bouncing down to the opposite corner. Bobby merely stared, fumbling in his pocket for his wallet. Bobby looked like it was all he could do not to put on a newsboy cap and say, *Gosh, mister!*

Remy looked back at his new companion and then at the bartender. "It looks like we be losin'," he said. "How 'bout we get a couple old fashioneds for de *p'tite* and me?" The bartender nodded grimly and turned away to construct the cocktails as the girl continued.

"You two," she said, taking the glass that the bartender slid in front of her, "are a bit out of place."

"And why is dat?" Remy responded, looking down to see the old-fashioned appear. The bartender was staring for a moment, then looked away.

"Last I checked every eligible bachelor I ever knew was off shooting all the eligible bachelors of Europe."

Remy cleared his throat. "Dat's all de rage dis year, ain't it?" He looked back at Bobby, who was chalking up for another embarrassing loss to the old man. "Let's just say me and my friend got nowhere to be for a while."

The auburn-haired creature cradled her glass and hunched her catlike shoulders. She smiled out from underneath the hair that fell over her face before pushing it back again. "That's just fine," she purred. "Fine, fine."

"I'm Remy. Dat over dere is Bobby."

The girl extended what might as well have been a paw and said, "Kathryn."

"So," Gambit said, leaning on the counter, "you work in de factory?"

The bartender's hand came swiping with a cloth under Gambit's elbow and the man growled, "Everybody around here works in the factory, son, don't you know that?"

"Ain't from around here," Remy growled back, looking at the bartender briefly.

"It's true," the girl said. "Everybody that ain't in the army works the factory—most everybody, anyway. 'Cept maybe old Earl there." She pointed a dainty finger.

"Earl?" Gambit turned.

"The old man who's sweeping the floor with your brown-haired friend. Your friend wouldn't be a hustler, would he?"

Gambit laughed, "Bobby? Bobby ain't no hustler, he just a really bad pool player." In the background, someone was telling Bobby to put more English on it.

"We'll see," the girl said, "if he suddenly turns real good when they start betting."

Remy nodded. Inside his pocket, the Tracker was humming away. He looked at the clock and saw that they still had an hour and a half to midnight, when, enough information or not, he and Iceman were going to pay the factory a little visit. "So what does everybody who ain't in de army make for a living?"

"Oh," she said, "well, most of us gals are making forks and spoons. Not exactly Rosie the Riveter, but it's the last thing we expected before the war started."

"Huh," said Gambit. "Silverware. I can t'ink of worse t'ings to manufacture." He had worked in a factory once, briefly, in Baton Rouge. Hot sauce. Even now the smell of red chiles, falling in the gears and burning, came to his nose and stung his eyes. He had lasted four weeks, working in the heat and the wafting smoke of burning chiles. Gambit downed the last of his drink and took the girl's hand again, raising it up and kissing it lightly. "It's been a pleasure, Kathryn."

Kathryn pouted, still holding his hand as Remy slid off the barstool and looked at Bobby, raising a hand to get Iceman's attention. She purred again, "Leaving so soon? The evening's just getting started."

"Yes it is, *p'tite*," Remy said with a grin, "but I'm sure you have an early morning. Maybe I'll see you."

"Nothing else to wait for in this town," she said, and as Remy took a last look he couldn't help but notice what a perfect specimen of redhead he was forgoing because he wasn't supposed to engage the locals.

Remy joined Bobby, who was leaning on the pool table with his palms flat on the rim. Remy leaned in near Bobby's head. "Girls and old men," he said. "Girl at de counter says it's a silverware factory."

Bobby frowned as the old man sank the eight ball again. He pointed at the old man. "You're lucky I'm—ah—a good loser. I guess."

"Fi'dollars," the old man said, coming around the table with his palm outstretched. "You said fi'dollars."

"Yeah," Bobby said. He took his wallet out of his

snappy tan vest and flipped it open, and extracted a five-dollar bill. "Sorry I can't let you hustle me more."

"Ain't no hustler," the old man said, only barely looking wounded as he pocketed the five. "You're just a lousy pool player."

"Dat's why I never let him out," Remy said, patting Bobby on the shoulder. Remy waved at Kathryn, the lovely redhead, as he and Bobby made their way past the smoky tables and the old men and lonely women, and out onto the rainy streets of 1944 New York.

Behind him, the bartender quickly went to the phone.

"My God," Bobby said, as they tugged their coats around themselves and felt the rain hitting their faces, cold and stinging. "Did you see that? I felt like a piece of meat."

Remy grinned. "And you spent your time wit' de old men. You're a very model of a modern X-Man, Icicle Lad."

"Hey, I saw you making time with Ann-Margret's twin. We're supposed to keep 'interac-*shone*' to a minimum." Bobby's rebuke was intended to be an imitation of Remy's accent. It failed.

"I'm not de one who spent five dollars."

"I already thought of that," Bobby said. "And I checked out the money. The clothes-maker is a pretty nifty little Shi'ar machine. The money is even correctly dated. That five dollars will pass without incident."

"I don't know," Remy said. "Five dollars can

change history. Say he goes home and decides to spend it on—''

''No,'' Bobby said, ''it'll pass without incident because it'll dissolve. That's the cool thing. The money is extremely unstable.'' Bobby chuckled. ''It's like Spider-Man's webbing. By the time the guy gets home he'll have a pocketful of lint.''

Remy laughed. ''You just ripped dat guy off.''

''The guy was a shark.'' Bobby said. ''Anyway, it was easy money for him. Don't be thinking about perpetrating any major fraud, though—that money is supposed to be for nickel-and-dime stuff.''

''Fair enough,'' Remy said. ''But if we go back home and de White Queen is president or somet'ing, I'll assume it was your fault.'' He pulled the Tracker from his coat as they turned a corner. The item chirped as he flipped open the case, and he watched the rain mottle the golden veneer. ''At least I got to talk to dat *p'tite*. Dis way,'' Remy said.

The X-Men turned a corner and made their way through an alley, coats flapping in the rain as they jumped over cardboard boxes and scattered junk. They spilled out onto the sidewalk of the next avenue. Before them, across the street, stood a gigantic squarish stone building. The high, dirty windows with steel gratings over brown glass reminded Remy of refineries he had seen in Detroit—fascist looking, oppressive, monotonously gray and brown.

''So,'' Bobby said. ''You're powerful enough to send strange time-virus equipment through the timeline, and you hide it in a spoon factory?''

Remy flicked his cigarette into the street and watched the rain take the paper away as they walked across the street and began moving north alongside the factory. There was a security house in front, bordered by a high chainlink gate that stretched across the length of the factory and disappeared on either side. The factory was cradled by open lots on either side, and what appeared to be tenement buildings on either side of those. "Not a lotta empty spaces," he said as they passed the guard tower. Inside, the guard was talking on the phone, and did not look up. "Be tough to sneak in. I'm t'inkin' it ain't no spoon factory at all."

They turned left at the next block and came around the back, standing in the shadows of the tenements behind the factory. The back of the factory was even less cheery than the front—here was a gigantic gray wall, a few of those brownish windows toward the top, and a single gray door with no knob.

Iceman looked the building up and down and said, "I could build an ice bridge and go through the roof. There's got to be a—"

Remy was already walking across the rainy street. "You been an X-Man since you were a teenager, *oui*?"

"Yeah." Bobby walked a few steps behind Remy until they came up on the sidewalk, making straight for an iron door at the back of the factory.

"So I'm t'inkin' dat your formative years've been spent fightin' folks like Magneto an' all dat." He stopped at the door and reached up a gloved hand and quickly unscrewed the lamp over the door, then casually crushed the light bulb inside. The glass tinkled in the rain as Remy reached into his coat, fished around for a moment, and produced what appeared to be a pipe-cleaning set.

"So?"

"So all I'm sayin'," Remy said, looking to the left and then to the right as he folded out a long metal spike from the pipe cleaner, "is dat sometimes de easiest way—de good ol' gypsy street way—" he grunted for a moment as he stuck the rod in the lock and jerked it around, feeling for tumblers; presently he heard the familiar sound of metal knocking against metal as the lock opened to his will "—is de best way."

Bobby sighed. "You may have a point."

Remy tugged on the wire and the door slid out a few centimeters, so he could get his fingers on the side of the door and pull a bit. "Door ain't been used in a while." He grunted as the rusty hinges whined and the door scraped against the frame.

The door was just coming free from the frame when a whistle split the air. Bobby and Remy looked in the direction the sound had come from; a flashlight shone in their faces. "You there!" the man behind the flashlight bellowed. Remy made out the shape of the security guard he had seen on the phone, running toward them with a flashlight in one hand and a pistol in the other. "Stop right there!"

"Rent-a-cop," Remy grumbled.

"Hello, officer," Bobby said, stepping toward the approaching watchman, holding out his hands. "What seems to be the problem?"

"Just step away from the door, boys," the guard said. He wore a policeman's hat, but underneath Remy could make out the pronounced lines and crow's feet on the man's face. Everybody young was at war. "Got a call there was a couple a—"

Bobby's eyes glazed for a moment and Remy watched as the very air surrounding Bobby's hands swirled white, as if soaking up energy. Suddenly there was an audible *crack* in the air as chunks of ice formed at Bobby's fingertips. The ice swelled up and flew forward at the guard, a stream of frozen rain slamming into the man's gun hand. The gun began to fall and froze in the air as Bobby flexed his fingers, the ice congealing up the man's arm and sticking him there. The man began to scream even as the barrage stopped, his arm stuck in a frozen chunk that started just below his shoulder.

"We don't mean to be any trouble," Bobby said, as he fired another bolt at the guard's feet and froze them to the floor. Now the man was silent, wheezing with fear, and Remy could swear there were particles of ice swirling in front of Bobby's eyes. He was about to congeal entirely.

"Sometimes the street way is the best way, huh?" Bobby said, looking back with a wry smile and very icy look. He said to the rent-a-cop, "Like I said, we don't want any trouble. Now, don't move, or you might break something."

The rain was coming down in sheets now, pelting the guard's frozen limbs and leaving rivulets in them. Remy was sliding the door open as Bobby said, "My friend and I are going to go about our business."

"I don't think so," came a voice from above, as a sheet of steam shot past Remy and Bobby and the street lit up like Christmas. The rumbling voice was deep and strangely resonant, almost—synthetic?

Remy looked up and saw what appeared to be a giant ball of flame in the sky. No—*two* of them, steaming in the rain, flaming like Roman candles. Remy pulled out a pair of Jacks as the air around Bobby swirled and slammed into him, covering him with a thick layer of ice from head to toe.

"Who de hell is dat?" Gambit asked.

The crystallized being that had a moment before been Bobby Drake smiled an icy smile. "I don't believe it," he said. "It's the Human Torch. And Toro, I think."

"Torch is wit' de FF—"

"No, the *original* Human Torch," Bobby said with a grin.

Then a jet of flame smacked him in the chest and sent him back against the wall, steam and ice flowing freely.

# CHAPTER EIGHT

O n about the ninth rendition of Neil Young's "The Needle and the Damage Done" played on harmonica by Peter Parker, Bishop let go of the bars he had been gripping until his fingers went pale and turned around, snarling. "Would you *please . . . stop . . . that.*"

Peter tilted back his cowboy hat and looked up from the harmonica he had managed to borrow from the deputy. He had his pointy-toed boots crossed and resting on the edge of the bunk, and he had to part the boots a bit to get a look at Bishop. Outside the bars, across the jail, the deputy was reading the *Tombstone Gazette* and only briefly looked up at Bishop's outburst. Peter tapped the harmonica in his palm a couple times and said, "I'll play something else. Do you have any requests? I should add that the only other song I know is 'Freebird.' "

Bishop exhaled deeply through his nose and sounded like an ill-tempered bull. He turned back around to face the bars while Peter played a few notes and then skipped right to singing, *"Byyyyyyeee, byyyye, Freeeee-biiirrrrddd."*

"Cartwright," Bishop said.

*"Byye, byyyye—"*

"Cartwright, if you don't shut up I will cram that harmonica—"

Spider-Man laughed. "C'mon, Li'l Joe. How many times are you gonna be in an actual Wild West jail, complete with a harmonica-playing bunkmate?"

"After I'm done I think you'll find playing the harmonica to be an entirely new kind of experience, Cartwright."

"Okay, okay," Peter said, leaning forward, gingerly letting the harmonica dangle between his thumb and forefinger. "Holding out the instrument, setting it down. You really are a tough nut, Bish," Peter grumbled, as he leaned back on the bunk, folding his arms. "*I'm* the one who's risking being late for dinner."

"You're not acting like it."

"There's two possibilities about that, Li'l Joe. Either I'm an idiot and I'm completely unaware of the situation, or I like to pass the time by making light," Peter observed. Mary Jane was at home waiting for him even now. He kept having to remind himself that time was ticking away in 1998 just as much as it was here in 1867. They had already killed two hours in Tombstone, an hour of which they had now spent in the Tombstone jail, which was a nice enough place, but hardly where one would choose to spend a full third of one's vacation. "With all due respect, I think you could cut me some slack. *You're* the one who said to surrender to the cowboy without a fight."

Bishop turned around again, keeping his voice low. "If I must remind you, Cartwright, this is no alternate timeline we're making here." He stabbed at the ground with his finger, punctuating his words. "This is *your* timeline. Cable told us not to interfere with history. We have to find the packages and get out of here—we've probably involved ourselves too much already, just by virtue of finding ourselves in this court system." Bishop paced a little bit, then looked out the square, barred window at the sun. "Anyway, it'll be dark in an hour. I think we can break out then. We'll have spent only three hours so far, that'll leave us three hours in which to work. Oh, and we'll need to get the Tracker back.''

''Fair enough,'' Spider-Man said. ''But while we're in jail I think I'll pass the time as best beguiles it. I could do a rousing rendition of 'Whipping Post.' ''

Bishop turned around and groaned audibly.

''Okay, how about 'Bad Company'?'' That suggestion was met with the type of look that people are talking about when they use the phrase *if looks could kill*. Peter pulled his hat down over his face.

After a while he asked, ''What are you thinkin', Bish?''

Bishop snarled into the bars once again. ''I'm wondering what I did to Cable that made me deserve you for a partner.''

''You're going to hurt my feelings here in a minute. And we all know what that means, don't we, harmonica lovers?''

''Shh,'' Bishop said, as the jailhouse door opened, casting a beam of bright light into the room. The deputy hopped up, bringing his hat down in a respectful manner.

''Why, Miss Carter, what a sight fer sore eyes,'' he said.

Peter sat up straight and looked past Bishop and through the bars to see the pretty blonde who had just come through the doorway. She wore a long brown skirt and a white cotton blouse. For a moment the door remained open and she was an angel, surrounded in rays of light that filtered through her hair and seemed to seep from sparkling blue eyes. ''Good

God,'' he whispered. ''That's the woman in the picture.''

The woman smiled at the deputy as she shut the door behind her. In her arms was a basket with a quaint checkered cloth over the top, and Peter's nose twitched with the smell of fresh bread. ''Deputy Kelso,'' the woman said, ''hope you're not working too hard guardin' your latest guests, here.'' She tilted her head toward Bishop and Peter, who had risen to stand beside the X-Man. Peter hung on the bars next to Bishop and felt himself staring.

''Say, Li'l Joe,'' Peter whispered.

''What?''

''Is it okay to stare at a woman if your wife is a hundred years away?''

Bishop actually smirked at that. Peter had heretofore thought him incapable of the expression. ''Why don't you ask her when you get back?''

''Right.''

''And how are you boys doin'?'' the woman drawled, as she turned to the two prisoners and walked toward the cell. Peter took off his hat and brought it down in front of him, feeling like Tom Sawyer. Bishop kept his on.

''Just, ah, just fine, ma'am,'' Peter heard himself say.

''Brought you boys some supper,'' she said, indicating the basket. ''Deputy, you mind opening up this cell for me for a moment?''

''Oh, sure, Miss Carter, absolutely,'' the deputy said. It was amazing, really, how well she controlled people. The deputy was falling over himself finding keys to open up the cell door for her, nervously smiling as he did so. Peter had the profound suspicion that she'd make a great bank robber. Deputy Kelso left the cell door open and Miss Carter waltzed in and set the basket down on the simple wooden bench against the wall next to Peter's cot, and immediately began to pull out a pair of plates, a few utensils, and the aforementioned supper.

Peter had a moment's panic about the supper he was running the risk of missing, but squelched it when he realized how incredibly hungry he was. He'd just pretend to be hungry later. "Is that sourdough?"

"Sure is," she said, laying out a hunk of bread on each plate and a thick slab of butter between. "Can't have you boys starvin' in the jail just 'cause ol' Two-Gun thinks yer Carter boys."

"And," Bishop said, tilting his head, "who are you, again?"

The woman turned around and held out her hand, which Bishop took and shook gingerly. "Nancy Carter," she said. "I teach school here in Tombstone, but sometimes I do a favor or two. 'Specially where my notorious brother manages to get a couple folks in trouble. Matt says he don't figure you for the Carter-Gang type. Lookin' at you two now, I think I see what he means."

Peter nodded. "Thanks for the vote of confidence," he said. "And, ah, thanks for the supper." He sat down on the bench as Bishop did the same, and the two looked at the bread for a moment. Peter had the impression they were each sizing all this up for a trap of some kind. Then they just decided to go ahead and eat. "So, ah," Peter said, swallowing a hunk of bread. The butter had honey in it and the effect on his throat was like fresh milk; he felt the dryness just smooth out and roll away. *Gosh, Miss Carter.* The door was opening again and Peter saw two more figures enter the jail. "So if your brother is Clem Carter, who sent you, who told you we were here?"

"That'd be me," came a masculine voice, and Peter looked up to see a tall blond man in a dark blue suit, and even a hundred years from home, Peter knew this just had to be a lawyer. At the chiseled-featured man's neck was a nifty bolo tie attached with a genuine Italian cameo. Tombstone Lawyer was stylin'. "Name's Matt Hawk," he said, as he waltzed into the cell. Behind him strode the sheriff, who Peter had met briefly when the burly, red-haired officer took him and Bishop off Two-Gun's hands and threw them into their cell.

*Matt Hawk. I know that name*, Peter thought. *Why do I know that name?*

The dramatically named lawyer was carrying a satchel, which he set down on Peter's bunk and sifted through for a moment. The man looked up briefly and cast a long glance at Nancy Carter, who was busying herself with packing up some of the picnic items. She met Matt's gaze and Peter suddenly felt as if there were entirely too many people in his cell. "Hello, Nancy," Matt said.

"Matt."

The lawyer looked at Peter and Bishop. "I reckon you boys are my clients for now, seein' as how there're no other lawyers in town. I've convinced Sheriff Busey here to let you boys out on PR."

"PR?" Bishop asked.

"Personal recognizance," the lawyer nodded. "Meaning we're hoping you'll stick around for as long as we need you to, but we're not gonna hold you in jail."

"Matt," said the sheriff, his sunburned face glowing under his red hair, "I don't know that that's such a good idea."

"Aw, Charlie, I know that," Matt said. "But that's your job. You're a sheriff. If I let you have your way, you'd never let anyone wait for trial."

"I'm sorry," Peter said, "but I'm not sure what we're being charged with."

"The charge," Matt sighed as he tossed a sheet marked COURT ORDER on Peter's bunk, "is conspiracy to commit armed robbery of a stagecoach."

The sheriff nodded. "Leastways that's the way it looked to Two-Gun."

"Yeah," Matt Hawk said, nodding. "Well, the Kid's a little overzealous sometimes. It's a tough town; so I guess he does what he feels he has to. But I'm not as convinced you need to be held."

Peter smiled, but not too widely, finally placing the name, kicking himself for not having done so sooner. Even if he hadn't read up on the Two-Gun Kid's history just that morning, he knew a secret identity when he saw one.

"Now," Matt said, "I don't figure you boys for the Carter-Gang type, but Sheriff Busey is a little concerned about these . . . items," he said, as he reached into the satchel and pulled out the large round recall device. Peter was still wearing the straps—he had managed to convince the sheriff to let him just unhook the metal device when the sheriff demanded to know what it was. That had saved him the trouble of revealing the Spider-Man suit underneath. The device thudded against the bunk, followed by Peter's web-shooters, which glistened bright and silvery. Next came Peter's pocket watch, the face of which had been popped up to reveal the mysterious Tracker screen underneath, beeping away. Matt surveyed the haul for a moment and then said to the sheriff, "Charlie, ya wanta get me that shotgun?"

Charlie stepped out and appeared a moment later with Bishop's disguised plasma rifle in hand, and handed that to Matt.

Matt hefted the gun and said to Bishop, "This yours?"

Bishop nodded. "Yes."

"Heavy. Mighty funny cartridges in there too. Here." He popped open the magazine and let the plasma cartridges fall on the bunk, then gathered them and dropped them back in his satchel. Then he tossed the weapon to Bishop. "You get your ammo when you leave. Now, what is all this stuff?"

Peter looked down at the Tracker, the recall device, and the web-shooters and said, "Souvenirs."

"Come again?"

Peter looked at Bishop, who merely sighed and closed his eyes in unmasked derision. "Yeah," the wall-crawler said, "Li'l Joe and I just come in from the World's Fair."

"World's Fair?" Matt blinked. "In New York?"

"Yes, sir," Peter said. "These here are souvenirs from the Jules Verne exhibit."

"Jules Verne exhibit," the sheriff repeated, as if these were three words he had never heard before.

Matt looked at the sheriff. "He's a writer. He's, ah, French."

"French," the sheriff repeated.

Matt nodded, staring at the items. He scratched the back of his neck dramatically and finally said, "Well, they ain't weapons, Charlie. So I figure my clients and I are probably okay to go on that."

Sheriff Busey curled his lip for a moment and finally said, "Matt, you sure you wanta just let these boys walk?"

"They're walkin' with *me*," Matt said, patting Peter's shoulder. "I'll keep an eye on 'em. I'm figuring a couple guys hauling French souvenirs are probably good payin' clients. Right, boys?"

"Absolutely," Bishop said.

"And how do I know you ain't runnin' from somewhere *you* need to be?"

Bishop looked as if he were suppressing a snarl. But then, he always looked like that. *Let it go*, Peter thought. *We need out of here.*

Matt stepped in and said, "Charlie, tell ya what, I'll check and see if there's descriptions for 'em back East. We'll make sure everything's on the level." He was already guiding Peter and Bishop out of the cell, quickly putting the items back into his satchel. "Don't you worry."

"I think you're bending over a little too far backward, Matt."

"That's me," Matt said, as they walked quickly out of the jail. As they got outside Matt stuck his head back in and shouted, "Trust me. Oh, and Nancy? Always pleasant seeing you."

Peter and Bishop stood in front of the jailhouse

and looked at the dusty streets, feeling a bit like children waiting for a parent to return. When Matt reappeared at their side he touched them both on the arm and said, "Let's walk. I wanta put some distance between us and Charlie in case he's tempted to change his mind."

A few minutes later they were sitting in a quaint saloon run by a pleasantly plump lady who lavished a great deal of attention on Matt Hawk. As she brought them a round of drinks and disappeared again, smiling broadly, Peter observed, "You have this town wrapped around your finger, counselor."

"I do my job adequately. I've helped a few o' these folks out of scrapes."

"Does everyone in this town need a lawyer?"

"I like to think of myself as a last best friend," Matt said, taking a drink. "Now. How's about you fellas tell me the truth."

"The truth?" Bishop asked.

Matt's eyes twinkled. There were lines baked into his cheeks, and they gave him the appearance of a wizened old man and a young heartthrob at once. "Jules Verne exhibit," he said. "Mr. Cartwright, there's no World's Fair in New York this year."

Peter and Bishop traded glances and finally Peter started, "Well . . ."

"Two-Gun tells me that you were watchin' that wagon train pretty hard. And more than that, he tells me there's something mighty strange about it. Maybe you two can start by telling me a little something about what my friend saw back there." He tossed his satchel to Peter, and Peter set to pulling out the various devices and replacing them on his person. Bishop pocketed his shells casually, remaining his stoic self.

Peter leaned in. "Your . . . friend . . . saw a lot more than you let on back there at the jail."

"I keep his confidence pretty close."

"Yeah," Peter nodded. "Okay. It so happens that Joe and I are agents of the federal government, and that wagon train is of particular interest to us. It's . . . more than it seems."

"Mister," Matt said, "I saw three wagons turn themselves over and right themselves again. I saw people fire guns I've never seen before and give the Carter Gang a scare I don't think Two-Gun could ever dream of."

Peter enjoyed listening to someone else casually talk about himself in the third person. "Right. I hope you'll understand if we can't tell you any more about all that. We do appreciate your help in getting us out of jail, though, because we are a bit short on—" he paused for a moment, looking past Matt and out the big window that said SALOON and across the street to where the lovely Nancy Cartwright had stopped on the curb; he stood and reached out his hand and shook Matt's "—time. Thank you again, Mr. Hawk. But we have a schedule to keep."

Peter and Bishop rose. As they stepped away from the table, Matt sipped his beer and raised an eyebrow. "Government agents. I liked the World's Fair better. I'll be seein' you boys real soon."

"I'm sure," said Peter.

Once they were on the street again Peter made for the street corner where Nancy Carter still stood. At the corner was a man with a tall, bulky camera, a few props, glass plates, various chemicals, and a big sign that said, PICTURES 25¢—REMEMBER YOUR LOVED ONES. As Peter and Bishop got closer they overheard the man pleading with Miss Carter. "Aw, c'mon, Miss Carter. Just one picture."

"Oh," she said, grinning, "I shouldn't."

"For free, o'course," the photographer said. "Just havin' the picture to show oughta bring in clients. What say?"

"Yeah, what say?" Peter yelled as they came closer.

"Cartwright," Bishop hissed, "what are you wasting time with now?"

Peter took Bishop by the shoulder—which was something of a strain, even for him—and leaned in. "Think, Li'l Joe. That picture I found in the museum. This is the girl from the picture." He looked up at Bishop. "We have to preserve history, right?"

Bishop stared. "What if this is what gets us stuck?"

Peter shrugged. "What if it's necessary?"

The giant man furrowed his brow. "Fine."

Peter spun around and clapped his hands together, "Miss Carter?"

"Hello, boys," she said. "Back in action, I see."

"Actually," Peter said, "I was hoping that you would allow your stunning portrait to be taken with a couple of friendly out-of-towners."

She tilted her head. "And why would a couple of out-of-towners want to have a picture taken with an ol' grade-school teacher like me?"

Peter smiled, but he felt the gravity enter his eyes as he realized she might actually say no. "We want to be remembered when we're gone."

Nancy Carter looked at Peter and Bishop, maybe even perceived that they were pleading with her, just a little, not enough to scare her away but just enough to convince her. "Why, all right."

"Excellent," the photographer said. "If you two gentlemen would just stand on either side . . ."

Peter put his arm around the Nancy as the cameraman disappeared under a black hood to focus. Peter glanced at Bishop's glowering, mountainous form, and back at the camera. Then the photographer removed the lens cap and counted the seconds of exposure. Those seconds seemed to last forever, because Peter realized how very, very long it would be before that picture came to him again.

A quarter hour later the sun was going down and Bishop and Peter were topping a hill on the way out of town. "They're camped a couple miles out," Peter said, watching the Tracker. "We need to hurry."

Suddenly the sound of horse's hooves cut through the air and the two men turned around to see a man riding toward them. Peter made out the red mask and tall hat immediately. "Two-Gun." Next to the Kid, following close, was a second, riderless horse.

Peter held up his hand as the Kid slowed and brought his horse to a halt next to them. The bright blue eyes shone in the rising moonlight. "I hear you boys're lookin' for a wagon train."

"Yes, we are," Bishop said, eyeing the empty horse.

"You," Two-Gun pointed at Peter, "hop on. Li'l Joe—or whatever your name is—you take this'un. And treat her right—she belongs to a friend." The second horse was white, with brown spots, and looked big enough to handle Bishop's weight without any trouble.

"Absolutely," Bishop said, as he came around and put his boot in the stirrup, swinging up onto the back of the filly. "Mind telling us why you're helping us?"

"Why should I be the only one who ever answers questions around here?" responded the man in the mask. The Two-Gun Kid looked over his shoulder at Peter, who tried to make himself comfortable on the back of the horse, putting his hands on Two-Gun's hips. "Let's just say this is my territory and I wanta keep close track. Now I know you got some sorta newfangled compass there, so tell me where to go."

"Northwest," Peter said. "And I figure we have a little over one—"

"Hyah!" Two-Gun called, whipping the reins, and the two horses started at a walk, then increased to a steady, fast clip.

After another twenty minutes of riding, Peter found himself lying at the top of a ridge next to Bishop and the Two-Gun Kid. They had left the horses about a quarter mile back, so their equine silhouettes wouldn't be visible to the wagon train, which, they now saw, lay before them next to another bend in the river.

"They're camped and circled," Two-Gun said. "I see two campfires. Looks like they got sentries posted at every corner."

"I count eight," Bishop nodded. "Maybe another eight inside the circle. This is not going to be easy."

Two-Gun looked at Peter. "So all you want is to get this . . ."

"Package."

"Right. This package. You want to steal it from them?"

"Well . . ."

"No, no, that's fine, they ain't human, I know, so don't worry about sellin' me there. But what's the big deal?"

"Let's just say it's extremely dangerous," Peter said.

"Extremely," Bishop repeated.

"All right." The Kid nodded slowly. "But I take it you don't know what this package looks like."

"That's . . . true," Peter said, bringing up the Tracker, "but this thing's led me this far, I'm hoping I can figure out the rest."

"Seems to me that whatever they guard the most," Bishop whispered, "is probably what we want."

"Well, there's four wagons," Two-Gun said. "It's gotta be on one of them. I don't mind telling you, though, I'm not sure how much my six-shooters are gonna help against those guns they got."

"This is our problem," Peter said. "You've done enough already."

"Bull," Two-Gun responded. "We're just getting started. I can hold my own. I just wanted to make you aware of just how outmatched we are here." Down below, the denizens of the wagon train were sitting around the campfire, oddly still, the perfect rendition of a bunch of regular robotic Joes on a wagon train.

"Consider us aware."

Peter sighed and began to remove his overcoat, letting it fall behind him. He turned over and removed his boots and pants to reveal the blue-and-red Spider-

Man suit underneath as Two-Gun stared, then began to remove the shirt.

"Son, what in hell—"

"I'm going down there," he said.

Two-Gun sized up the wall-crawler and said, "What do you plan to do, show 'em yer longjohns?"

"You laugh," Peter said, "but these longjohns are a lot easier to work in than that duster." He winked, then pulled a piece of cloth out of a hidden pocket on the red stripe around his waist and pulled it over his head, feeling the comfortable and familiar warmth of cloth pinning down his ears, his vision brightening in the eyepieces of the mask. Next he slipped on his red gloves, and the transformation was complete.

"I have no words," Two-Gun said.

"We call him Spider-Man." Bishop curled his lip. "Humor him."

"Being nice is just beyond you, isn't it?" Spider-Man flipped over again and arched his back, looking over the ledge. "Here goes nothing."

Over the ridge and stepping lightly in the darkness, the web-slinger was suddenly on his own, and liked it. Humans walked on two legs, and Peter Parker had been born to be a human, a gangling head balancing above a neck, walking like people walk, with arms swinging as counterweights to the constant balancing act that was the inelegant human walk. The spider was different: the spider moved as one entire piece, all portions together, feeling out and sliding forward. Peter Parker had received the bite, and he had learned to move as a spider does—or as close as his human body would allow—his weight distributed evenly, no part of his body out of place.

There was a sentry by a gnarled tree, a six-foot fellow with a hat pulled low. As Spider-Man crept close his spider-sense buzzed back in his brain: *Danger—this man is not what he seems.* There were other sentries posted thirty yards away on either side.

Spider-Man scanned the tree next to the sentry, making out the shape of a nesting grackle. The wall-crawler began to roll and flexed his fingers, the tips of them touching his web-shooters, and a line of webbing flew at the tree. The webbing smacked into the grackle's nest; the black bird squawked, rising into the air, and the sentry turned to look at it. Spider-Man rolled a few more times, came up on his toes, and sprang, coming over again on his hands and pushing again, lightly, as if he weighed nothing, and his body flew through the air and landed ten yards within the sentry line, all in the moment the sentry had looked away. The sentry saw the grackle fly out of the tree and flutter before nesting again, then swiveled his head back to its prior position.

The earth was a web of countless points and weights, and Spider-Man crept low, feeling his way until he reached the nearest wagon, crawling in underneath and taking refuge for a moment in the dark spot between the front and rear wheels underneath the chuck wagon. He looked around at the vehicle, expecting to see the disguised but complex rigging that had been so useful to the wagon train back at the battle with the Carters. In fact, looking across at the next wagon, and all of them, Peter could feel the alienness of them, the distinct tinge that came from a thing disguised. There was no such rigging here—this was just an old chuck wagon, a battered wooden monstrosity most likely stolen and used as a model for the high-tech engines that the sentries guarded so zealously.

*Who is doing this? Who has access to that kind of technology and time travel?* Spider-Man rattled off a short list in his brain of technologically gifted megalomaniacs and decided he was wasting time trying to discover the culprit. He pulled out the Tracker device and watched the arm sweep around. There was little time left.

The Tracker had increased in brightness until the swiveling arm had to change color again to stay contrasted. Spider-Man watched the bright spot on the screen light up and looked across at one of the chuck wagons, and nodded to himself. That had to be the one. However, there happened to be eight men sitting stonefaced at a campfire in the middle of the circle.

The wall-crawler stared at the men around the campfire. One of them idly stirred the coals with a stick—except there was nothing particularly idle about his movements. Another man casually drank from a tin cup, except that he had all the casualness of Bishop. Spider-Man thought of those displays one finds at Macy's around Christmastime, little robot elves doing casual things like darning socks, or whatever elves did once the rush was over. It was just a programmed movement, and the more casual the movement was supposed to be, the odder it looked. Never mind that every one of them wore a low-slung hat and he had yet to see an actual face or hear an actual word uttered by the silent crowd; these guys, Spider-Man was now certain, just weren't human.

Spider-Man crept backward outside the wagon circle, and decided the best way to get to the wagon with the package in it was walk along their tops. Outside or inside, he'd be too easily seen, but with any luck they wouldn't be routinely scanning the roofs of the wagons.

The chuck wagon is a vehicle built for travelling in extreme heat. The top is mostly cloth: there are generally six or seven heavy wirelike rods moving from the front of the wagon to the back, giving the wagon its rounded form. All of this is covered over with a cloth, heavy enough to keep the sun away from the people inside, although usually light enough in color to reflect more heat than it absorbs.

Spider-Man sprang up and felt his toes land on the rearmost wire. He balanced there for a second, his toes dropping through the cloth, lowered his body, and stretched forward to touch his fingers to the fourth wire down. He stayed there for a moment, gauging just how he was going to be able to move on these things.

Then he stopped thinking and listened to his spider-sense. He started to move, touching fingers and toes to the wires and reaching the front of the wagon, flipping through the air and landing on the next wagon. He heard the wagon creak audibly as he did so and winced, berating himself for forgetting that even if he could move like a man on a web, he still weighed one hundred and sixty-five pounds. He had to get over this wagon and the next before reaching his target. *Don't let that happen again.*

This next wagon he moved over more gracefully, getting a better feel for the distribution of his weight over the tiniest points on the wire, springing from the front to land deftly on the rearmost wire of the next, no sound emanating from it. Perfect. The package was in the next wagon; all he had to do was—

Spider-Man was stepping forward when his foot stopped on one of the metal cords and he felt his spider-sense sing out and scream up and down his spine. Even as his toes touched the center of the rod he could feel the flaw in its manufacture—it was just a mockup, not enough that it would collapse but just enough that it would . . .

*Snap.*

Spider-Man gasped and felt his foot plunge through the tan tarp as the rod broke at its soldering point and gave underneath him. He felt himself falling through the roof of the wagon, cloth ripping loudly as he went through, banging his shoulders on the rods, the one that had split tearing a gash in his side. He could not suppress a brief yelp of pain as he crashed into the storage space underneath, his spider-sense wailing in his brain. The wall-crawler slammed into the wooden floor of the chuck wagon and looked around—it was empty. He had begun to creep (*no one heard that no one heard that*) forward when he heard a strange hum from outside, like someone switching on a nuclear device, and Spider-Man could actually envision the "men" around the campfire swiveling their heads toward the chuck wagon and rising as one.

He moved forward toward the front entrance, calming himself, finding his equilibrium, and as he touched his fingers to the floor he heard a charging whine and a tiny, audible *klikt.* Immediately after that, a bolt of plasma tore a chunk the size of a tractor tire out of the side of the chuck wagon, ripping through the other side after grazing Spider-Man's back, and disappearing in the distance.

Spider-Man sprang through the roof and up into the air, hitting the rod on the next wagon and jumping again as one of the sentries charged up and fired off another round. "Bishop," he cried, "I think I got their attention!"

He landed on the outside of the target wagon, hearing the tracker in his belt beeping as if excited by having found its mate. Spider-Man heard that charging whine and looked forward, seeing a shape step from behind the tree, levelling a very large and decidedly non-nineteenth-century weapon at him. He began to spring again as he heard the bolt fly, heard the plasma burst searing the air. As Spider-Man landed seven feet to the left he saw the plasma burst he had heard punch a hole right through the sentry, and he watched tiny particles of what might have been gears and wiring flying and melting as they spat out of the hole.

As the man fell forward, Spider-Man saw Bishop come into view, reloading the magazine of his disguised plasma rifle with a vicious *ker-chunk* sound. Bishop, with Two-Gun close behind, stepped to the man that Bishop's fire had just torn in half and looked down. The hole through the man was fizzling brightly, popping with tiny arcs of red and blue.

"Androids," Spider-Man said. "I knew it."

"Who would send—"

"Bishop!" Spider-Man exclaimed. Suddenly his spider-sense was singing the *Carmina Burana* in his brain and swirling around that android and he ran forward and grabbed Bishop and yanked him into the air and past the tree, slamming him to the ground. Two-Gun dived to join them as the android exploded, sending a minor shock wave through the air and burning the grass near them. Spider-Man sat up as Bishop shook his head gruffly. "Wow," the wall-crawler said, "someone's very worried about leaving evidence."

"What in hell are these fellers?" Two-Gun asked, as a pair of sentries came running.

"It's a long story, pal," Spider-Man said. "Just try to stay alive." He turned to Bishop. "Bish—we're dealing with a master—Dr. Doom, maybe, someone who knows robots and time travel, and is very comfy with both. What I'm saying is," Spider Man cocked his head, "don't make any mistakes. He won't allow for it."

Bishop nodded. The chuck wagons began to move apart as more sentries came running. "Let's just get the package."

And suddenly, the engines began to whine, and the heroes began to move, and the sky lit up with plasma fire.


Blaquesmith craned his neck at the four sets of lines on the monitor as Professor Xavier spoke, his chair whirring as he swiveled.

"Bishop and Spider-Man?"

"Very near the package," Blaquesmith said. "They're right on top of it. However, they are moving around quite a bit; I believe they have encountered resistance."

"Wolverine and the Beast?"

"Heading in the right direction. Iceman and Gambit also seem to have met with resistance. It is safe to assume that every one of our teams has been anticipated and met with force." He sighed.

"Why can't we follow their efforts on the monitors?" Professor Xavier asked. The laboratory was quiet except for the two men, both studying the Time Displacement Core intently.

"I was afraid of this," Blaquesmith shook his head, his bulbous eyes blinking slowly. "But this is an unusual endeavor. The Core is diverting too much power to keeping the timeline together, and with every move our teams make, there is tremendous potential for a shift in the entire timeline. In essence, the points at which our teams lie are . . . amorphous. Constantly reshaping. There's just not a steady picture to lock on to, even had I the power to divert to doing it. The best we can do is follow the lines and the raw indications—and I'm only using the power it takes to do that because we must lock on to the homing mechanism on their recall devices when the time comes." He tapped his cane on the timelines, showing the moving shades that represented the packages and the teams.

The Professor looked at the screen and tilted his head. "Hm. What about Cable and Storm?"

"Moving toward it," the Askani wizard said, "but it's being moved as well. They're chasing it."

The Professor indicated another strange blip that had appeared on the screen. "What is that anomaly on the Cable and Storm timeline?"

Blaquesmith pointed a bony finger and wagged it. "This is a mystery that concerns me greatly."

"What is it?"

"I have no idea. But I think it may be . . . another team."

"Another . . ."

Now Blaquesmith sucked in air, ragged and deep, and his eyes swiveled outside his head, rolling back. "Or . . . how . . . how?" He reached out a long, leathery hand and touched his finger to the screen. "Just a dot, but I *know* you, don't I, I can *feel* you, can't I?"

The Professor wheeled forward alongside Blaquesmith, who was humming softly to himself. "Blaquesmith. You know this team?"

"It may not be a team. It may be but one. But whoever it is, I sense . . . no, I can say it, I sense *her*. Oh, Nathan, oh no, oh no, not now. Not when so many lives are at stake."

"Who is it, Blaquesmith?"

"Someone Cable wants to find very badly," Blaquesmith said, "and who could not have been found at a worse time."

Suddenly their was a hiss in the air of the laboratory and Blaquesmith looked over his shoulder. "What . . . ?"

The Professor swiveled around as the air itself began to shimmer and spin with thin bands of color and light, spinning around, and Blaquesmith could see shapes beginning to congeal.

"We're under attack," Xavier said.

Suddenly the first shape took form, the boots hitting the concrete floor as the whole body congealed, a man in a green-and-purple padded suit, a metallic green mask covering his face. Behind the masked man a team fell into place, popping out of the ether, gigantic plasma guns whining to life and charging up. Blaquesmith threw a force shield of energy around himself and the Professor, hoping it might provide even the slightest defense against the army of ten troopers who had just invaded from nowhere.

"Not you," came the voice of the green-masked soldier in front. "You're incidental," he hissed.

"Who are you?" asked the Professor. "What business do you have?"

"We serve Kang," said the man in front as the troopers fell in and surrounded Blaquesmith and the Professor, leveling their weapons at the two. "And we have come to relieve you of the Core."

On the monitor the teams blinked away, unaware of just how close to being lost in time they were.

# CHAPTER NINE

"This way," Wolverine said, as he jumped over a fallen tree and immediately sprang into the air again. "Quicksand there; look out." He hit the ground moving, his head swiveling slowly and smoothly, the animal senses reaching out. Logan stopped and looked around, nostrils flaring.

The Beast came up behind and stopped, looking around, scanning the depths of the prehistoric jungle. Within seconds they were joined by the boy, who said a few unintelligible words in the language of his tribe. There was a heavy thudding of earth and suddenly the Devil Dinosaur appeared behind them all, the massive red head swooping down as if to join them in their conversation.

Wolverine was staring into the woods and glanced at the Devil Dinosaur. "I'm tryin' to pick up the girl's scent," he said to the Beast. "But right now about all I can smell is Red Ryder here."

"I suggest you try to ignore our protoiguanodon compatriot," the Beast said, and it was always odd to hear that smooth, almost fey voice coming out of a man who looked like he belonged more in these prehistoric times. "That girl is risking the lives of billions because she thinks the Tracker is *pretty*."

Wolverine squatted near a strange, leafy tree and sniffed. He closed his eyes for a second, and in his mind there were two of him—two forms of one man, hovering over a river of inky darkness. One was Logan the man, and he had claws but they were tools, and he drank beer and smoked cigars and listened to Japanese water music for relaxation. The other was Logan the not-man, Logan the beast: the creature snarled and stayed low, leg muscles tensed, nostrils flaring. He could see the heat pouring off Logan the beast and felt the hot blood that ran in that creature's veins. He opened his mind and ripped the hinges off the doors that kept his senses at close to man level, and watched as Logan the beast jumped and shoved Logan the man down, making him disappear into the inky blackness.

Now Wolverine leaned back and curved his neck, closing his eyes and sniffing loudly. On the wind there was a piece of her, the girl's scent in the tiniest fleck, the smallest jot of perspiration left on a leaf, carrying on the wind. He snapped forward and opened his eyes. "This way." And when he moved, he exploded into the brush.

The boy turned his furry visage to the Beast and uttered something in that language of his, and the Beast merely shrugged. "Let's go." As the Beast disappeared into the brush, the boy shouted something to the Devil Dinosaur and was up and in the hands of the bipedal creature, pointing in the direction the two had gone. The red dinosaur roared, breaking into a steady, ground-shaking trot, moving through the brush-laden valley.

Wolverine watched the leaves and fingery tree limbs fly toward him and disappear as he moved, an animal on two legs, jumping, sometimes falling forward to use his arms to push himself over a fallen tree, always reaching out for the scent. He topped a hill and came upon a river and stopped, roaring profanities at the heavens.

"What is it?" the Beast flipped down from behind and stared at the water.

"Lost it!" growled Wolverine. "She went in the

water here, for some reason. Scent's all gone; I don't know if she went downstream or up.''

The Beast put his furry hands on his hips and scanned the area. ''Sun's coming up,'' he observed, absently. ''Well, we could follow the river that way, toward the *big* volcano. Or this way,'' he turned, surveying the river as it twisted round a wooded bend and disappeared, ''which seems to lead to the rock wall of those volcanic mountains over there.'' The Beast cursed. ''What on earth is she doing? How much time do we have?''

Wolverine brought up his wrist and glanced down at his watch, which looked decidedly odd, this feral-acting fellow consulting his Rolex. ''We got forty-five minutes to save the world.''

The Beast sighed deeply. ''I fear we won't find the girl in forty-five minutes, much less consult the Tracker anew and discover the whereabouts of the package.''

Now the boy and Devil Dinosaur appeared behind them and the former leapt from his riding place in the latter's claws. He landed and asked a question, and the Beast merely pointed one way, then another, and shrugged, the pantomime of a befuddled blue furry man.

The boy looked at his dinosaur partner and in each direction. The rock wall around the bend he dismissed, shaking his head vigorously, waving his arms and stomping. Then he pointed toward the dominant volcano in the other direction.

Wolverine scowled. ''This is ridiculous.''

''He seems to think the girl would not go to the cliffs, so the place to look is the big volcano.''

Logan crossed his arms. They were running out of time. "Great," he said.

They began to follow the river in that direction, Logan reaching out for a scent.

"Anything?" the Beast asked.

"Nothin'."

A scream split the air from what must have been a half mile away, and the entire party turned in their tracks, back toward the rock wall. The boy exclaimed something that sounded like recognition. "That's her," Hank said.

They rounded the bend in a matter of minutes and came to the cliff and a set of caves that resembled the ones in which the boy and his folk lived. From the clearing of rock and dirt at the front, a series of crude steps had been carved, leading into the various caves. "What is this?" Wolverine asked the Beast, as the two hopped up on a rock near the cliff, looking down into the plazalike area before the wall. There was no one in sight, merely the series of carved caves protected only by height. "I catch the scent o' the girl," he said. "But . . . is this another rival tribe?"

The Beast clicked his tongue, scanning the area. The screaming had stopped. "If this is a rival tribe, I don't think it's an even match."

"Why?"

"Remember the caves our folks lives in? These caves here are at least three times taller."

Wolverine looked at the caves again and nodded. "You're right. But . . . there ain't no other scents. 'Cept for the girl, there's nothin' here."

The Beast shrugged as the Devil Dinosaur lumbered up behind, towering over them and breathing loudly. "It stands to reason that . . ."

Suddenly a frightful scream echoed through the valley as the girl burst from one of the caves on the second level, clutching the Tracker in her hand.

"That's our girl," Logan said. "And she seems to have somethin' in her mouth."

"Fur," The Beast said. The girl was screeching madly, tufts of dark fur spitting from her mouth. A roar of annoyance and pain came from behind her as she hit the steps and jumped to the plaza below, rolling. Now her captor emerged, and the Beast gasped audibly. The pursuer was gigantic, his head touching the top of his cave, at least fifteen feet tall, with a dark, furry chest as wide as the Devil Dinosaur. "My God," he said, "that fellow's as big as a Sentinel."

"He ain't alone," Logan said, as the sound of more roaring came from the caves, and now three more of the gigantic creatures emerged. The first giant jumped and landed behind the girl and the whole area shook with the concussion as the other three leapt, landing beside their fellow.

"If I'm not mistaken," the Beast said, "they seem to want our little friend's prize."

"Yeah, well, we *need* that prize," Logan said, springing. Behind him he heard the Devil Dinosaur roar as his master shouted for him to advance.

"All right," Wolverine said, his claws snapping out. "You guys are all wrong." He rolled between the legs of the first one he saw as it lunged for the girl, who clutched the Tracker close to her. "Somethin' just ain't right." He sprang up on the shoulders of one of the creatures, half expecting to catch a whiff of the fur, the oils that should be heated and baking into raw, never-washed skin, the tiny creatures that would live in the matted flesh and fur, and half knowing before he grabbed on to the giant shoulders that no such scent would come. He wrapped his boots around the giant creature's neck and it roared, reaching back to grab at him. Wolverine slashed at the back of the creature's head and felt adamantium tear through fur and flesh and *metal*. "I *knew* it!"

"Eh?" the Beast shouted, as he confronted one of the giants and tried to jump and headbutt the thing. He felt his forehead smack against a fleshy nose, the nose squashing, and was astounded at the sensation of striking the skull underneath. The Beast fell back and jumped aside, flipping to avoid the furry claw that swiped at him.

"They're androids!" Wolverine shouted. "They ain't real! And they want the Tracker!"

The Beast turned and looked at the girl, who stared at him with fear as he lunged at her and snatched the Tracker from her hands. He popped it open and studied it quickly. "Of course," he muttered. "The package is here, Wolverine, they're guarding the package!"

"Someone," Wolverine said, as he jumped up on one of the giants' chest, "knew we were comin'." He wrapped his legs around the giant's neck again, this time hugging the creature from the front. "Say *ahh*," he growled, plunging his claws into the giant's open mouth, feeling the adamantium rip through the fake teeth and the palate. He gave his claws a giant tug and pushed off the creature's chest with his legs, and felt the lower jaw come with him. Wolverine struck the ground and looked up to see what resembled a caveman with no lower jaw, and the faceplate fell forward, hanging there. The face was a mess of fur and wiring and revolving artificial eyes. The giant took a moment to regain its equilibrium, and Logan saw the eyes swivel down at him. Stooping, it began to swipe a giant furry hand at him when Logan saw a huge red iguanodon mouth close over the giant's head and shoulders.

The Devil Dinosaur reared back, swinging its red head back and forth with the heavy robot clamped in its jaws. The boy leapt free of the dinosaur's shoulders as the giant was torn in half by its own weight, its lower body nearly squashing the girl as it hit the ground.

The girl stared at the fallen giant, the twitching legs and lower torso torn open. There were brilliant snakes of wiring and cables writhing on the ground, and as she crept close, her eyes grew wide and she reached out to touch the brilliant showers. As she did so the lower body began to shriek with a high-pitched whine and the cables began to melt together and flare brightly.

"My dear," said the Beast, "you're too curious for your own good." He plunged down, slamming into the girl and knocking her back, rolling with her as the dismembered robot exploded in a brilliant conflagration.

Nearby, the boy watched this and immediately turned to his dinosaur, shouting a quick order. The dinosaur still had the upper half of the giant in its mouth, and now it fell forward, spitting the head and arms out, sending them crashing against the rock wall.

Wolverine found himself near the collision and dived for cover behind a nearby rock as the thing blew, sending a sheet of fire up the rock cliff and blackening the wall.

The Beast stared at the mess that had been the first creature and realized he was still holding down the girl. He shook his head, looking down at her, and she smiled, touching his face.

"Please don't misunderstand," he said.

She touched the Beast's face with her fingers and then screamed, kicking him and rolling him to the side as one of the giants stamped on the area where they had been lying. The Beast looked at her. "Misunderstand all you want," he said, and sprang at the giant's head. Wolverine, he reflected, had managed to pull that other one's face off; surely the face and neck would be weak points. Hank McCoy roared and plunged his clawlike right hand through the fur that surrounded the giant's neck, feeling the material rip out of the way, and found cables underneath, throbbing with power. He managed to get his fingers around them and pushed off with his feet, leaping away, and the giant howled with the closest approximation to pain the Beast had ever heard. He hit the ground and the cables were still in his hand, ripping down the front of the giant, tearing chunks from the android's neck and chest. The giant screamed and clawed at its chest as the Beast gave another yank and a sizable chunk of machinery came bursting from the android's chest. Suddenly, the giant emitted a horrendous shriek and the Beast saw the popping cables inside begin to boil and shine.

"Haywire," the Beast said. "If I didn't know better," he shouted at Wolverine, giving another yank to the cable and sending the giant tottering toward one of its last two fellows, "I'd say they're unstable." The giant crashed into its brother and the two androids fell back against a wall. There was a moment's pause, followed by the sound of crunching metal, and suddenly the two giants erupted in flame and fire, and after the conflagration had passed there remained nothing but dust.

"I'm gettin' the package," Wolverine said.

"In that cave," the Beast told him, as the Devil Dinosaur tore into the fourth robot, taking the right ankle in its mouth and stepping on the left, ripping the whole android asunder. The boy cheered as the thing roared into flame and the dinosaur jumped free. "They were guarding it," the Beast said, stopping to stare at the piles of unidentifiable mess that had been the androids. *We come looking for the package. There are androids guarding the package. The androids are strong, but let's face it, they're not really all that . . .* He looked up to see Wolverine disappearing into the cave. "Wait!" The girl crept up beside him where the Beast sat with legs akimbo, and she nuzzled his side with her head.

Wolverine emerged a moment later from the mouth of the cave from which had come the androids. He held something up in his hand—a golden device that the Beast didn't get a very good look at. "This is it," Wolverine said. "It's . . . an arrow."

The Beast stared at Wolverine and at the rocks, ignoring the furry girl nuzzling him and the giant red dinosaur breathing behind him. "Logan, I'm not sure that we have this right."

"What?"

"Well, the . . ."

"How much time do we have?"

"Not much, but . . ."

"What?"

"It's just a feeling. Something's not right about this."

"You'll have to do better than that, bub," Wolverine said. "We came to destroy this thing. We fought like hell to get to it. And we gotta destroy it or the whole timeline will be lost, millions o' lives, and all that."

"Yes," the Beast said. "But it was . . . easy. Perhaps—if only there was another way. We could take it back with us, have Blaquesmith examine it."

"Hank," Logan said, hefting the golden device, "we're runnin' outta time. From what we know, this thing will unravel the timeline if we don't destroy it before it does its thing, whatever that is. All right? Now you prefer we let it go off back home?"

"No, but—"

"Yer thinkin' too hard, Hank," Wolverine said, tossing the arrow into the air. His claws popped out and he thrust them forward, splitting the arrow in half, sending the pieces trailing down to the rock plaza below.

The pieces of the arrow danced on the rock for a moment, the air boiling, and for a moment it looked as though the rock wall itself began to bend toward the energy that was sucking at the pieces.

"Are you telling me," the Beast muttered to himself, as he watched the air split and rip black and reveal nothingness, "that this isn't what this thing is *supposed to do*?"

Suddenly the rip sealed, and from the arrow poured a wave of brilliant light that swept through the plaza and knocked Wolverine off his feet, and even the Devil Dinosaur tottered back. And then, suddenly, it was gone. Every trace of the arrow they had come to destroy, as well as every trace of the androids.

The Beast stared at the blackened ground. "I don't feel good about this at all, Logan."

"Don't matter," Wolverine said. "We got sent on a mission, a very clear one, and you're talkin' guesswork. Ain't no way o' knowin', Hank, and that ain't enough to risk the world."

The Beast stood, brushing his coat of fur. The girl still clung to his arm. "I suppose you're right. But I fear we may have hurt more than helped. I just have no really good reason for it."

The two men stepped to the center of the plaza and looked at the Devil Dinosaur and its master. All were stunned at what they had seen, and the boy was staring at where the androids had fallen. He looked at the Beast and Wolverine and gestured, clearly beckoning to them to return to his camp.

The Beast shook his head, and then looked at the girl, who was still staring, enchanted, into his eyes. "Ah—my dear. Um."

"Never seen you actually speechless before," Logan said. "You wanta hit that recall device before we're stuck here? Unless," he smiled, "you *want* to be stuck here."

"You have to go," the Beast said to the girl. "Go.

Move along now." He gingerly pried her rather strong fingers from his upper arm and held her hands with one claw while pointing in the direction of the camp with the other. "Go."

"You know," Wolverine said, "you could stay. I guess I don't have to tell. I can just picture the little furry children you'd have."

Ignoring Wolverine, Hank shouted, "Go!" He looked at the boy, who stepped forward to take the girl by the arm. He was about to push her and just couldn't bring himself to do it. Instead, when the astute boy took the furry girl by the shoulder, the Beast hastily hit the recall device on his chest, sighing deeply. "Good-bye," he said. The air shimmered around them. He looked at Logan, who was laughing as he disappeared from view.

The Beast could hear Wolverine still laughing as the blackness hurled around and came up in a wall around them, and he felt lost and without being and suddenly, no time later, no time at all, Wolverine was still laughing, and a room was coming into view.

The air shimmered again as the two men popped into Blaquesmith's laboratory. A plasma burst lit up the room and the Beast saw ten green-and-purple-suited troopers firing on Professor X and Blaquesmith. The laugh died in Wolverine's throat as he jumped to avoid the incoming blast that tore a nearby flower pot to flaming pieces.

"What the flamin'—?"

*Hank! Logan!* came the telepathic voice of Charles Xavier, who was huddled in the corner with Blaquesmith. A force field surrounded the two while Blaquesmith stared at the monitor. *They're here to destroy the Core!*

"Welcome back," came Blaquesmith's weak voice, as the Beast and Wolverine plunged into the ten attackers. "I suppose it just wasn't crowded enough in here already."

# CHAPTER TEN

Iceman howled at the night sky as he soared upon the ice ramp that he built as he moved along. *"I can't believe it I can't believe it!"*

"Would you *please* quit sayin' dat," Gambit spat, watching Bobby zip into the air to dodge the Human Torch's blasts. Gambit took what appeared to be an eight-inch metal bar out of his coat and flicked his wrist. With a loud *crak* his staff popped and extended.

There were two of the flaming attackers in the air—one of them, the one that Bobby insisted was called the Human Torch, was a faceless ball of orange flame. With him was another, smaller male, who flew differently. The smaller firethrower flew in what looked to be a less . . . *calculated* style. While the larger male tended to fly carefully timed figure eights, swooping in at Bobby and shooting off bolts of flame with what Gambit would have to call digital timing, the smaller one flew more like Bobby moved on his bridges—with artistry, and even what appeared to be a sense of fun.

The Torch fired off a bolt of flame and Gambit used his staff as a pole vault to dodge it. There was little question which one was more dangerous. Gambit fished in his pocket for a playing card and pulled one out, flashing it before his eyes, feeling the potential energy crackle in his palms. He could see the eyes of the Suicide King fire up and crackle as he wound up and let the card fly. He saw it catch the smaller Torch in the shoulder, exploding when it hit the wall of fire that surrounded the kid. (It had to be a kid. Had to be.)

"Hold on!" Iceman was shouting, even as he shot out his ice bridge and kept on fighting the Human

Torch, matching every fiery blow with an icy one. "We don't need to be doing this."

"Surrender or pay the consequences, saboteurs," cried the Torch, except that it was hardly a cry, more of a nearly inhuman shout that rattled out from a throat that didn't sound right at all.

"Oh, for cryin' out loud," Bobby said, avoiding the fire bolts, "can't a bunch of super-powered, tights-wearing roustabouts ever meet without trying to pulverize one another?"

"It appears not." The Torch's next blast shattered Iceman's bridge. Bobby, flipping in the air, reached out his fingers and sent a pulse of ice. The ice formed another ramp and he hit it and slid, building the ramp up as he moved, finding his feet again and surfing once more into the air.

"Listen to me!" Iceman cried. "You're a hero! You're the Human Torch! You gotta help us!"

The two fire-users continued their barrage of heat and flame. "Surrender!" came the voice again. Steam was erupting from the streets and from the air, the rain not even penetrating. Gambit could only dodge so long.

"Okay," Gambit growled, "if yer gonna be dat way." And now Remy LeBeau bent down and touched his palms to the street, feeling the heat and the concrete and the rocks. He felt the mass, the billions upon billions of tiny molecules of matter, and called to them, exciting them, hearing them begin to spin faster and faster, taking the potential energy of the surrounding twenty feet of concrete and giving that potential energy *life*.

Suddenly the street exploded, chunks of concrete

flying into the air and smacking into the Torch and his partner, who were barely able to put up enough forceful fire-blasts to keep themselves from grievous injury. Gambit watched the two men fly back and slam against the wall of the tenement on the other side of the street, and Iceman wasted no time in pinning them there, laying layer after layer of ice upon them.

Iceman was flying forward, slinging ice, calling out and slamming ice over their snuffed-out, smoking forms, "I *told* you . . . I *didn't* . . . want to *fight*." Now he pushed forward and heaved one more ice layer across, and when he stopped, he stood on his ice bridge, leering at his burned-out quarry.

The Torch and his partner were pinned to the wall and encased in ice, with only their heads protruding from their encasement, halfway up the wall. Without the fire that had surrounded them they looked like any other humans—the older one was blond, with chiseled features, the younger a brown-haired teen-idol type; Gambit reflected that they could just as well have been Captain America and Bucky. Iceman turned around and looked at Gambit. "You okay?"

"A little barbecued, but alive-and-kickin'," Gambit said. *Mon Dieu*. He had forgotten how Bobby could lay it on if he really wanted to. "You gonna introduce me to your friends?"

"This," Iceman said, "is the Human Torch. He's *something* of a hero of mine."

The Torch spoke, his voice a strange, unnatural thing. There was something . . . *artificial* about him. "You have me at something of a disadvantage, Ice-Man."

"Good guess." Bobby smiled. "Iceman it is. My partner here is Gambit. And Gambit, this young fellow over here is Toro, fiery boy wonder."

"D-don't call me th-that, Ice Cube," the kid spat.

"Now," Bobby said, the cold air swirling around him. "I know very well that you two are just waiting to heat up and bust out of that ice. I don't expect it to hold you. What *I* want to know is, are you going to help us into this factory, or am I going to have to pin you here again?"

"What do you want with the factory?" the Torch said. "FBI tipped us that there were a couple of gentlemen asking around and casing the joint. Then we find you breaking in."

"Not to mention how you f-f-froze that security g-g-guard," Toro said. Gambit looked over to where the guard had been and saw that he had, in fact, managed to get away—there was a puddle of water where his feet had been pinned, and it occurred to Gambit that he must have been freed by Torch and Toro's heavy heat offensive.

"Sound pretty cold, there, Toro," Bobby said. "Now, I know that your mentor isn't gonna get cold. But we can't all be androids, now can we?"

The Torch and Toro both stared at Iceman, with not the smallest tinge of fear. "What do you want?" the Torch asked.

"There's something in that factory," Iceman said. "Something very, very dangerous. And my partner and I have less than an hour to find and destroy it. Now, can I let you guys down? What do I have to do to convince you that I'm one of the good guys?"

"Letting us d-d-down would be okay," Toro chattered.

"Just burn on out, I won't rebuild it," Iceman said, standing on his platform like a conqueror. "Then let's talk." And as the two men erupted in flame, Iceman slid on down to wait for them next to Gambit. "Well," he muttered, "I think we've managed to go pretty far afield of Cable's admonition not to involve the locals."

"Dey started it," Gambit observed.

Iceman did his best to boil the story down in the safest manner he could express it to the Torch and Toro, but the fire-android was not completely satisfied. "You two are . . . like us."

"Yes," Iceman said, "but from a different time."

"You have fairly similar powers, actually," the Torch observed, scratching his fiery chin. Gambit wondered if that was a programmed action or if it actually itched. "That blast that Gambit brought out of the ground—what's the nature of this power of his?"

Gambit folded his arms before him and leaned against a wall. "It's called interkinetic energy. I . . ."

"Convert potential energy into kinetic energy, very interesting," rattled the Torch, in that strange almost-human voice of his. "I've read theories about that being possible, but I never imagined a human could do it with his mind."

"You guys should join the Invaders," said Toro, who apparently had decided that Gambit and Iceman were "neat."

"Or the Liberty Legion?" Iceman cracked. "No,

thanks, I did my time in teenage super-groups. Besides, we're on something of a timetable. We're here to get into the factory—and we were nearly in, too, before you guys came along.''

"There's been some strange reports here,'' the Torch said. "While Cap and Bucky and the rest are on special assignment, Toro and I were sent to guard this factory.''

"It's not a spoon factory, I take it,'' Iceman said.

"No, it's a munitions factory,'' said Toro. "I think everybody pretty much knows that. But the night shift has entirely changed its roster in the last week and we've been watching them. They, ah, don't act normal.''

"How do you mean?''

"He means,'' smiled the Torch, "they act synthetic. I try not to take that personally.''

"You're a remarkably well-adjusted android,'' Iceman said.

"There was nothing to adjust to,'' the Torch said. "I was born an android. I didn't know I was different until somebody tried to kill me for it.''

Gambit and Iceman were silent for a moment. "I understand,'' Iceman said.

The Torch passed a flaming hand through the air, dismissing the issue. "So this package—you say it's going to destroy the world?''

"Yes.''

"Then let's go get it.''

A moment later they were standing by the door as Iceman held the Tracker before him. The sweeping arm on the display revealed a few shapes representing larger masses inside the factory, and he pointed at them, the Torch labelling them as he did so.

"Those are bomb casings. There's an airplane-parts section here in the north side; those are landing gear parts stacked there."

"The package is here." Iceman pointed to the pulsating blob in the southwest corner. "It seems to be inside a large, dense mass."

Toro sighed. "That's the safe."

"Safe?"

"For plans, orders, that sort of thing."

"All *riiight*," whistled Gambit. "We be crackin'."

"I think he's right," Iceman said. "Gambit and I will take the safe and get the package. You and Toro cover us until we're done."

"Do you need to take it anywhere?"

"Just destroy it. If you get *your* hands on it," Iceman said, "just destroy it. This thing will kill more people than you can possibly imagine if it's allowed to do its job."

"All right," said Torch, as the rest of them stepped away from the door. "I'm still not one hundred percent sure about you two, but I'm willing to go along for the time being. I warn you, though, at the first sign of any kind of betrayal, no amount of ice—or exploding sidewalks—will be able to stop us."

"Understood," Iceman said, trying, Gambit thought, a little too hard to sound reassuring.

"Good," the Torch said. "Let's go."

Inside the factory, forty women worked slowly and deliberately at the jobs they had taken over in order to guard the Time Arrows. There was the sound of forty humming, ratcheting eyes and swiveling necks as every single one turned to watch the metal back door melt off its frame before a flaming man burst through and into the air.

As Toro burst in, followed by Gambit and Iceman on his bridge, forty rifles fired forty bursts of plasma.

Iceman felt his bridge burst out from under him and iced up another one before he dropped six feet. "Something tells me we were expected."

"That would be an accurate observation!" shouted the Torch, as he flew around the room, dodging the plasma fire.

Toro was singed by a bolt and dipped behind a metal press. He shot a blast of flame at one of the guns, which promptly exploded.

Iceman noticed two things after that. First, that the explosion of the plasma gun was thorough—there weren't even pieces left, it was completely destroyed without a trace. And second, that the explosion had also caused abrasions in the skin of the hands of its wielder; abrasions that made the skin peel back to reveal wiring.

"Androids!" Toro shouted, having noticed the same thing. "These women are all androids!"

"In dat case, we can cut loose," Gambit said.

If the Torch took offense at Gambit's remark, he didn't show it. He flew right through one of the factory workers, melting the front of her rifle as he passed. He felt the machinery melting around his body and looked back to see the crumpled heap twitch and blow, followed by the detonation of the plasma rifle. He released a heavy blast of fiery air, circling and sustaining the explosion. "Be careful, Toro!

These androids are highly unstable. They're basically just walking bombs.'' He swooped down to join Toro behind the press. ''Destroy them but contain the blasts. We don't want the whole factory to go up, if we can help it.''

Toro nodded.

Gambit jumped and flipped over a plasma burst as Iceman swirled around him, avoiding the fire and trying to cut him a path. The safe was twenty feet away, blocked by a series of metal tables and at least ten androids who had fallen in line in front of it.

Iceman saw one android's rifle charging up and heard the *klik* before the burst, and he laid on hard with ice, encasing the rifle and the android both in a sizable chunk. The whole chunk sat there on the factory floor and shook as Iceman continued to pile on the white, and he didn't stop until he saw the block of ice crack and turn black inside, falling to chunks. ''Man, these things are unstable,'' he said.

Gambit saw two androids coming at him, guns blazing, and he dodged one burst and managed to slam his staff into the first android's neck. He felt a moment's pang of reflexive guilt—these things looked so *human*, except that in those artificial eyes was nothing, absolutely nothing. ''Dey're walkin' bombs,'' he said, as the head tore from the android's shoulders and he sent the headless mechanical woman crashing into her neighbor. The second android's gun went off and obliterated half of the first, and the explosion that followed reduced them both to unidentifiable soot before Iceman even had time to contain the fireball that shot out.

"This is crazy," Iceman said. "I've seen Danger Room programs with more resourcefulness."

"Just get me to de safe," Gambit said, dropping and rolling under one of the androids, sending her crashing into Iceman's ice bridge. Iceman wasted no time in tearing through her with missiles of ice that could punch through the side of a tank. "And be careful where you aim dose t'ings, *homme*!"

Gambit jumped under one of the tables, reaching out and charging it up as he did so. He heard the flash of kinetic energy released by the charged-up metal take out two more androids even as he reached the safe.

The safe was four feet tall and four feet wide, a typical metal cube, most likely reinforced with concrete on the inside. A combination lock made up the most of the safe's front, and he pressed his ear against the door, swiveling the black circular grip, listening for tumblers. "Been a while since I done dis," he said, to no one in particular.

"Gambit!" Iceman cried, as he shot a rifle out of an android's hand, too late to stop her firing it. The plasma burst flew out of the rifle barrel and Gambit looked away from the safe to see a bolt coming for his face. He jumped aside and saw the burst slam into the safe. For a moment he hoped that burst might have opened the safe *for* him, but he cursed when he saw that the fire had had the opposite result. The front of the safe was a melted mess, the heavy black grip and numbers hopelessly fused, the very door of the safe soldered to its body.

Gambit pulled out a joker and threw it, watching the sparks fly from the card as it caught the artificial woman in the face and split her head in half. "You did dat on purpose!"

The woman exploded, and Gambit could have sworn he saw a mocking smile coming from the android's halved mouth. Iceman contained the explosion and then shouted, "Get out of the way!" As Remy stepped back, Iceman shot a sheet of ice at the safe, not a thick sheet, but very very cold, and Remy felt the air temperature around him drop dramatically, the safe changing hue, turning brighter with the cold and frost. Iceman turned off the ice but continued to pour on the cold until, satisfied, he stopped, lowering his hands.

"Now," said Bobby, again putting on his weak impersonation of Gambit, "we be crackin'."

Remy gave the safe a good low kick with the bottom of his foot and watched it shatter into a thousand pieces, tiny fragments of cold metal spreading across the floor like chunks of agate. "You, *mon ami*, are one dangerous man."

In the middle of the gemlike chunks of frozen metal was a frosted piece of gold, long, with jeweled, blinking fins and a barbed end. "It's an arrow," Remy observed.

Iceman looked back and saw the Human Torch and Toro zipping into the air, melting hell out of the last few androids. "I don't get it. We were expected, but you'd think they didn't expect anyone very powerful."

"What," Toro said, lowering himself beside Iceman's bridge. "You think this was easy?"

"Iceman," Gambit said, hefting the arrow, "we be runnin' out of time."

"Right. Do your thing."

Gambit felt at the golden metal and was amazed at the energy inside there, the destructive force that beckoned to his brain and danced when he drew it out. He felt the arrow charging up eagerly, shaking in his hand, and when it was charged up as much as he could muster he threw it into the air against the far wall. "Contain it!" he cried.

Iceman's blast of ice caught the resulting explosion head on and for a moment the blasts fought for space, and Gambit saw the air ripple and swallow some of Iceman's onslaught, the whiteness disappearing into nowhere. The arrow disintegrated and the flash burst through the room, zipping out and back inward and disappearing as quickly as it had come. Iceman continued to pour on the ice a few more seconds before he stopped, lowering his hands. "Huh."

"Yeah." Gambit nodded.

"Something's not right."

"I know." Gambit pointed at his watch. "We gotta go, or joinin' de Invaders is de best we can hope for."

"Right," Iceman said. "Torch? Toro?"

The fiery partners were still staring at the ice-covered safe where a moment before reality itself had been split open. "Yes?" The whole factory was a mess of black soot and wrecked airplane parts. The Torch had an expression on his face that was half bewilderment and half resignation. *Why do cosmically destructive things always happen on my watch?*

Iceman touched his recall device and smiled as the

air began to shimmer around himself and Gambit. "See you in the funny papers."

And they were gone as quickly as they had come, leaving the Torch and Toro behind to explain all that had just happened.

# CHAPTER ELEVEN

A burst of plasma flew past Spider-Man's shoulder and he felt the air crackle as it passed, ripping the tree to shreds.

"Which wagon is the package in?" Bishop cried.

"The second one there," Spider-Man responded, grunting as he hit the ground and sprang at the android that had shot at him.

"I'm going for it." Bishop fired a round at one of the advancing forms and followed his own blast, lowering his head and running at the attackers.

Spider-Man sized up the android and heard the rifle charging up for another shot. The android aimed at him and he feinted to the side, dropping, rolling again, and springing. The wall-crawler slammed into the android's chest, knocking its hat off and grabbing it by the gun arm as he heard the mechanical *klik* that always came right before discharge.

"You . . . buddy," Spider-Man grunted, wrapping his legs around the android and putting all of his strength into bending the android's elbow, "are one strong hunk of metal." A shimmer began to emanate from the barrel and Spider-Man looked down to see he still had it in line with his own chest. "Not . . . yet . . ."

Bishop was making his way toward the coach and looked back, kicking an android out of the way and firing a round, tearing off a mechanical arm. The arm fell to the ground and twitched. "Cartwright! Get away from that—"

"Not . . . yet . . ." said Spider-Man, forcing the android's arm up, trying to ignore the pain as a mechanical fist pounded at his shoulder. He kept his hands on the android's wrists, the two tottering, and looked in the robot's eyes. They were cold, like a mannequin's, no thought or desire at all. Just a killing machine doing a job. He relaxed his legs and then brought them in again, slamming his knees into the android's torso, pushing the wrists just an inch farther . . . farther. . . . He felt the elbow crack and swivel and the gun barrel aim up as the blast came out. There was a roar and a flash of heat and bursting air in front of Spider-Man's face as the plasma blast ripped the android's face off and sent its head flying backward. Spider-Man felt the arm let go of him and the android began to twitch violently. He jumped to the ground and grabbed the android's spasmodic free hand and looked around, finding another target. There was an android taking aim about ten yards away, and he swung his android violently, sending it spinning. His android crashed into the other as that mechanical assassin's barrel emitted its blast, ripping the first android's upper torso in half. The two androids fell and tumbled together for a moment and Spider-Man sprang clear as the headless creature exploded underneath the second one. There was a moment's pause before the second creature blew, too, sending shrapnel flying. Spider-Man surveyed the mess as the two forms, what was left of them, shook and quivered and fried themselves into oblivion, disappearing into a sheet of burning grass and melted dirt.

"Bishop," Spider-Man said, "I hate to ruin a decent gag, but my name's not really Cartwright."

"Fair enough," Bishop said. He had made it to the wagon and was tearing at its canopy. "Where is it?"

• • •

The Two-Gun Kid was out of his league. He looked around at the army of strange sentries and felt the handles of his revolvers in his hands. *Who am I kidding?* But that Spider-fellah had managed to get one of those artificial men to blow its own head off. Spider-Man didn't use any weapons, so he and Two-Gun were in about the same boat. These guys were like clocks, they were pretty tightly wound: it looked as though all you had to do was figure out some way to tear up the gears a little bit.

One of the androids was headed for Two-Gun and the gunslinger didn't waste time firing, but dropped and rolled, hitting the artificial man's legs, feeling the heavy machinery kick him in the ribs. But the android toppled forward and Two-Gun sprang up behind it, jumping and landing on the android's back. The android was lying facedown on the ground and now tried to get up, but Two-Gun kept him pinned, wrapping his legs tight, riding the robot like a bronco. "You stay down, mister, this ain't gonna hurt a bit." He drew his right gun from its holster.

The android was still holding its gigantic plasma rifle and tried to aim it up toward Two-Gun's head, but Two-Gun brought the barrel of his right six-shooter down and blew off the android's thumb. The digit flew into the air and exploded, disappearing into fiery dust. Now he holstered the weapon and grabbed the rifle, hefting it. *God almighty, thing's gotta weigh seventy pounds*. There was a bolt on the side, and as he rocked, trying to keep the android down, he drew back the bolt, shoved it forward, heard it ratchet into place. Lowering the barrel, he levelled it at the android's head. *Klik*.

The barrel cracked and spurted and the plasma bolt roared as Two-Gun felt himself thrown back like a rag doll, slamming into the ground. He looked up to see the rifle lying near the android, and the headless automaton was shaking, pounding its fists into the dirt, faster and faster. Suddenly the thing raised itself up on its arms like it was trying to get up and exploded, flying apart, clothing and pieces whizzing past Two-Gun's head.

"Whoo-ee!" Two-Gun yelled. Now the plasma rifle the android had been holding, caught in the blast, jumped a few times on the ground and then burst, sending out a blast of green and red.

"Yeah," Spider-Man yelled as he landed on the shoulders of the android that was lumbering toward the Two-Gun Kid. "They blow up real good." He kicked at the android's arm, pushing the barrel toward the ground, while he twisted and gave the automaton's head a good, solid yank. The head came loose in his hands and he held it before him, springing away and landing. Two-Gun rolled out of the way as the android exploded, followed quickly by the explosion of the android's rifle.

"Those rifles'll blow as soon as they're gone," Two-Gun yelled.

"I noticed," Spider-Man responded. The head in his hands was biting at him, the tongue flying back and forth, the eyes swirling wildly in mechanical sockets, and Spider-Man reared back and heaved the head as hard as he could at the next android he saw. The head tumbled through the air and slammed into another android, who actually seemed to blink as the head exploded, tearing that one in half.

Two-Gun ran right at one of the androids and fired both pistols point-blank into its right eye. The thing staggered for a moment and Two-Gun saw it bringing up its weapon and he wondered if his guns would be any good at all. They were. Even before the arm came all the way up, Two-Gun was rewarded with yet another explosion to avoid.

"I don't know, son," Two-Gun said. "I get the feelin' they blow up *too* good." He watched the rifle that had been in the android's hand hit the ground. *Klik.* A plasma bolt fired off as the rifle burst into a million unidentifiable pieces. The burst flew past Two-Gun, searing the rim of his hat, and he turned around to see Spider-Man spinning in the direction of the bolt. "Look out!"

Spider-Man hesitated at that warning, then caught the plasma burst full in the chest. The thing he wore on his chest caught the brunt of the impact, the metal circle slamming back with the force. He hit the ground and rolled end over end, crying out in pain as the hot metal burned through his costume and into his flesh.

"I got it!" came Bishop's voice, as he blew hell out of another android and came out of the chuck wagon holding something. The device was about three feet long, shimmering gold, with a long hook on the end, and crystal fins surrounding it. It was an arrow. Bishop drew the thing back, hurled it at one of the androids, and watched it catch the android in the eye, driving back and piercing out the back of the android's head. Bishop raised up his plasma rifle and fired at the twitching android and its head blew, followed quickly by the roaring concussion as the rest of the automaton followed. The arrow took flight and sailed back past Bishop and stuck in the side of the chuck wagon, burrowing deep.

"I thought that would have destroyed it," Bishop said, but then the arrow began to shake where it rested, embedded in the wood. The whole shaft shook, the golden metal shimmering wider and wider as the whole thing vibrated faster and faster. There were three more androids standing and each one of them stopped what it was doing and swiveled its mechanical head.

"Get down!" Bishop cried, as the Time Arrow split down the middle, crustal fragments flying off and tearing at his flesh from ten feet away.

Bishop rolled and looked at the burst of golden light and saw it roar and spit an energy he had never seen before. The air around the Time Arrow split and cracked like glass, the wind picking up and swirling, and Bishop watched as the thing exploded, ripping a hole in the air, and inside the hole was roaring and endless eternity.

A shock wave of energy flew through the air, arcs of golden power reaching up and over the wagon train, grabbing each frame and android, zipping through the entire area, and Bishop found himself pinned to his spot, staring at the powerful eruption.

The clouds overhead rolled and suddenly the Time Arrow exploded, and every point touched by the arcs of energy went with it, the wagons bursting into countless pieces of unidentifiable dust, the androids roaring into nothingness.

And in a moment that might have been an eternity, it was gone.

Bishop lay where he had fallen, looking around. He saw only the prairie and the campfire, which lay exhausted by the force, smoking gray. The very ground burned and smoked. Bishop coughed. There was still one chuck wagon. That one must have been natural to *this* time. Of all the other anachronistic items, there was no trace, aside from some very fine ash. *Probably unidentifiable*, Bishop thought. *Whoever's doing all of this is efficient.*

Bishop looked around. "Two-Gun! Spider-Man! Are you all right?"

Two-Gun was getting up and nursing a nasty cut to his cheek where a piece of shrapnel had hit him, but he looked okay. "I'm—I'm all right," he said. "But I think your buddy over there . . . ain't."

Now Bishop looked past Two-Gun and for the first time noticed the fallen form of Spider-Man, who lay on his chest, sprawled like a rag doll, his arms and legs twisted in various directions. Bishop and Two-Gun ran to Spider-Man's side.

"Doesn't look like anything's broken," Two-Gun shook his head as he reached down to turn the wall-crawler over, "but he took a hit to the chest."

"Nooooo," Spider-Man murmured, and Bishop could hear the pain in his partner's voice. Spider-Man lifted his head and turned over with Two-Gun's help, groaning loudly. "Oooohh, nooo."

Bishop scowled at the smoking mess on Spider-Man's chest. "You okay?"

"Get this thing off me," Spider-Man said, and he helped Bishop pull the leather straps off his arms. The metal disc slid away from his sternum and Spider-Man looked down at the black spider that was still visible on the cloth there in the center of a round, darkened patch. "Looks like someone left the iron on," he murmured, wincing with pain.

"Well, I don't know what that thing you were wearing was," Two-Gun said, "but it looks to me like it saved your life."

Spider-Man rested his forearms on his knees and gave a bitter laugh from beneath his mask. He nodded, looking at Bishop and then at Two-Gun. "That was our recall device," he said.

Bishop winced. He hoped Two-Gun had no idea what Spider-Man was talking about—but, honestly, that was the least of their problems. What they had feared had come true. He reached over and picked up the burned-out metal shell, letting the smoking leather straps dangle from his hands as he held the thing up.

"It would seem," the big mutant said, "that we're stuck here."

Wolverine ripped through the torso of one of the troopers, who screamed in pain and bitter anger and kicked at him with a heavy boot. Logan rolled with the kick, finding his balance, and as he spun he saw the air shimmering. Someone else was coming in.

"Well, well," came the voice of Gambit, as he materialized and Logan slammed into him. Gambit rolled with Logan and the two tumbled and hopped up as Iceman emerged from thin air a few feet away. "You t'rew a party and didn't invite your favorite Cajun?"

"Nothin' personal," Wolverine said.

Iceman looked around in wonder. "What in hell is going on?" The laboratory was in chaos, with a full-fledged battle in progress. There were ten troopers in green-and-purple armor—nine, after Logan had taken out that last guy—now pitched against four X-Men, not counting the Professor and Blaquesmith.

*They're trying to destroy the Time Displacement Core*, came a telepathic burst from Professor X. *You must not let them!*

"Charley," Wolverine shouted, as he jumped at one of the troopers, pointing the trooper's gun at the ceiling as it went off, "stop screamin' in our heads, fer cryin' out loud!"

The Beast's fur burst into flame as one of the troopers shot at him and barely missed his shoulder. Hank McCoy growled and grabbed the man's arm, pulling the trooper close to him, so that he breathed into the man's face. "When you do that," he growled, "I would prefer that you smile." The man screamed as the Beast roared, baring gigantic fangs, but rather than tear out the trooper's throat, which of course McCoy would never do, the Beast flung him through the air and into a standful of glass flasks, his head smacking nastily into the wall behind. The trooper collapsed in a heap, bleeding from a number of superficial wounds.

Gambit grabbed one of the Erlenmeyer flasks and, feeling the charge run into it from his fingers, threw it over McCoy's head and at another of the troopers. The thing exploded with energy, the trooper's eyes rolled back in his head, and he fell unconscious.

"Iceman," Gambit cried, "block de Core!"

"On it," Iceman said, sending a sheet of ice

through the room, drawing a neat icy line along the floor. As he poured on the cold, the ice wall grew, drawing itself up from the floor in front of the Time Displacement Core. When the wall had reached the ceiling, Iceman began to pour on the layers, and he was pleased to see that when one of the troopers managed to get off a shot at the Core, the plasma burst slammed into the wall and crept through the entire structure, but did not break through. He poured on more ice, repairing the shield. "You guys keep me covered," he cried. "I'll keep it shielded."

Blaquesmith looked up from underneath the table in horror. The force field that protected them was eating up precious power reserves—reserves they could ill afford to spare—but as burst after burst slammed into it and dissipated, the old wizard knew that they had to leave it up.

Suddenly the monitor began to beep rapidly and loudly, and Blaquesmith craned his neck to get a look. "What on Earth?"

There was a shimmering on Spider-Man and Bishop's timeline, the form representing the recall device sputtering and fading. Then, suddenly, the form disappeared from the line, remembered only by the alarm that continued to report. "Askani Risen," Blaquesmith cried, "Spider-Man and Bishop's recall device has left the screen!"

"Gone?" the Professor asked.

Blaquesmith hung his head, barely audible over the bursting plasma bolts that were making a charred wreckage of his laboratory. "They are lost."

The air began to shimmer in the middle of the

room and Logan shouted, "Heads up! More comin' in!"

Blaquesmith founded himself hoping against hope that somehow it would be Spider-Man and Bishop, and the disappearance of the recall device was merely some odd glitch.

It was not. Nor was it Cable and Storm, whose recall device still flared on the monitor screen.

The form that stepped out of thin air was laughing from beneath a solid blue mask, and was dressed from head to foot in a metallic purple cloth. In his gloved hands he held a device Blaquesmith did not recognize, and his chest shook as his laugh grew more enthusiastic.

Professor Xavier's voice filled every brain in the room. *Kang.*

"Yes," said the man behind the mask. "And this has been very amusing." Logan roared and tore at one of the troopers, sending him flying back, and Kang idly stepped out of the way as the man flew past him. "But I think it has gone on long enough."

"He got somet'ing in his hand!" Gambit cried, swinging his staff, and he saw the staff stop, frozen above the item Kang held, the staff embedded in a force field that now rippled as it dissipated the energy of the blow.

Kang pressed a button, and the entire room screamed.

Logan felt a sound shoot into his inner ears and bring him to his knees a half second before everyone else heard it. He roared in pain as Bobby fell beside him, clutching his ears. The sound shook the entire room, and Kang continued to laugh. The troopers watched, probably shielded by earplugs. Iceman was shaking so hard Logan could see cracks shooting through his temples, ice flaking off of his head as he slammed into the ground.

Charles Xavier was losing control of his defenses. *Sonic . . . blast*, he thought loudly.

"Oh, Charley," groaned Logan, "please . . . I beg you . . . shut up. . . ." Logan began to feel the pressure in his ears exploding and saw the world swirling around him, the pain bringing the curtains down. He heard a crack and looked over to see one of the troopers blasting a hole in the ice wall Bobby had put up. The chunks of ice flew melting through the room, falling on the X-Men, who clutched their ears and groaned.

"Now," Kang said. "I think this Time Displacement Core has been operational long enough."

# CHAPTER TWELVE

In the dense woods of Northern Britain, Cable stared down into the eyes of Aliya, his wife. His dead wife. "It can't be," he cried, rolling over, reflexively taking his hands off of her, as if to let the illusion go free and hopefully plague him no more.

Storm came zipping through the woods and stopped, hovering above the two. Following shortly came the Black Knight, who had replaced his dark, shining helmet. "Nathan!" Storm called. "Are you—?"

"Go after the package," Cable said, turning to look at the wind-rider and the Knight. "Remember the mission."

"Who is this woman?" the Knight demanded. "And who are you?"

"Nathan," Storm tilted her head and ran her eyes over the strange woman, "is that who I think it is?"

Cable's bionic eye flared as he rasped, "Storm, please, go after the package. Explain what you like to the Black Knight."

The African woman hovered on the air, the leaves fluttering on the ground underneath her. "We shouldn't separate."

"Would you please give me some time here?"

Storm and Cable locked eyes for a moment, and she seemed to be studying him. She took another long moment to study the woman who sat on the ground next to Cable. The auburn-haired warrior was watching Cable, though, mouthing something, and then she shot a glance at Storm, clearly waiting for the X-Man to be gone.

Technically, Storm had rank here. She and Cyclops led the X-Men—while Cable was a valuable ally and associate, he had no authority with the team, and she was under no obligation to do as he said.

Cable hoped, however, that she would do as he *asked*.

Finally, Storm turned to the Black Knight. "Sir Percy, if you will—I think we should pursue that cask. Don't get lost, Nathan," she said.

"I'm certain," Cable sighed, looking back at Aliya, "that you'll make sure I don't."

When the Black Knight and Storm had disappeared in the direction the android knights had run, Aliya sat up and crawled to a nearby tree, sitting back against it. "All right," she said slowly. "All right. Suppose you explain who you are, now," she said.

"I am Nathan Dayspring," he said, "as you know. I am Askani'son."

"No." She shook her head violently, her jaw quivering, the voice barely a whisper. "You died. You died in my arms at the hands of Stryfe—"

"And so did you," answered Cable. He closed his eyes and tried to slow his blood, taking it all in. "There's—there isn't time to grapple with this, Aliya. I am . . . just as shocked to see you here as you are to see me. And at any other time I would be doing everything in my power to discover what trick some illusionist is trying to play, but, Aliya, I sit here and I can *smell* you, I can feel your presence echoing in my mind, it's *you*," he said, whispering, "Askani Rising, it's *you*."

The woman staring back at him was older than he remembered, just as he was, and the years had not been kind. There was a harshness that competed with the natural luster of her eyes, and a few wrinkles had begun to invade the once-perfect smoothness of her face. Her right shoulder, barely visible under her green plates, was a matted mess of untanned scarring. She had grown to be the warrior she had always promised, perhaps more. Now Aliya bent forward and crawled toward Cable, and suddenly she grabbed him, clenching her fingers hard around his shoulders, and pressed her lips against his. She lingered in the kiss for a long time before pulling away, breathing over him, her eyes closed.

"And it is you," she said gruffly, her hand running to press against her stomach. "God, I can't stand it, I can't stand it, Nathan, what are you doing here, why *now*?"

"Someone has sent a package into the past, at four distinct points on the timeline. We're here to destroy them."

Aliya nodded slowly, absorbing this. "Of course. Of course, we're on the *same mission*! Oh, my ... aaarrgghh! Of all the ... do you have any idea how many times I have searched for an alternate Nathan that *survives*? Nathan, Nathan, I don't have *time*, we only have a few hours, maybe *less*."

"I know the search," he said with a nod. "And there were times I searched the monitors looking for an alternate Aliya, and I felt you, reaching out across time, somehow, I knew it." He looked around. "Is there— Are you alone? Did any other Askani come with you?"

"You—" she shook her head. "You don't understand, Nathan. A lot has happened since you've been ... gone. We lost," she said flatly, the edge in her voice palpable. She brushed her eyes with the side of her rugged, calloused right hand. "We lost very *badly*. Stryfe, he *slaughtered* the Askani, and you were gone, and I was left to travel to the past alone. But things have gone from bad to, to just *terrible*, Nathan. And all the time I've been alone, finding help where I could, Blaquesmith managed to join me, but it's . . . if only you had been there; I was never the strategist that you were."

"Nonsense," he said. "I remember the battle you led when I was sick."

"This isn't *battle*," she rasped. "I can handle battle. But you have no idea what it's like to be *alone*."

Cable closed his eyes, sighing deeply. "I do know."

"You brought a team, didn't you? This is the first of four stops for me." She looked around desperately, and then laughed, "Blaquesmith will have my head if he finds out I've been wasting time with you."

"Wouldn't be the first time." Cable smiled. Her laugh was infectious. "Aliya, Aliya . . . if I'd only known where I could find you."

"You wouldn't—you wouldn't like it." She cleared her throat, brushing back her hair and nodding, graceful in every movement. "That woman you were with. Is there . . . something . . ."

"She's, ah," Cable danced, "she's a member of the X-Men."

Aliya's eyes flashed and she shrieked, jumping to her feet. "The *X-Men*?"

Cable stared. "Yes, what . . ."

"And do *you*, Nathan Dayspring, count yourself one of these *X-Men*?"

Cable put a metal finger to his lips and arched his

eyebrow. "Why do I get the impression that I shouldn't answer that?"

There was rage in Aliya's eyes, rumbling and volcanic, and for a moment she bit her lip violently before closing her eyes, spreading out her hand, finding some calming place within her to spread through the rest of her and return whatever poise had enveloped her before. "Of course," she shook her head, "of course, you're in an alternate timeline, maybe it's—maybe it's different."

"The X-Men, some of them, and Spider-Man and myself have come to the past to find the packages that threaten the timeline."

"This Spider-Man—is he an *X-Man*?" she asked, not able to mask the disgust that the word held for her.

"No, he's a nonmutant, ah, mutation, I guess," he answered. "Why are you so concerned about the X-Men?"

Aliya leveled her hands, as if spreading out a cloth over a table. "Let's put that aside, shall we, Nathan? I . . . Nathan, I don't have *time*. Maybe it's different, and I don't care, I don't care, here you are, I don't care if you're riding with *Apocalypse*," she sat down, putting her hands to his face, "here you *are*."

Cable took her hands in his and took them away from his face, holding them. "We—" he knew what he was going to say was crazy, insane, idiotic, all of that, but here it was "—we have a mission here, and we have to destroy that package, but . . . that's it." He shook his head. "There are teams heading for the other three points, you don't need to go there. Help us finish this, Aliya, and you don't have to go back where you came from if—if you don't want to.''

She shook her head, ''What are you saying?''

''*Come with me*,'' he whispered forcefully, ''come back to my world. Or, or, we could stay *here*.'' He looked around. ''Ever dream of serving King Arthur? Or we could go somewhere else together, another timeline where there's neither of us, or *anything*, Aliya, think, we don't have to be apart ever again.''

Aliya sat down beside him and leaned against him as he cradled her in his arms, smelling her hair as she nuzzled his chest. ''Blaquesmith would miss me,'' she smiled.

''He's a resourceful old wizard,'' he whispered into her hair. ''He'll probably build an android just like you, only nicer.'' He blinked, the tears welling up in his eyes. ''I've searched so long.''

''I know.''

''A thousand possibilities,'' Cable said, ''a thousand worlds where the wars we have fought need not be, where there is peace, we can find one . . . it doesn't matter where.''

''It doesn't matter where,'' Aliya repeated, looking up and bringing her lips to his, ''it doesn't matter where.''

There was a crackle in the air and he sound of leaves fluttering as Storm emerged from the trees, hovering in the clearing, the Black Knight appearing right behind her. Cable looked up in barely masked annoyance as Storm cleared her throat dramatically. ''Nathan, we've found it.''

The Black Knight spoke. '' 'Tis true, shining one! The artificial men have stowed their treasure in the castle of the late Morgan Le Fey.''

"It's not far," Storm said, "we saw it down the hill outside the woods. But we must hurry."

"We have *six hours*," Aliya and Cable snapped nastily.

Storm pursed her lips, folding her arms before her, floating like the goddess she had once been and speaking like the team leader she still was. "I might *remind* you, Nathan, that *you* were the one who told us about the dangers of wast—" She stopped, toning it down. "Losing track of time."

Cable looked at Aliya for a moment and considered holding her until the world unravelled like a ball of yarn. He sighed. "All right." The pair began to stand. "Morgan Le Fey's castle?"

"Aye," said the Knight.

"Let's go," Aliya said, picking up her rifle and slamming back the bolt. "We have a job to do."

"I couldn't have said it better myself," Cable said.

Within minutes the four were perched on a hill on the west side of the wood, overlooking a large castle. The dark structure brooded with an inky gloom that seemed to seep from the rough-hewn black battlements. "As I told your ally Storm," the Black Knight said, "this castle that lies before you was once held by Morgan, the sorceress."

"Morgan is dead now?" Cable asked.

"That she is," the Knight replied. "Well—not *dead*, exactly."

"How do you mean, 'exactly'?" Aliya asked.

"Her forces were conquered by we who serve Arthur. Merlin the Magician banished the wounded Morgan to an ethereal life, bounded by the walls of the castle you see before you. She can never leave it, and I would not really call her alive.''

''But I take it she is . . .''

''Oh, yes, certainly,'' the Briton nodded. ''She can kill you. She's just dead. In a manner of speaking. It doesn't stop her—we just generally avoid the place.''

Cable nodded. ''The androids are holed up there, and took the package with them.''

''Yes,'' Storm said, ''I watched them ride to the moat. They were even aided.''

''Aided?'' Aliya asked.

The Knight turned to look at Cable and Aliya through the eye holes in his helmet. ''The drawbridge was lowered for them. I can only conclude they have allied themselves with Morgan Le Fey.''

''The not-exactly dead.''

''Exactly,'' the Knight intoned.

Below, Cable could make out the moat that surrounded the dark building, and he pointed at it, and at the drawbridge that lay closed against the front wall on the other side. ''I wonder how we get across that?''

''Very carefully, I should say,'' the Briton chuckled. ''Great magic is there, by which I mean a number of . . . creatures. Swimming I do not recommend. And it is, if I recall, a thirty-foot leap.''

''I could fly into the castle,'' Storm proffered, ''and open the bridge from the inside.''

''You'd be alone.'' Cable shook his head. ''And we don't know what kind of force they'll counter with, especially with this extra problem of this helpful ghost.''

"Doesn't have to be alone," Aliya said. "She could carry someone."

"Too heavy," Cable shook his head, thinking, "I weigh two-hundred and fifty pounds, and the Knight's got this heavy ..." He stopped. "You mean *you*, don't you?"

"Storm, isn't it ... *X-Man*?" Aliya asked. "How much can you carry?"

Ororo Munroe smiled. "Up to about two hundred. How much do you weigh?"

Aliya's eyes narrowed. "I'm light enough for you."

Cable looked at Storm and Aliya and back down at the castle. "I don't know ..."

"Nathan," Aliya countered, "what are you worried about? This is what I came for."

"I know, I know, it's just ..." What could he say? *"I'd rather you just sat this one out, I don't want to see you get killed again"? Who am I kidding?* "Be careful."

"Always," Aliya answered. "I've been doing just fine by myself, you know." Her eyes softened for a moment and she leaned in and kissed him quickly. "But I appreciate the thought."

"Ready?" Storm asked.

She nodded, standing, tapping her plasma gun. Storm dropped and hovered behind Aliya, putting her arms under Aliya's knees and shoulders and grunting a bit as she lifted Aliya off the ground. She seemed to be straining, and bobbed a bit, then Aliya adjusted herself, putting her arm around Storm's neck. Storm seemed to find her balance and lifted up again, beginning to move forward, rising as she did so.

As the two began to move off, Aliya in Storm's arms, Cable called, "Don't drop her."

Storm didn't dignify that with a response.

Gliding on the winds, Ororo Munroe looked down at Aliya and flew a little bit higher, mentally calling to the winds to support them. "So," she said, in the lovely, musical voice of hers, "you are Aliya."

"Yes," Aliya said. Ahead of them, the battlements slowly enlarged in view. They were nearly over the moat. "You're a . . . teammate of Nathan's?"

"Not exactly. We are allies in a similar cause, and we have worked together on several occasions—such as this."

"And what cause would that be?" Aliya asked.

Ororo did not answer right away. Was Aliya testing her? What other cause would a mutant be fighting for in these difficult times? *Homo sapiens and homo sapiens superior* had been at odds, despite the best efforts of the X-Men and like groups, for years.

*But then*, Storm thought, *these times are not the same for us as for her.*

"The fight for justice in a world that is constantly unjust—particularly toward mutants."

"Interesting." Aliya was keeping her voice neutral.

Below them the moat bubbled black, and Storm could see strange, iridescent white things slithering in the shadows.

"We have arrived," Ororo said as she circled above the battlements, scanning for a place to set down. "Look for guards," she said. "There may be armed resistance."

The design of the castle was cryptic: the structure appeared to be at most four stories high, but from the roof Storm could see the shape in which the castle stretched out—dark stones set off in a checkered arrangement with dark granite, so that the pattern sparkled and caused a strange, shimmering black-and-white illusion. The whole affair cast the illusion of swirling on an axis.

"What is it?" Aliya asked.

"If I had to guess," said Storm, "I would say it's a nebula. Though these people have never *seen* nebulae."

"I think we can assume that this Morgan Le Fey has."

The wind tapered off as Aliya dropped the last four feet to the stone battlements of what seemed to be the west wing of the castle. Storm lit beside her and the two surveyed the roof. "There." Storm indicated a dark spot on the raised tower in the center of the nebula-shaped roof. "That looks like a door."

They stepped along the smooth stones, following the snaking arm of the nebula on which they had landed, until the two women came to the dark wall in the center. There was a six-and-a-half foot doorway there, and the wooden door was heavy black oak. Aliya found it to be locked from the inside.

"Like the saying goes," Aliya observed, "we can do it nice, or we can do it rough." She charged up her plasma rifle. "Personally, I prefer rough." The barrel erupted, and the door was blown off its hinges by the blast. The flash lit up the spiralling staircase within, and Aliya and Storm listened at the door for a moment after it went dark. The blast echoed through the castle and died.

After a moment Storm said, "I don't hear any running guards."

Aliya nodded. "We're probably walking into an ambush. If nothing else, they probably heard me blast the door. Do you— Wait." She held up a hand. "Do you hear that?"

Ororo craned her head into the doorway. "Yes." Coming from deep within the castle was a song, sung by one voice, high and airy, in a language that Storm did not know. The sound was magical. Storm said, "That must be Morgan, ghost or not, serenading us."

"Let's go," Aliya said, leading the way down the spiral stairs, listening as the song grew the tiniest bit louder with every step. Aliya let out a gasp and then shuddered. "Something just . . . touched me."

There was a shape there, for an instant, something ethereal white, that zipped past Storm and Aliya and passed back into the wall, as a lilting chuckle filled the stairwell.

*You bring the Knight*, the voice said. *You bring the Knight*.

The two continued to step down the cold stone stairs, until they reached the bottom, and found themselves standing at another wooden door. Storm reached out to touch the wooden handle on the door. "Cold," she said, though she did not pull her hand back. Her mutant powers granted her a certain immunity to changes in temperature.

*Yes it's cold*, came the whispery voice of Morgan Le Fey. Storm looked up to see a gray, ethereal head push through the wood, long hair touching on transparent shoulders. Transparent, yes, but *thick*, somehow, as if both solid and ephemeral at once. She moved her mouth, but the sound came from the walls: *You're looking for something?*

Aliya nodded, slowly. How does one talk to a ghost? "We're looking for a . . . package. In a wooden casket."

*Of course. There are strange nonmen here who harbor this treasure. And you bring the Knight?*

"Which knight is that?"

The ghost shot out of the doorway and clamped her icy and suddenly very solid grip around Aliya's throat, pinning her back against the stone stairs. *I am dead*, the ghost hissed, *but I am not an idiot. Bring the Black Knight and the treasure is yours.*

Aliya glanced at Ororo as the ghost relaxed its grip and sank backward into the doorway, a pair of glowing eyes remaining. "Should we deal?" Aliya asked.

"I think we should simply continue as we planned," Ororo said.

Aliya smiled and kicked at the door—and nearly lost her balance as the eyes on the door blinked—and the door swung wide open with a long, mournful creak.

A plasma blast split the air and slammed into the stone wall, just clipping the edge of Aliya's braid. "Get down!" Aliya shouted, rolling out of the stairwell and onto the floor. Even as the room spun she took in her surroundings: inky black tapestries of demons and princes, and those in between, hung by tall, broken stained-glass windows that looked out on nothing, because someone, probably Morgan, had had the windows bricked up long ago. A mustiness thick with decay and damp dust filled Aliya's nose and threatened to choke her as she rolled, coming up behind a feasting table overrun with cobwebs.

There were medieval knights armed with plasma rifles, firing at her.

Ororo did not "get down," as Aliya had instinctively shouted, but rather lifted herself into the air, sticking to the high ceiling.

Aliya jumped up and looked at Storm. "Where's the drawbridge?"

Storm pointed at the hallway at the end of the room and said, "It must be through there," and took off in that direction. She gathered the wind around her as she did so, and watched one of the androids rock off balance in her wake. As the knight fired its rifle at her she dipped, dodging the blast, and the whole castle rocked as the plasma bolt slammed into the stone walls. Ororo dropped and, passing it, kicked the android, grabbing the rifle from its hands as she kicked its helmet off. Storm then thrust out a hand and hit the android with a bolt of lightning, blowing its head off. She threw the rifle down in disgust. At Aliya's surprised glance, she said, "I cannot stand guns," then moved into the front hall.

Behind her, a woman who absolutely loved guns was firing away, the concussions filling the air and shaking the house with each blast.

Ororo zipped into the hall and spun around near the ceiling. Her eyes came to rest on a great door of dark wood, nearly twenty feet high, with an intricate rigging of wheels and pulleys attached to the corners. Next to the door was a great wheel with wooden handles, and wrapped with great, thick ropes. She dropped next to the wheel and heard Aliya shouting from the main room, "I can't find it!"

Ororo put her hands on the drawbridge wheel as the ghostly Morgan popped out from the center of it. *You bring the Knight, now?*

"I . . . cannot . . . move this," she said, exasperated. She raised an eyebrow at the smiling ethereal woman sticking out of the wheel. "Are you stopping me from turning this wheel?"

*You bring the Knight now?*

Storm considered. "If I lower the bridge, the Knight will come."

*Very well, then.* The beautiful ghost laughed, and Ororo heard a clamp slide free, and suddenly the wheel was turning in her hands. The pulleys jumped to life as the ropes sailed through, and with another mournful creak the gigantic door began to pry itself away from the top edge, falling forward.

As the door opened up, Ororo saw the moat below, and the unnamable things crawling in the inky water, snapping excitedly at the sound of the lowering bridge. As it fell farther, she saw the waiting forms of the Black Knight and Cable.

Ororo looked over her shoulder and heard one of the androids exploding as two more ran into the front hall.

Cable and the Knight were already jumping onto the bridge and running across it, and as they hit the doorway, the Knight seemed stunned, grasping the edge of the wall and freezing in his place. "Oh, dear Lord, she's looking for me."

Cable turned and looked back. "Morgan?"

Ororo joined them at the doorway. "It's true," she said. "The spirit in this house desperately requests an audience with the Black Knight."

Cable winced as he heard Aliya cry out. "Aliya!" He looked back at the Knight, who still stood in the doorway. "I can't ask you to continue if you're walking into a trap, Sir Percy."

"Nonsense." The Knight shook his head, shivering as he stepped forward. "I'll not abandon you in your quest."

The house shook as Aliya shouted and fired off another round. "Your choice," Cable said. "Storm! Let's find that package and get out of here."

Cable ran to the end of the room and peered in. Aliya was under the cobwebby dining table, and she stuck her head out and shouted to Cable. "Nathan!" she fired off a round and ducked back, shouting, "Glad you could make it."

"You shouldn't have engaged," Cable said, running toward the table. There was an android dropping to its knees to peer under and get a shot at Aliya, and Cable grabbed it by its helmet and hauled the robot sideways. The android slid along the edge of the table and fell, bringing a candelabra with it, dust filling the air. Cable ducked underneath.

"What are you talking about?" Aliya asked.

"You should have waited for us before you started fighting. The whole point is to find the package, not to get yourself killed."

Aliya's gun clicked and fired, the blast flying past Cable and tearing through another of the android knights. "They didn't give me much of a choice." She loaded in another cartridge and looked around.

"There's that singing again," she said. The air was filled once again with the lilting song of Morgan Le Fey.

"What is that?" Cable asked.

"Morgan. She wants the Knight. Would you believe she said she was willing to trade?"

Cable looked down at the Tracker he held in his hand. The lines on the grid were wavy and unreadable. "I can't even get a lock on it. You mean the ghost knows where the package is?"

Another plasma bolt from one of the androids split the air and burst the wooden table leg nearest Aliya. "They're as bad with those guns as they were with swords."

"All they have to do is wear us down," Cable said. He was holding the tottering table from underneath. "Here," he said, "give me a hand."

Cable pressed hard on one side of the table and it tipped over, sending musty place settings flying through the room. The table clattered forward and came to rest and Cable and Aliya ducked down behind it.

"Perfect cover," Aliya said.

"Thanks. You have enough ammo?"

"What," she asked, "you think I came here expecting to borrow cartridges from you?" She pumped off a round and sent an android into oblivion, the following explosion rocking Le Fey's dining hall. "Actually, I could use a couple more rounds."

"Here." Cable reached into his vest and pulled out a handful of cartridges. He practically shivered as their hands touched briefly, and he shook the electricity off, cursing at the Tracker. "Where in hell is it? We should be right on top of it, and yet . . ."

Aliya gasped. Cable glanced her way and saw the cause of her outburst, as a pair of ethereal-but-solid misty hands reached up from the floor, brushing her face, and disappeared into the bricks.

A plasma bolt from one of the androids tore a hunk of wood from the tabletop and Cable peered over the table to see one of the robot knights walking steadily toward them, powering up his weapon again.

Storm flew overhead and cried out as the misty air swirled about her, and she unleashed a lightning bolt, splitting the android down the middle. Wires melted and the robot knight exploded, the concussion rocking Aliya and Cable's cover.

Aliya was staring at the floor, shaking her head. Now she dropped to her knees, brushing madly at the bricks. "Nathan, these are—these aren't stones."

"Huh?" Cable looked down to see Aliya scratching half an inch of dust and muck away from square stones that covered the floor, and now saw what she meant. Aliya scratched away and suddenly two beams of light poured through the stained, thick . . . "Is that glass?"

"Doesn't feel like glass," she said. "But those are . . . *eyes.*"

Cable looked down at the transparent bricks, stones, glass, whatever, that Aliya had uncovered and saw a woman's face, the eyes and nose and mouth, frozen and staring, wide eyed, the light shining up from the floor. "But I've seen her flying around." Aliya shook her head.

" 'Tis her ghost you saw," came the voice of the Black Knight, as he dodged plasma bursts to crouch down behind the table. The Knight grabbed a plate from in front of the toppled table and came around, digging into the paint and dust that layered the floor. He and Aliya and Cable vigorously brushed away more and more muck, revealing the figure underneath. "Merlin enchanted her here, and here she lies, encased in the magic that bound her."

Storm sent a heavy wind into one of the androids, spinning it out of control, and when the robot knight crashed into one of its fellows she brought more lightning down, destroying the two together. She flipped through the air, avoiding the blast that followed, then came to hover over the tabletop. "That's all of them, Nathan," she said.

"We have another problem," said Cable, as he stood up to stare down at the frozen figure encased in the magical block. He looked at the Tracker and then back at the woman, as the singing filled the air once again.

There, below the floor, the open-eyed woman lay in perfect repose, her mouth closed even as her ghost ran about the castle. And in her hands was the casket.

Aliya scowled. "She did it on purpose," she said. "I don't know how, but the casket is in her hands."

The Knight shook his head. "The ghost cannot break Merlin's spell. That block in which she lies has been her tomb for five years. She could not have pulled the casket into her own hands." He turned to them, taking off his helmet so they could see his eyes. "She plays tricks. She can move things about. But she cannot break the spell that holds her. What is within is within."

Cable ran his fingers though his silver hair. "But

we saw you fighting with the androids in the woods, and they had the casket. Our Tracker *led* us there.''

Storm, who had had some significant experiences with the forces of magic in her time, said, "Nathan, even a technological wonder such as Blaquesmith's Tracker is not enough to keep us from a good spell. It was here all along.'' Was that passive form smiling at them from beneath the magic ice? "We were bewitched into thinking the package lay with the androids so we would follow them here.''

"You were bewitched,'' the Black Knight intoned, "so that *I* would follow you here.''

"So whoever sent the package here,'' Cable said slowly, "actually had the foresight to encase it in the hands of this magically trapped woman so that we couldn't get to it.'' Cable looked at the Tracker. "We don't have time for this.''

Aliya nodded. "Knight, how do we get it out of there?''

"Out of there?'' he shook his head. "Surely you jest.''

*Jest . . . not . . . jest not . . . so little tiiiiiiiime*, sang the voice in the walls. *Hello, Percy, it's been soooo long.*

Cable looked at the Knight. "Sir Percy, you must understand. We came here to destroy this thing.''

"You can blow the castle to kingdom come,'' the Knight responded, "but it will not affect that block in which lies the sorceress. Your prize cannot be reached.''

*Not true, not true, listen to you!*

"Fie on thee!'' cried the Knight, into the air. "I will not set you free, not after the time it took to put you where you belong!'' The wind swirled about them violently as the ghost only chuckled from the walls.

"Sir Percy," Cable said, "people . . . a lot of people, more people than you can possibly imagine, are going to die if we don't destroy that thing in there. Do you understand? There has to be a way to get it out.''

"Just the package," Aliya said, "just the casket, and whatever lies within.''

"You don't know what you're asking," Percy said. "This woman is *dangerous*, she nearly destroyed Arthur before she was encased here.''

"You know how to break it, don't you?" Aliya asked.

"Percy, that *box* is dangerous!" Cable roared, putting his hands on the Knight's armored shoulders, "Don't you understand? None of this is going to be here, none of it! Tell me how to—''

"You cannot do it," Sir Percy hissed. "None of you can. Only *this*," he said, lifting the black blade he held, "only *I* can free her. Don't *you* understand? You're asking me to set free this *witch* because you tell me that *box* in her hands is more important.''

"Yes," Storm said, still hovering in the air. "Yes, that is what we are telling you. We cannot make you do it, Percy, but we came here to destroy that item, and we must pursue every avenue in order to do that.''

The Black Knight furiously kicked the table and sent it clattering across the room. "If you lie," he said, "I will hunt you down, each of you. If you secretly serve Morgan and—''

"You know that we do not," Cable said quietly. "We don't want to be here any more than you do. And I wish I could say that I can't ask you to do this, Percy, but I must ask you. There is no longer a choice."

"Whatever spirit sent that package, she used. She always uses. She is the best at using. She always will be." The Knight's back was turned to them, and he bowed his head for a moment, holding the black sword out and kneeling before the cross of its hand-guard and heft. After a moment he stood and turned. "Get out of the way."

Cable, Aliya, and Storm all moved to the wall and watched as Sir Percy of Scandia stepped to the foot of the frozen sorceress, holding his sword aloft. "O spirits who counsel Merlin, who inhabit this land, the lake, and this sword, O hear me." About him, the mist began to swirl, as the laughter and singing of the spirit in the walls grew in intensity. "Bewitched is this ground, and trapped within is she who deserves to be so! Merlin cast this spell, and now does this spirit beg for release! O spirits, with heavy heart do I beseech you, guard me and this enchanted blade, and strengthen me as I grant the wish of the evil one!"

The Black Knight gasped, his cloak flying as the wind sailed around him, and his muscles tensed, and in one great arc he brought the sword back and flying forward toward the enchanted ground, crying, "Now!"

The tip of the magic blade sang out as it crushed the ethereal block, and he brought it up again and down and repeated, "Now!"

The wind whipped and chunks of icy blue magic exploded from the ground and Cable, Aliya, and Storm fell back, stunned by the shock. Cable felt something slam into his chest and he looked down as the wooden casket clattered to the stone below, falling open to reveal a thick golden arrow.

"There!" cried the Black Knight, over his shoulder. Before him, a form was rising, all bluish white, her eyes glowing widely, her mouth pulled back in rapturous laughter. "Your quest is finished! Do your work and begone!"

Cable and Aliya fired once, sending two plasma bolts into the arrow. There was a whistling crack on that side of the room as the golden arrow exploded, splitting infinity wide open and sucking the air around it into the void. As quickly as it had started the explosion vanished, taking with it the remnants of the arrow and the fallen androids.

And Cable and Aliya and Storm looked to the other end of the hall, where the Black Knight held up his sword, howling at the sight of the risen sorceress.

*At last, you fool*, she said. *It's been so long, Percy.*

"Begone, I say!" Percy said, looking back at the three. "Your work is done! This is my battle to fight. If you speak true, it is a small price to pay."

"We can't just leave you," Aliya said, standing next to Cable.

"Go! This is not your place!" the Black Knight said. "Would that I had never seen you!"

The sorceress hung in the air and smiled at the three. "Leave us, children. There will be time for you later."

"I think we've done enough," Cable said.

"You're right, Nathan, we have to go," Storm said. "Whatever we have set loose on Camelot, we still have the timestream to save. But we will die here if we wait any longer."

Cable looked at Aliya. "What are you going to do? You can come with us."

"I can't," she said. "My recall device sends me back to my time."

"Destroy it," he said. "You'll be caught up in ours, maybe, and—"

"Nathan," Aliya put her hands on Cable's chest and said, "I'll find you again. But I can't. . . . We have a job to do, and look at you, you're watching out for me, and I can't even concentrate with you around. I'll find you after it's over. Now that I know you're there, we'll figure out a way. I promise, my love."

"I will search for you until the end of time."

"Nathan . . ." Storm said. The laughter of the sorceress was filling the air.

"Hit the recall device," Cable said.

"Hey, *X-Man*," Aliya called to Storm, "you take good care of him."

"You have my word," Ororo said. Aliya stepped back, and nodded, and touched her recall button as Storm did the same.

And as the three shimmered out of the space and into the void, Cable called out, "You can't stay lost forever."

And all that was left in the castle of Morgan Le Fey was the Black Knight, who had a long battle ahead of him.

• • •

Kang the Conqueror watched his foes writhing in agony and turned to see an image of Lireeb the albino shimmer to life below him. "Master? I thought perhaps you would like to know that the four—*all* four—Time Arrows have been destroyed."

Kang saw Cable and Storm shimmer into the room. They immediately made for the troopers and then fell to their knees in the screeching agony of the sonic disrupter. Kang, laughing heartily, turned to Lireeb's glittering holographic image. "Thank you for the report."

"Excuse me," Lireeb said, "but I should think this required more comment than that."

"I prefer to let actions speak for me. Such as the action of them watching, helpless, motionless, while my troopers destroy their crude approximation of a Time Displacement Core." Kang gave the sonic disrupter to one of his troopers, then stepped toward Lireeb's image. "Finish these meddlers off here, then report back to me. I still have my Ravonna to find. Lireeb, bring me home."

And as Kang began to fizz and disappear, Wolverine looked up from the ball he had curled into and felt the blood flooding into his eyes, and the animal inside of him howled and drank pain and licked it clean.

And he began to move.

# CHAPTER THIRTEEN

S pider-Man cursed loudly, kicking the earth with his toe. "I can't *believe* it!"

"What's the problem, son?" Two-Gun said. The gunfighter put his hands on his hips and surveyed the campsite, which lay a smoking ruin by the river bend. "Looks to me like you done what you come for."

"Yeah," Spider-Man said. "Except that there's one small problem." He kicked the ground again. "We can't go home!"

"We—" Bishop looked at Two-Gun and touched his chin, trying to decide how to proceed "—we were afraid this might happen. That device Spider-Man had on his chest was our—our homing signal, you might say. And now it's destroyed."

"How were you gonna send a signal when you ain't near a telegraph station?" Two-Gun asked.

Spider-Man sat down by the campfire in the center of the dark ring that had been the wagon train. The fire had been blown out by the explosion; all that remained were the cooking utensils used by the prop-conscious androids and a few smoking coals. "It's something the government gave us for the mission. We were afraid this might happen. We had a . . . warning."

"You can speak straight, son," said the Two-Gun Kid, as he sat down beside Spider-Man. "I've seen you boys fight. Those web-shooters on your wrists are nothing the government could give a field agent even if they wanted—the same goes for that gun your partner carries. And as for these wagon riders," he said, "I think we both know they ain't from this part of the world. More like," he tipped back his hat, revealing a bit of blond hair, "more like something Jules Verne would think up. I'm thinkin' you boys are from some other place, in some entirely different . . . time."

"Don't answer that," Bishop said.

"You don't have to," Two-Gun smiled. "I don't want to know any more than I already do."

Spider-Man ran his gloves over his head. "You're a smart man, Bishop, I'm sorry. I'm really, really sorry."

Bishop scowled. "Much as I'd like to blame you for this, Cart—Spider-Man, I know you didn't walk in front of that blast on purpose." Then he sat down at the campfire with the other two and rested, taking off his hat and setting it on his knee. "We knew the risks."

"How can you be so easygoing about this? We're so far from home, we might as well be dead."

"We saved countless lives, Spider-Man," Bishop said. Behind him, the stars were twinkling brightly. "I grew up listening to stories about the X-Men, and how they were willing to lay down their lives for the rest of mutantkind and even humanity, which hated them. From the moment I heard the first story about Cyclops and Phoenix, I knew that I would die to be like them. If I have done so, it is only because I sought that destiny. We did our duty, Spider-Man. I'm prepared to die for that."

Spider-Man sighed. "I believe you've got to be the most morose man I have ever encountered."

Two-Gun listened to the two strangers talk and then broke into the conversation, clearing his throat. "I hate to break up you guys' mourning, but I for one am hungry, and I know you boys didn't have much o' that supper Miss Carter brought. What say we go back to town, rustle up some grub? You can try to think your way out of this, or whatever you want, on a full stomach.''

"Oooh, nooo," Spider-Man moaned again, falling backward, "I promised my wife I'd be home in time for supper."

Two-Gun sighed deeply. "Well, I can't speak to that," he said slowly. "But I can get you boys a nice plate o' ham and beans, and maybe we can—"

Spider-Man shot up where he sat. "Plate."

"Excuse me?"

"The plate!" Spider-Man looked at Bishop. "I know how we get home! God, what am I thinking, it was there all along!" The wall-crawler started looking around the burned-out campfire, and shoved away some dirt, uncovering a metal dinner plate. "Look at this!"

"Yeah," Two-Gun said. "That's a plate, all right. I take it you have those where you come from?"

Spider-Man brushed his hand through the air, ignoring the gunslinger. "Bishop, remember? This is what I find! I mean, I will!"

Bishop stared. "But that's how we got here in the first place."

"No, but—" He bobbed his head in either direction dramatically. "Well, yes, it is. I know. But that was . . . before. Wasn't it? I mean . . ."

"Excuse me, but what are you talking about?"

"Gimme a knife," Spider-Man said, holding out his hand.

"I'm not sure I want to do that."

"Just—for heaven's sake, I want to carve something. Do you have a knife?"

"Yeah," Two-Gun was reaching into his breast pocket. He fished out a penknife, which Spider-Man snatched greedily. The wall-crawler set to work immediately with the knife, grinding the blade into the bottom of the plate. When he was done he held it up to show to the other two. It said:

CABLE!
IT'S JUNE 26, 1867, AND WE'RE STUCK HERE! SEND HELP TO THE PLACE WHERE IT ALL BEGAN! HOPE TO SEE YOU SOON!
YOUR PAL,
WEBS

"Now that," Two-Gun said, taking back the knife as Spider-Man handed it to him, "that's right nice. What exactly is this about?"

"A theory," Spider-Man said, as he hopped up and ran toward the chuck wagon. He dropped to the ground and shimmied underneath it. "There's a compartment under . . . here." He searched the underside of the wagon for a moment until he found the indentation where a piece of wood could slide back, unlocking the drawer that came right out in his hand. It lowered down on a pair of metal slides. Spider-Man attached one of his spider-tracers to the plate, dropped the plate in the drawer, slid it back up into place, and slid the lock back, where he knew it would remain. He shimmied out from under the wagon and stood up.

"Now," said the wall-crawler. "All we have to do is go back—"

"—to the place where it all began," nodded Bishop. "I've got you. But, Spider-Man," he shook his head, standing up, "I have to tell you, I think you're getting your hopes up for a mighty long shot."

Two-Gun added, "Which I have yet to understand in the slightest."

"Send *help*," Spider-Man said.

"Yes," Bishop said. "And they *did*."

"Ah-ha!" the wiry hero countered. "But we weren't actually *stuck* then. See? We are now."

"And how exactly is Cable going to know that?"

"What do you mean?"

"I mean," Bishop said, "he sent us. He's already *seen* the note. It's real nice that you remembered to carve it, but that just means that we get sent here in the first place. What more can he do?"

"Ouch. You being a real downer, here, Bish," the web-slinger said. Finally he shrugged. "Look, I know it's a long shot, and I know it's riddled with paradox. But see—we're not *help*."

"You'll get no argument from me," Two-Gun agreed.

Spider-Man continued, "We're *us*. Surely, if they can send us, they can also send a recall device."

Bishop chewed his lip, staring off onto the dark horizon. "You're telling me you think Cable is going to send us a recall device."

"I'm *telling* you," said Spider-Man, "that we can't lose anything by trying. And what's more, we *still* only have our six hours, so we better hurry."

Two-Gun broke in. "I'm sorry, you lost me a *looong* ways back there. Hurry where?"

Bishop and Spider-Man both turned and shouted at Two-Gun, "To the place where it all began!"

Spider-Man nodded. "The place we started. Um, where was that?"

"I arrested you about three miles from here."

"Then let's go," Spider-Man said. "And if we're lucky, I might still be home for dinner."

In the winery, Logan turned over and saw red spots flowing over his eyes as his fingernails dug into the hardwood floors. The sonic weapon screeched and pounded in his ears, and he felt his teeth chattering and grating together with the pulsing sound.

Just beyond his grasp, through the red blur in his vision, he saw the air shimmer as Cable and Storm came into view.

Logan watched them, as if in slow motion, the sound pounding in his eyes and ears, threatening to shut his brain down, while the animal inside him growled and writhed in anger and agony. *Turn it . . . turn it . . . take it . . . around . . .*

Cable and Storm fell to their knees, screaming, Cable reaching for his plasma gun as he did so. Logan heard a distant *ker-chunk* as Cable slammed back the bolt, but he was clutching at his ears, and his arms were shaking. He dropped his weapon.

"Don't lose control!" Logan cried. "Keep . . . keep . . ." he snarled, barely able to find words, the red spots growing.

Cable was seizing up, his eye shining, and now tendrils of metal stretching out from his metallic arm were beginning to cover his body. Cable was losing control of the techno-organic virus that he kept in check at all times. Logan snarled again and tried to rise, crawling toward the trooper who still held the sonic disrupter. The trooper turned the disrupter up another notch and Cable, writhing in agony, fell, metal surging over his body.

*Must stop them* . . . came Charles Xavier's voice in Logan's head, and Cable looked up through the metal that was covering his face and seemed to hear it, underneath and layered over the crunching shriek of the disrupter. *They're going to* . . . *destroy the Core* . . .

"No!" Cable cried, holding out a metallic hand toward the trooper. "No! You don't know what you're doing!"

"I have my orders," said the man behind the mask, and he nodded to the troopers behind him, who turned their guns on the Time Displacement Core once more.

Icemen cried, "No," as he crawled to his knees and shuddered, wrenching ice from his shattering palms and covering the core.

"It's madness!" Cable cried, the metal lashing around his tongue and numbing his speech. "Madness! Your master is a madman! We're trying to . . ."

"I have my orders," the trooper said. One of the troopers behind him fired on Cable and the metallic man fell back, the plasma arcing over his body.

Suddenly a cry came from where Storm was hunched over, and she raised her head against the pounding sonic shriek and her white teeth and glistening white eyes seemed to glow, and the air itself began to swirl as she buffeted the troopers with wind. Every spot of moisture in the air came to her and pounded the troopers in the laboratory, knocking them back.

• • •

Cable rolled over, feeling the virus taking his body, piece by piece, trying to shut out the numbing sound, feeling metal stretching down his esophagus and gagging him, metal wrenching through his teeth. He looked up at the monitor where Blaquesmith and Professor X were huddled. *Cable* . . . came the telepathic voice of the Professor, who strained to look at him, the sweat pouring down his bald head. *Spider-Man . . . and Bishop . . . they're lost . . . their recall device . . . gone . . .*

Metal seized Cable's heart and he felt the organ grow sluggish, beating away and bruising, pain shooting up and down his body, *No, not now, keep control, keep control.* . . . He would think about something else, anything else . . .

Cable slammed his metal hands into the floor and howled in pain, the metal on his left searing nerve endings half-metal and half-human. A plate flashed in his mind, metallic and spinning, and he slammed his fists into the floor again and howled once more, *Back! Back!*

He saw his fingers flash red and pink and the metal moving back, ignoring the pain, concentrating on the metal.

*Plate.*

The plate spun in Cable's mind and he looked up past the Professor at the homing monitor and the plate was spinning, and he saw the words there, *We're stuck . . . send help . . .*

"They need . . . another recall device . . ." he grunted, slamming his fists into the floor, and he watched as the viral metal pushed back up his good arm, the pink flesh shining and bruised underneath.

Two-Gun slipped off of his horse and stood beside Spider-Man and Bishop, who were staring at the ground.

"This the place?" Spider-Man asked.

"You tell me," Bishop responded. The gigantic mutant put his hands in his pockets and swiveled on his heels, looking to the ravine up above, then to the bend in the river. "There's where the Carters fought the androids."

"Nuts," Spider-Man said. "I don't know. It was a crazy thought."

Suddenly the sound of horses filled the air and Two-Gun dropped to one knee, looking up the hill. A pair of riders came over the ridge, and stopped for a moment.

Spider-Man turned and stared. "Who are they?"

The rider in front looked back over the ridge, then back down at Two-Gun. He whipped his arm in the air, firing off a shot.

"That," Two-Gun said, "is Clem Carter."

"Two-Gun Kid!" cried Carter, as he whipped the reins and broke into a run. "It's time to settle a score."

"Not now," Bishop growled.

"Shouldn't be much trouble," Two-Gun said, as a tuft of sand exploded nearby. The bullet whizzed off into the distance. "There's only two of them."

Spider-Man's felt his spider-sense run wild and he looked up the ridge, as six more riders topped the hill, following Carter's signal. "Not anymore."

Bishop looked around as the riders sped up. "We're wide open here; we need cover."

"Right!" Two-Gun cried, grabbing his horse by the neck, "Get your horse down!"

"What?"

"Get it down!" the gunslinger said, putting his arms around his horse's neck and pulling. The horse reared back, snorting fearfully, and Spider-Man felt sure that the animal was going to knock Two-Gun's head in. "Easy, girl, lay down! Down!"

The horse finally buckled as Two-Gun dragged at her, dropping to her knees and hitting the ground. Sand flew around the animal as Two-Gun crouched behind it. The gunslinger got out both guns and then looked over his shoulder in horror. Bishop was struggling with his own horse. "Get that horse down for cover, son!"

"Trying..." Bishop said, struggling. The horse was rearing back, howling in protest. The riders were closing in, now seventy yards away. "C'mon," he said, yanking at the horse, "c'mon."

"Get it down!" Two-Gun said, as he fired from behind his own horse at the oncoming riders. "You're wide open, get it down!"

"Trying..." Bishop snarled, and the horse kicked him in the stomach, staggering him back.

Spider-Man heard a shot ring out, and suddenly the snarling beast was falling, slumping to the ground, its brains shot away.

"You shot the horse!" Spider-Man said to Two-Gun, horrified. The Kid barely looked up as he fired off another round in the direction of the attackers.

"This ain't fun-'n'-games," Two-Gun growled.

"Now, you two get behind that carcass and gimme some support here."

Bishop crawled up behind the fallen animal and Spider-Man did the same. What was he going to do? Web them? *Maybe.*

The riders stopped fifty yards up the hill and the man in front called out, "Two-Gun! Some friends o' yours hit us pretty hard today."

"Ain't no friends o'mine," Two-Gun called. "You come back to settle with them or with me?"

"With them wagon trainers," Carter called.

"Well, they done gone," Two-Gun called, resting against his horse. The filly breathed smoothly, quietly waiting for her master to ask her to get up again. "You're out o' luck."

"Well, then," Carter said, "I reckon I'll take it out on you."

Cable crawled along the wooden floor, slamming his fists as he did so, clenching his teeth against the sonic onslaught and the technovirus. Iceman had built a solid wall around the Time Displacement Core, and Cable had to crawl over one of the fallen troopers and around to get behind the ice wall and near the TDC. He heard the ice spattering on, wet and cold, and some of it landed on his body and stuck to his metallic joints. He didn't even feel it. Cable reached up and ran his hands along the front of the Core, searching for the storage chamber that held the recall devices. He had another one. Didn't he have another one? Surely he had another one.

He felt his hand touch something metallic and round and he laughed, feeling metallic saliva strike the front of his teeth as he spat the laughter out. His ears were beginning to bleed, and he could feel the pieces of metal in the blood that flowed. He reached up for the keypad, barely able to see the monitor, isolating Spider-Man and Bishop's timeline. He slapped a button and the front of the Core emitted a thin, strong beam, and Cable grunted and tossed the recall device in the beam's path.

Cable laughed again, painfully, as the recall device shimmered in the beam and disappeared. The laughter died in his throat as Iceman's wall began to crack again, bursting where a plasma blast had struck it. Suddenly something powerful hit him from behind and the floor swooped up and kissed him.


Spider-Man winced as a bullet tore a chunk of horseflesh out of the dead animal that was his shield, and warm blood rained down. The horses were closing in, and he heard one of them squeal loudly as Bishop blew one of the animals out from under a member of the Carter gang.

Spider-Man rolled several times and jumped up, firing off a web-line, catching Clem Carter in the shoulder and sending him sprawling off his horse. He hit the ground and rolled, the horse moving forward, and Spider-Man had to jump into the air again to keep from getting trampled.

"Helllooo," Spider-Man called, flipping onto the back of the riderless horse and over again, landing on another horse. This horse had a rider, and Spider-Man straddled the animal's back, face to face with the gunman, in the small space between the pommel and the neck.

The cowboy growled, striking Spider-Man across the chest with his hat, as if he were a bug. "What in tarnation—"

"Didn't your mother tell you not to play with these things?" Spider-Man said, feeling the web fly out and attach to the man's pistol. He flicked his wrist and the gun came free, flying back into Spider-Man's hand. "You boys shouldn't play so rough."

Spider-Man broke open the gun and let the bullets fall to the earth, then crumpled the gun in his hand. He tossed the hunk of metal in the man's face as he hopped to his feet on the back of the horse and leapt away.

Spider-Man hit the ground and fired off his webbing in two directions at once, catching the right hands of a pair of gunmen closing fast. The force of the webbing threw the men back. They fell from their horses, each screaming bloody murder. "I promise," Spider-Man shouted, "you get to keep the hands. You just can't use them for an hour."

The web-slinger saw the air shimmering on the ground as reality itself opened up and spat out a recall device. Spider-Man nearly tripped on the thing and cried out, "Yes!" and then had to roll out of the way as a horse threatened to grind him into the dust. He watched the horse's hoof kick the disk, sending it flying into the midst of the Carter Gang.

The air cracked from behind Bishop's horse as the mutant's gun discharged. "Spider-Man, what have you got?"

"We have a recall device!" Spider-Man cried, leaping into the air, and kicking one of the Carter gang in the chest. He and the gunman rolled and

Spider-Man webbed the man up and leapt after the device, only to see it struck by a bullet.

"Get it!" Bishop said, as Spider-Man saw the disk skitter off like a crab, flipping under another horse.

"Working on it," Spider-Man said, leaping once more, bullets flying around him.

Storm howled and buffeted the trooper with wind, sending the trooper toppling back, and threw herself over the fallen Cable. She turned him over and watched his face, unconscious, shaking, the metal pouring over his body. "Nathan! Wake up!" But it was all she could do to produce any sound, as the sonic screech shook her own body. She held him to her, shaking herself now with rage and pain, and looked back to see the ice wall around the Core shatter. The trooper unclipped something from his belt. She heard a distant whirring sound and watched the grenade in his hand grow a pair of drill-bit legs.

*A grenade . . . he has a grenade.*

The trooper drew back and threw the device, and Storm watched it tumble through the air, landing on the Core. Where it landed it stuck, and the two legs drilled in, and it resembled a shiny black metal tick, biting in.

The trooper kept one hand on the sonic disrupter as he drew another device from his belt. This one had a cover on it, and he flipped the cover open to reveal a button.

"Detonator!" Storm cried. Below her, Cable shook, the metal overtaking him.

• • •

"Hyah!" Two-Gun cried, as he fired into the air. Clem Carter had crawled on his horse again and now was shooting back at Two-Gun, who fired off another shot. "Get on outta here, boy!"

Clem Carter knew when he was beat. He called out to his men, one by one, watching them find their horses where Spider-Man had knocked them off. Out of seven, five had lost the use of their gun hands, two had bad gunshot wounds. Once Clem was satisfied that his men were on horseback, he whipped the reins. "Let's go, boys! Two-Gun, this ain't the last! You can't keep your weird friends around you all the time!"

"Get on out!" Two-Gun cried, as he patted his horse and watched her rise up. "You're lucky we don't chase you back!" But by that time, the Carter Gang was too far gone to hear him.

Spider-Man came running with the golden disk in his hand. "I got it! Man, this thing nearly got trampled to bits, but I got it!"

The trooper's laughter filled the air and Logan heard it over the sonic screech and locked on to the laughter. The red spots in his eyes swirled and his fingernails dug into the floorboards. His vision began to clear for a moment and he saw the trooper's gloved finger inching toward the detonator button.

Wolverine roared and howled, the sonic screech shaking his body and brain as he leapt through the air, his claws slicing forward. He saw the trooper look up in shock as Logan's claws tore through his shoulder, sending him spinning.

The healing factor was kicking in and Logan felt

the animal blood pumping in his veins, the hot breath pouring out of him, the red spots in his vision becoming *his*, this pain *his, turn it around*. He roared and slashed at the trooper's faceplate. The trooper brought up his legs and kicked once, slamming his metal boots into Logan's chest, and Logan felt himself crashing into the chunks of ice on the floor. He rolled over and saw the trooper's eyes, there behind the metal mask. The trooper grinned and reached for the fallen detonator.

"I reckon this is good-bye," Two-Gun was saying, and Bishop nodded serenely. "This is a little more excitement than I prefer for one evening."

"Me too," Spider-Man said, his head jerking in that odd, arachnid way that it did when he was in costume. "I wish we could stay and ... explain ..."

"But we'd have to kill you," said Bishop.

Spider-Man and Two-Gun looked at Bishop as Spider-Man held up the recall device.

"He is kidding, right?" Two-Gun said.

"You can never be sure," Spider-Man said, as he touched the disk and the world split open.

Logan didn't know what he did next, couldn't feel it, couldn't talk about it, except that he was flying through the air and slashing, and there was a blur in the air, a strange mist, an unpleasant stench, and every chunk he tore and every piece he ripped through and every howl he emitted could do nothing to change the fact that he could not stop the trooper's finger from closing on the button in his hand.

A screech, a burst, and Logan felt himself torn loose from the trooper's sagging frame as the Time Displacement Core belched fire and exploded.

# EPILOGUE

**K**ang's laughter echoed through Limbo for hours as he watched the monitors, watched again and again as the Core exploded.

"It's just . . . so *pathetic*," he said. "So deliciously *incompetent* of them."

"Feeling a bit impressed with ourselves, are we?" Lireeb said, pouring Kang a goblet of wine.

Kang glared at Lireeb, then turned his attention back to the monitors. "Those poor fools. You can always count on heroes to make things easier. They're like dominoes, really: I line them up and give them a push, and there they go! Falling this way and that. Amazing. They actually thought they were doing me a disservice, and all along they were working *for* me. Getting them to detonate the Time Arrows—that was a masterstroke, if I must say so myself."

"How, exactly, did destroying the arrows help your plan along?"

Kang smiled. "The Time Arrows had only begun to do their job, powering up, laying the first few seeds of temporal destruction. It took a bit of extra effort to actually set them off. Of course, it would have been easy to send my androids to do that for me, but it was so much more entertaining to see these," he licked at the word, "*heroes* do it." He laughed again. "I sent them bait and they took it, hook, line, and sinker. How were they to know with their pathetic, antediluvian equipment that Immortus's weeding devices had a failsafe requirement, and had to be triggered in a two-step process? After all, destroying timelines was not something he took *lightly*." Kang finished off his wine and looked at his servant. "This is not a qualm I share."

"So I'd noticed," Lireeb said with a sigh. "More wine?"

"Call out!" Cable groaned as he crept to his feet. He reached out his arms and concentrated, wincing, as the metal flowed back. He felt it flowing away from his heart and lungs, away from his esophagus. After a while he was whole, or as whole as he ever could be—the one same arm still covered in the lacing metal scarring of the technovirus.

Around him, the X-Men were rising, brushing dust and wood off their faces and bodies. "Call . . ."

"I'm here," Logan said, as he stood up, panting, He was covered in something unpleasant. "Those troopers are gone."

Storm touched Cable on the shoulder. "I'm here."

"I'm okay." Bobby coughed, the water dripping off him. He had received a nasty cut on the brow, and his forehead froze over to stop the bleeding. "Looks like Gambit's coming around."

Gambit looked up and muttered something in French.

Hank McCoy had fallen next to Professor Xavier and Blaquesmith, and all three were coming awake. "All . . . present and accounted for."

"They blew up the core," Cable said. "Blaquesmith, they blew up the core!"

Professor X was pulling himself up onto his chair and he shook his head. "Bishop. Spider-Man."

Cable shook his head. "I sent them a recall device." He looked at the monitor. "There's no sign of them on the monitor." He stared at the Core, which was cratered out in the middle. "Blaquesmith, can—can you fix this?"

Blaquesmith craned his leathery neck and rose, limping over to the busted Core. He sighed deeply. "I can rebuild it, I think," he said finally.

"Maybe they're out there, where we sent them. Maybe we can build another one and bring them back."

Blaquesmith shook his head. "You said so yourself: they are not on the monitor."

Bobby touched his forehead and winced. "Then where are they, if they're not there, and they're not here?"

"Lost." Blaquesmith shook his head and sighed. "Lost."

*Itsy, bitsy spider . . .*

Spider-Man and Bishop felt reality open up and swallow them, and they fell into the gap between.

*. . . went up the water spout . . .*

Icy cold nothingness flew past Spider-Man's fingers and he looked over and saw Bishop, hanging there, falling, and Bishop was far away, and there were voices in the nothingness and visions swirling. *This isn't supposed to happen.*

Mary Jane flew by, and she was young, she was the teenager he had first seen on his doorstep years ago, and she split into a thousand shards of nothing, and Spider-Man fell, and Bishop fell, spinning through the howling nothingness.

*Down came the rain, and . . .*

And Uncle Ben—the one Peter Parker had not been able to save—flew by and disappeared, and

Aunt May flew by, crying softly, the cry muffled in the whistle and howl of the gap in reality. Spider-Man closed his eyes and saw through his eyelids, and the world was full of stars, and the stars were black and space was white. And Spider-Man saw a spider glowing red that tumbled down a line toward a radio-active pole.

*. . . washed the spider out . . .*

And space and time ripped and howled through the man that moved over the world like a spider on a web, washing through him, howling, and he was howling, and his eyes were bright and looking back on himself . . .

*Up came the sun, and dried up all the rain . . .*

Space splitting and Spider-Man splitting a spider and a man dancing on a radioactive web and the gap between space and time tore open—

*. . . and the itsy bitsy spider . . .*

—and he was tumbling through nothing that was turning white and the white was ripping in two and there were trees poking through and ground ripping through the nothingness and congealing.

*. . . went up the spout again!*

And nothingness flashed and the air shimmered icy hot against Spider-Man's covered skin and Bishop was standing next to him and they both collapsed on the concrete.

*Concrete?*

He didn't know how long he'd been lying there, but Spider-Man felt Bishop nudge him in the side with the toe of his boot. Spider-Man sat up, rubbing his head and looking around. "Where?"

"Not where we should be." Bishop sighed as he looked around. The mutant looked woozy, but it didn't shake the look of steely resolve he always wore. "But not bad, all things considered."

Spider-Man's vision defragged and came together as he looked past Bishop to see buildings he had known all his life. "We're in Manhattan," he said. The web-slinger heard the sound of laughing and turned his head in that direction, to see a man standing on a street corner making balloon animals and selling them to a gaggle of squealing school kids. He leapt to his feet. "It's . . . what time is, it, it must be about noon . . . yesterday, or today?" he rambled, then grabbed Bishop by the collar, leaping into the air. "Who cares? We're in Manhattan! We made it!"

A scream ripped the air and Spider-Man turned. There was a little girl pointing, and she was screaming, screaming like Peter Parker had seen people scream when they saw car accidents happen in front of them. Spider-Man looked around. "What is it now?" he asked Bishop, glancing in all directions. He even checked himself to make sure he hadn't lost a limb and not noticed, but then, she wouldn't be screaming at *him*.

*I'm your friendly neighborhood Spid—*

"Sponkie!" someone cried loudly, and the word was repeated, tumbling into Spider-Man's ears like a mantra, *sponkiesponkiesponkie*. And the little girl's mother came running, snatching the girl up, and the girl's balloon animal was falling and trampled underheel. And the mother was screaming, and Bishop and

Spider-Man looked around as people pointed at them and screamed and began to run.

"Oh, boy," Spider-Man whispered, as he got back-to-back with Bishop. "I think you were right."

"What?" Bishop said. There were sirens in the distance, and now a heavy machine-produced hum filled the air.

"We're not where we should be," Spider-Man said.

"Halt!" An amplified voice cut through the air. The machine hum grew louder and Spider-Man looked up to see a hovercraft buzzing toward them, slowing as it banked overhead. Someone in a yellow-and-black uniform was shouting through a megaphone. "You are in violation of the law!"

"Law?" Spider-Man held out his hands. "What the heck is this?"

"You are hereby ordered to surrender yourself to the authorities. Any attempt to escape will be answered with deadly force."

"Oh, my God," Spider-Man whispered, as the hovercraft moved between him and the sun and he saw the three men on board clearly. The man with the megaphone had hair that swept up at his brow like an owl's, and next to him, also clad in yellow and black, with a high, military collar, was a blue, furry man. The third appeared to be made entirely of ice.

"Wolverine!" Bishop shouted. "What in hell are you doing?"

"Takin' you into custody, bub," came the answer, as Logan snapped off the megaphone and said, "I'm sick'a this official-language garbage. Put 'em up, freaks, 'cause we're takin' you in.''

"But you're the X-Men," Spider-Man said, holding out his hands.

"And you are an unidentified augment!" Iceman cried. "Surrender and prepare to be taken into custody!"

"We can do this the easy way," Logan said, "or we can do this the hard way. Personally, I prefer it if you raise a fuss."

Spider-Man said to Bishop, "Run," as Logan stepped to the rail of the hovercraft, his claws snapping into place. Bishop was already turning to run and Spider-Man saw a shaft of ice slice through the air and stick in a tree. Spider-Man turned to see Bishop backing up, away from the approaching Wolverine. "Bishop, we gotta get out of here."

"But—"

"It's not them!" Spider-Man shouted. "Not yours, anyway! Let's go!"

"Right," Bishop said, raising his gun and firing. The hovercraft's engine split and whined and Spider-Man was already running. He looked back to see Bishop close behind as the engine of the hovercraft exploded and the three X-Men flew into the air, howling in protest.

Bishop was panting, pumping his gun as he ran. There were people screaming and leaping out of the way as Spider-Man made for the high-rises. "We've got to hide," he said. "I think I can get us someplace safe."

"You think so, huh?" Bishop said, panting, as they exited the park.

"This is my city, remember?" They ducked into an alley and pinned themselves against the wall as a man on an ice bridge slid past, followed by the uniformed Wolverine.

Bishop shook his head. "I'm not so sure."

## TO BE CONTINUED . . .

**TOM DeFALCO** entered the comic book industry in the summer of 1972 as an editorial assistant for Archie Comics. Learning his trade from the ground up, he pasted down character logos, proofread stories, and even served time as an occasional colorist. Within a few months, Tom sold the first of what would eventually become an avalanche of stories. Over the years, Tom has written for such diverse comic book titles as *Jughead's Jokes*, *The Flintstones*, *Scooby Doo*, and *Superman Family*. He joined the editorial staff of Marvel Comics during the early 1980s and eventually became the company's Editor in Chief. Tom has recently returned to full-time writing. He currently writes the monthly comic *The Amazing Spider-Man*, coauthored a novella with Stan Lee for *The Ultimate Silver Surfer*, and wrote short stories for *The Ultimate Super-Villains* and *Untold Tales of Spider-Man*.

**JASON HENDERSON** was born in North Texas and attended the University of Dallas, where he wrote his first book, *The Iron Thane*, in his junior year. After finishing his JD at the Catholic University of America, Columbus School of Law, in Washington, D.C., Henderson came back to Texas and now lives in Austin with his wife, Julia, an educational policy wonk. His other novels include *The Spawn of Loki*, the *Highlander* novel *The Element of Fire*, and the Hulk novel

*Abominations*. Visit Henderson's home page at http://www.flash.net/~jhenders.

**TOM GRUMMETT** started doing commercial illustration while working for the Saskatoon Board of Education's printing department. His first comics work appeared in the 1980 *Captain Canuck Summer Special*, and he went on to work on *The Privateers* and *The Shadowalker Chronicles*. In 1989, he started doing fill-in work for DC Comics, including issues of *Animal Man, Secret Origins, Action Comics*, and *Wonder Woman*. He has served as the regular penciller on *The New Titans, The Adventures of Superman, Robin, Superboy*, and, for Marvel, *Generation X*. Tom presently lives in Saskatoon, Saskatchewan, Canada, where he resides with his wife, Nancy, and their two children.

**DOUG HAZLEWOOD** has been inking professionally since 1985. After winning the inking category of the "Official Marvel Try-Out Contest" in 1986, he plunged into comic books full time. He has enjoyed stints on the critically acclaimed *Animal Man* and was a part of the death and resurrection of Superman on *Adventures of Superman*. Doug currently is the inker on *Superboy* for DC Comics. A native Texan, he lives in Victoria, Texas, with his wife and two children.

To learn the fate of Spider-Man and Bishop in the alternate present, as well as the X-Men's continued attempts to stop Kang's mad plan, don't miss . . .

# TIME'S ARROW
## BOOK 2: THE PRESENT
by Tom DeFalco & Adam-Troy Castro

Here's a preview...

It was the dead of winter: a bitterly cold day, redeemed only by the relative lack of any exacerbating wind. There was no snow on the ground, but the trees were bare, the pedestrians were hidden beneath warm hats and gloves, and every spoken word became visible as vapor dissipating in the air. Central Park was crowded, but only because the sun was shining, the weather was otherwise clear, and today's mercury level actually represented a substantial improvement over what New Yorkers had become used to in the past month. There were a lot of people, enjoying the wide open spaces of the park. But there'd be a lot of runny noses and chest colds to deal with later.

Peter Parker's clothes were itchy.

He wore battered snowboots, patchy corduroy trousers, a stained and oily goose down jacket, a wool scarf, and a black woolen cap over something that most passersby just naturally assumed to be a funky ski mask. It was actually his Spider-Man mask, and he wore it partially pulled up, exposing his nose and mouth. The gestalt was not an outfit designed to make him look prosperous, or even reasonably intelligent. He'd chosen the clothes because they were available, which is to say that he was able to nab them from a charity clothes drop. He did not want to know why they were itchy.

At that, he was much better off than his travelling companion, Bishop, who was larger and bulkier and more difficult to dress in clothes scavenged from storage bins. Bishop wore a tattered green sweater, a green military jacket, a pair of camouflage pants, a red wool cap, and an ankle-length trench coat with a rather disconcerting bloodstained hole where the heart would have been. He carried a hefty cardboard box, wrapped in a mesh of sticky gray webbing.

Together, they didn't exactly blend. But that was okay. Even in an alternate universe, this was still New York. Most people didn't even give them a second look.

But though they were all dressed up, they still had no place to go, for though this looked like Earth, it was not *their* Earth: not the one where Peter Parker prowled the rooftops in the guise of the amazing Spider-Man, not the one where Bishop fought for humanity as a trusted member of the uncanny X-Men. This Earth was a far stranger place . . . a far more dangerous place . . . and the two of them had been trapped on it since the Time Displacement Core dumped them here two days earlier. Oh, there was no reason to believe it was permanent . . . not when Bishop's teammates were back on the real Earth, and probably spending every spare minute searching for them. But there wasn't much they could do while they waited to be rescued, except get to know each other.

*Yeah. Right.*

All in all, Spider-Man missed Venom.

He said, "Hey, Bish. You know what really kills me?"

The massive X-Man rumbled, in a voice like a freight train waking up from a nap. "I most sincerely wish I knew."

Spider-Man managed to press on. "No. I mean it. Really."

"I know. And I'm sure you insist on telling me."

*Daredevil*, Spider-Man thought. *Captain America.*

*Reed Richards. Even (and I'd never tell him this to his face) the Torch. These are guys I get along with. If I was temporarily trapped on a parallel Earth with one of those guys, it wouldn't be that bad. We'd have stuff to talk about. But this guy makes the Punisher look like Jim Carrey. He could depress a Shirley Temple movie. What do they put in his breakfast cereal and where do I go to have it declared a dangerous substance?*

Spider-Man shook his head, determined to keep up the conversation at all costs, and said: *"Cats."*

Bishop stopped in mid-stride. "Cats?"

"Yes," Spider-Man said, with grim satisfaction. *"Cats."*

It was fun to watch Bishop's face at war with itself. The guy was usually one big scowl—except when he screwed up his attitude enough to attempt a grimace instead—and normally betrayed his thoughts about as much as Spider-Man's full face mask did. But now his emotions were churning visibly: the simple human need to ask battling the dread certainty that he'd be sorry if he did. It was only after a seeming eternity of conflict that Bishop slumped, surrendered to the inevitable, and said, "All right. What about cats?"

"Look at the skyline," Spider-Man said. "I take a serious interest in where all the tallest buildings are—"

"Naturally. You have to know your battlefield."

"—so I know the skyline better than anybody this side of the Tourist Information Board. And since we've been on our feet for the past two days, I've been paying close attention to which buildings are different."

Bishop was intent now. "I don't believe it. You actually sound like you're going to say something useful. Go ahead."

"Well, the first thing I see is that hotel, off to the south. Back where we come from, that's a Helmsley Apartment building: very elegant, very fancy, and very old. It wasn't the thirty-story mirror it is here. Over there's the Roxxon Corporate Headquarters. It looks exactly like it does on our Earth, but it's on the west side of the street instead of the east: meaning that though the architect was the same, they erected it on a different lot. I don't recognize that short building over there; my guess is that the skyscraper I'm used to never got built, which to me means that the corporation that owned it didn't prosper quite as much as it did where we came from."

"Or," Bishop mused, "that they built their corporate headquarters in another city, which would no doubt have any number of repercussions. Go ahead. What else did you see?"

"That the *Daily Globe* and the *Daily Bugle* have switched addresses. That the Baxter Building never got destroyed and replaced with Four Freedoms Plaza. That the Pan Am Building is still the Pan Am Building, which on our world it's not. That there are fewer *new* buildings, and that the older ones seem to be in slightly better shape. That there are still foreign banks all over Madison Avenue, which confirms that there's still a thriving international economy. That Damage Control, Incorporated, appears to be out of business, when back home they're the most lucrative growth stock since IBM. That the Trump Tower is here called the DeLorean Tower, indicating that a certain automobile company which failed on our world actually became a thriving success here. That Avengers Mansion was in the same place, but it doesn't seem occupied by Avengers . . .''

''And how do you know that?''

''Because back on our world they had a battle with some guy in a robot suit about a year ago. Well, that by itself isn't saying much, because they have fights with guys in robot suits all the time—but after this particular fight, the masons who fixed the wall couldn't match the color of the mortar. There's a whole section that looks slightly different, thanks to the hole left when Iron Man politely asked the guy to leave. Here, all the mortar's the same color. Meaning either that on this world Tony Stark employs a better breed of mason . . .''

''. . . or,'' Bishop mused, ''that the Avengers are out of the picture.''

''Exactly. Maybe they never occupied that mansion and therefore never invited attack by men in robot suits . . . maybe they were there once, and something happened to them . . . and maybe, for once, they broke up and actually stayed broken up, like the Beatles did. Then there's the matter of the weather.''

''I noticed it's cold,'' Bishop said dryly.

''Exactly. But what exactly does it mean to us, that it's cold here, when it's summer back home? Is it possible that this Earth rotates on a reversed axial tilt, making the summer months back home the winter months here? Or can it be that there's no direct correlation between the passage of time in one universe and another? Maybe the days we're experiencing here only correspond to, let's say, a number of hours back home. Maybe the whole reason the X-Men haven't summoned us back yet is that they haven't even had time to realize we're overdue!''

Bishop nodded with reluctant admiration. "You really do have a functional brain in there. I'm impressed."

Spider-Man, in response, gave a slight bow. "Thank Kyew."

"The only thing I don't understand is just what this has to do with cats."

"Everything," Spider-Man said. "Because that's the part I was talking about, the part that really kills me."

"Tell me."

"Well, with all these major differences, and all they mean to us . . ." Spider-Man hesitated.

"Yes?"

"Even on this world, *Cats* is still playing!"

Bishop stared. And stared. And stared some more. And emitted a not-very-pleasant sound somewhere deep in his throat: a sound that reminded Spider-Man of nothing so much as a gear grinding itself to slivers because somebody forgot to add the oil. "I really don't understand you," he said at last. "We're trapped on a world far from home, where we may have to stay if Blaquesmith can't call us back, where we may have to face dangers we're not even equipped to understand, and you make jokes?"

"Can you think of a better time?" Spider-Man asked.

Bishop shook his head and walked away.

Spider-Man, who followed close behind, knew the big guy had a point. Inside, he was frantic; it was impossible not to think of Mary Jane, and how desperately he wanted to see her again. He joked about it for the same reason he fired off wisecracks while fighting monsters like Carnage, or Dr. Octopus, or the Hobgoblin . . . because sometimes they were the only thing that kept him from being afraid.

He followed Bishop onto the Great Lawn, which, given the temperature, was only sparsely populated with pedestrians and diehard joggers. There was somebody flying a kite on the other side of the field, at the spot where stages were erected whenever somebody decided to do a concert in the park. The kid was flying it so high that it was little more than a speck in the sky. Spider-Man watched it bob and weave in the wind, and found he envied it; the need to keep a low profile had stuck him at ground level since arriving on this world, and he'd been denied the simple exhilaration of being able to travel across town at skyscraper height. He didn't miss it as much as he missed Mary Jane, but he still missed it. He wondered what Bishop missed. If Bishop missed anything.

And then he wondered about the one thing he'd tried so hard to avoid wondering about. Namely: why weren't they back home?

Spider-Man's adventures hadn't taken him time-travelling as frequently as, let's say, the Fantastic Four's—which was fine with him; he much preferred life as a friendly *neighborhood* Spider-Man—but he had been back and forth a little, enough to take it more casually than it merited. (He'd fought Martians in the future and Puritans at the Salem Witch Trials— after that, one's sense of awe tended to operate wonkily if at all.) When he agreed to go along on this trip, he hadn't devoted nearly enough thought to the kind of things that could go wrong. He hadn't wondered what Mary Jane was going to do if he wasn't able to find his way back.

But then he hadn't had much choice, had he? The whole mess had been dropped in his lap as suddenly as a fat lady falling from a theatre balcony.

Bishop was right. It was no time for jokes.

But Spider-Man knew no other way to stay sane . . .

He caught up with Bishop just in time to feel a certain buzzing sensation in the back of his head. "Uh oh."

Bishop said, "Another joke, web-slinger?"

"No." Spider-Man didn't bother to explain about his spider-sense. "Trouble. Somewhere up ahead."

Bishop's eyes narrowed as he scanned the trees at the other side of the meadow. It was true. Something was going on over there. All the people on the walkways were whirling around, reacting to something behind the trees. Something very startling, and very frightening, and very unexpected. Spider-Man heard their distant cries a second before he heard the source of the disturbance itself: a certain high-pitched humming—

—and then he spotted the lone figure moving through the air over the trees.

He was a tall, athletic young man in a warmup suit. He wasn't flying, at least not in any way that Spider-Man was used to. He was . . . running? No, *skating*. He moved in the rhythmic side-to-side manner of a pro hockey player going for speed, his legs driving hard against open air, treating it like solid surface instead of open space. It was obviously a physical effort for him; as he sped through the sky over the Great Lawn, moving faster than anybody skating across mere ice, his arms and legs pumped with the desperation of a man giving the race everything he had. Almost immediately after he cleared the trees he descended to within a few feet of the ground, and doubled over, now moving so quickly that most of the onlookers must have seen him as a blur; Spider-Man, who was used to people capable of moving even faster, caught a good look at his face as he passed by and saw that he couldn't have been older than sixteen.

About as old as Peter Parker had been, when he first became Spider-Man.

*Cripes! Was I ever that young?*

Bishop didn't flinch as the Air-Skater sped by, merely turned his head, to follow his progress. "He's terrified."

"He's not the danger," Spider-Man said. He knew it for a fact. His spider-sense was tingling stronger than ever now, but not because of the air-skater: because of something else yet to make its appearance from behind the trees.

And then he saw them.

Men and women in black uniforms. They looked like cops, but their uniforms were darker, and more severe, and cut along paramilitary lines. There were dozens of them, coming into view behind the trees; they moved quickly and professionally, but without any particular sense of hurry. Some carried slender weapons with transparent barrels; others carried little boxy machines with something that resembled a parabolic antenna mounted on the front. There were so many of them that the electronic beeping emitted from all those boxes was audible all over the lawn. As they fanned out over the lawn, the civilians in their path hurriedly got out of their way; Spider-Man did not need to be an expert in body language to know that the people seemed more frightened of this army than they were of the young man skating through the air. One look at their faces—and the terrified hunted expression on the face of the young man who seemed like a younger version of himself—and he knew why. He tensed up, ready to lend the Air-Skater a hand—

—only to stop when he felt Bishop's hand close tightly around his wrist.

"No," Bishop said.

Spider-Man stared at the hand encircling his wrist. It couldn't hold him here; not physically. He was stronger and faster than Bishop and could break the grip in the time it took to sneeze. But that would mean ignoring the urgency in Bishop's voice . . . "Bish, can't you see what's going on here?"

"I see," Bishop said. "Probably even better than you. I'm a mutant. I've been in that young man's position."

Spider-Man twitched his wrist, freeing it from Bishop's grip. "Then why—"

"Because this isn't our world," Bishop said. "It may look like our world, but we don't understand anything that's going on here . . . and anything we do to interfere runs the risk of making matters a thousand times worse. No. Painful as it is, the most we can do right now is watch, and learn, and figure out the rules, in case we need them."

Spider-Man didn't like it. It went against everything he stood for. And standing idly by while something wrong happened had once proved the single greatest mistake of his life. But Bishop was right . . . and so he remained in place, helplessly watching as the Air-Skater sped around in circles in the air three stories above their heads.

That was a bad sign. The kid moved much faster than the cops. If he wasn't fleeing the scene, it could only mean that he considered himself trapped . . . and that he'd chosen this the place where he was going to make his last stand.

*Come on, kid,* he prayed. *You may think you're alone up there, but you've got a rooting section.*

Most of the civilians had fled the Great Lawn; those that remained seemed either frozen with indecision or rapt with curiosity. Spider-Man saw a few taking pictures, and found himself wondering inanely whether any of them were stringers for the *Daily Bugle.* He saw a few others shouting at the Air-Skater, either taunts or words of encouragement. The cops took no notice, but just fanned out around the lawn, their weapons all trained on the Air-Skater. The officers who carried the little boxy machines didn't look at either the crowds nor the Air-Skater; instead they just kept their attention firmly riveted on their machines, obeying readouts that seemed the world to them.

"Cerebros," Bishop said.

Spider-Man glanced at him. "What?"

"It's a device invented by Professor Xavier when he founded the X-Men. He designed it to detect and track down mutants. He built his because he wanted to recruit allies before his enemy Magneto did. This wouldn't be the first time I saw somebody use the same basic technology to try to hunt mutants down. They're all focused on the boy right now, but it won't be long before somebody realizes he's not the only mutant here. We should—''

And then it was too late.

There was always one in every gang of thugs: a trigger-happy idiot who wasn't content to be one of the many faceless soldiers pointing a weapon, and had to be the big glorious hero who actually fired the weapon. Spider-Man hated those guys even more than he hated thugs in general. After all, a guy who can't obey the rules even as a hired thug is a guy you can't depend on for anything.

This one fired his shot from somewhere in the middle of the field. A burst of flaming yellow energy rocketed into the air and exploded next to the Air-Skater with a force that might have incinerated him. But his reaction time was almost as fast as Spider-Man's own . . . and by the time the fireball swallowed the place where he'd been, the Air-Skater was already twenty yards away, zigzagging so quickly that he seemed less a man and more a multicolored streak in the shape of a man.

Some people cheered. A hot-dog vendor some thirty yards away from Spider-Man and Bishop cried out, ''You go, bro!'' Somebody shouted, ''Do it again, fella!'' Somebody else yelled, ''Shoot him! Shoot him! Shoot the sponkie!''

Spider-Man was in agony. *Don't get cocky, kid. Keep an eye on the ground.*

Another half-dozen fireballs exploded in midair, lighting the sky brighter than any sun. The Air-Skater flew a ragged course between them, staying just one step ahead of the explosions, at times buffeted by them, but remaining unharmed. The last one detonated over his head, and the Air-Skater had to descend to less than ten feet over the earth to avoid the shock wave; he passed close enough to Spider-Man for the web-slinger to see that he was covered with sweat, and shouting in mingled fear and anger. He flew directly over the head of one of the cops, who was stupid enough to actually try to jump up and grab him; the glancing impact disturbed the Air-Skater not at all but sent the cop tumbling to the ground with what looked like a pair of broken wrists.

*Smart*, Spider-Man thought. *Stay low. Stay between them. They can't fire their weapons if you're that close.*

The Air-Skater seemed to realize that even as Spider-Man thought it. He descended to within a few short feet of the ground and skimmed the earth at dizzying speed, scattering the cops as he went. He didn't actually collide with any; he seemed to have way more self-control than that. Instead, he just picked his target, and let the normal human tendency to avoid rapidly moving objects do most of the work. Some cops fell all over themselves to avoid being run down. The ones that stood their ground were bowled over by the air pressure when the Air-Skater changed course at the last minute. Once, a group of twenty linked arms and rushed him *en masse*; he shot toward them, banked at the last instant, and, now moving almost parallel to the ground, skated through the air only inches ahead of their advancing line. Not all of them fell backward out of instinct, but because their arms were linked, those that did dragged their more stouthearted compatriots to the ground with them. It was like watching a row of dominoes fall all at once, and it was agony to watch, because Spider-Man knew it didn't solve anything. It wasn't helping the Air-Skater escape, or stopping the cops from getting up and going after him again.

Bishop cried out, "Cartwright!"

It took Spider-Man a fraction of a second to remember that this was the alias he had used with Bishop during their mission in the Old West. He had already told Bishop that that wasn't his real name, but perhaps the large mutant thought calling him by such an obviously false name as "Spider-Man" would be unwise under the circumstances.

He yanked his gaze away from the battling Air-Skater and saw what Bishop was so upset about. One of the police officers, a skinny fellow with a pencil-thin moustache, was standing only a few feet away, and staring at his portable Cerebro with no small amount of shock. The officer glanced in their direction with wide eyes and immediately went for a communication device strapped to his wrist. "Frants here! Code—"

Bishop crossed the distance between himself and the police officer in three short steps, and took him out with a single blow to the neck. The officer stiffened and fell to the ground without making a noise. In the chaos on the Great Lawn, nobody even noticed. Bishop crushed the portable Cerebro with a single stomp of his boot, then turned on his heels, and walked away as quickly as possible, grabbing Spider-Man by the arm as he went.

Spider-Man said, "You didn't—"

"He'll have a sore throat for a while," Bishop told him. "I try not to war against people who are only doing their jobs. But we may have to do a lot worse soon, if we don't get out of here now. The rest of them may be too busy to notice anything strange about their readings, but that won't last. They'll notice us and call for reinforcements. Maybe super-powered reinforcements, and probably lots of super-powered reinforcements."

The Air-Skater was up in the sky again, dodging another fusillade of exploding fireballs. Spider-Man protested, "We can't just leave him, Bishop!"

"And what are you going to do, if you take up his cause? What are you going to do, if we're summoned home while you're still fighting everything that's wrong with this world? Are you actually irresponsible enough to raise the stakes of a battle you know you might not be here long enough to finish?"

Spider-Man wanted to fight. He really did.

But his spider-sense was shrieking like an air raid gone rabid, and the air above the park was filling with police helicopters, some of which were equipped with what looked like high-tech weaponry, and some of which had larger versions of Xavier's Cerebro device mounted on their fuselage. They flew above the Great Lawn in tight formation, hemming the Air-Skater in, preventing any attempt at escape. With dozens of police weapons now aimed at him, and the whirling blades of the helicopters threatening to carve him into slices if he moved outside a very restricted airspace, the Air-Skater could only move in circles, like an animal probing for weak spots in its cage.

Loudspeakers broadcast the police ultimatum at a volume that must have been audible all over the park: *"Attention, the individual in the air! You are in violation of federal law! Surrender now and you will not be hurt!"*

Bishop pulled on Spider-Man's arm. "Come on. Before their Cerebros pick us up again."

And Spider-Man, hating himself, made a decision as difficult as any he'd ever known. "All right." *But I'm not done with this. I swear it.*

Spider-Man and Bishop were not particularly conspicuous as they fled the open spaces of the Great Lawn. All around them, the civilians who hadn't already run away—who had preferred to enjoy the spectacle of the Air-Skater making fools of the police—were also belatedly realizing that this had become a show too dangerous to keep watching. Spider-Man and Bishop were just two out of the dozens running away from the battlefield.

For Spider-Man, who could have hopped to the front of the crowd in three giant leaps, the act of will it took to keep himself down to merely human speed was not quite as difficult as what it took to restrain himself from lending the Air-Skater a hand.

They ran through a clump of trees and onto a paved walkway, just in time to hear a young woman shout, "Look! It's him!"

He and Bishop stopped just long enough to see that she was pointing at three men running toward the Great Lawn. Two of them were police officers clad in the same militaristic black uniform as the troops in the park; the third, leading them, was a tall athletic man in a strangely altered version of a costume that both Spider-Man and Bishop otherwise knew quite well. The one they were familiar with was a blue bodysuit with yellow trunks, gloves and boots, topped with a hood and a gleaming gold visor; this version had all of that, but the colors were yellow and black, and the uniform was padded and bulked up, with unidentifiable military insignia along one side of the chest.

"Cyclops," the young woman said breathlessly.

A kid stopping for rest near a tree said, "He'll stop that sponkie. You'll see!"

Spider-Man and Bishop glanced at each other. This wasn't good. Their Cyclops was the co-leader of the X-Men. He was totally professional in battle, and totally dedicated to Charles Xavier's dream of a future where normal human beings and super-powered mutants could live together in peace. If this world's Cyclops was here, now, then their own situation was more precarious than ever.

Bishop said, "See what I mean? You probably didn't have a problem fighting the police, but are you ready to take on Cyclops, and maybe the rest of this world's X-Men as well?"

"You've made your point," Spider-Man rasped. *But I'm still not done with this.*

He hesitated only an instant before joining Bishop and the rest of the fleeing spectators in the mass exodus from the park.

For Scott Summers, aka Cyclops, taking down the Air-Skater was a minor challenge. He was moving fast, of course, and there were a number of helicopters up there that would have been even more vulnerable to an optic blast than the boy himself. It would not do to miscalculate, and send the shattered remains of a chopper crashing down upon the people below; that might be acceptable behavior for movie directors, but not for the nominal leader of the X-Men's Super-Power Registration Enforcement Action Detail. Cyclops needed to be considerably more precise in his work.

Still, it was essentially just skeet-shooting.

All Cyclops had to do was stand unseen by the trees at the edge of the Great Lawn, watch the Air-Skater for maybe ten seconds, then activate the mechanism that controlled the ruby quartz lenses in his visor. As long as the lenses covered his eyes, his force-beams were contained; when the lenses were retracted, however slightly, the terrible destructive power was allowed to burst free. It was a power that, in another world, might have turned him into a brooding obsessive type, haunted by the knowledge that his eyes presented a potential threat to everybody around him; but that was precisely what this Scott Summers, a much different man, liked most about it.

He tracked the speeding figure from a distance, under conditions that might have challenged the world's greatest sharpshooters, then fingered the controls in his palm to open his visor just a tiny notch. The force-beam left his visor at the speed of light, piercing fifty yards of open space to strike the Air-Skater in his solar plexus. The impact immediately knocked the breath from the fugitive sponkie, who emitted an astonished "Whuuuufff!!" He spun out and crashed into the ground, tearing a twenty-foot furrow as he went.

The two cops accompanying him both whistled in appreciation. "One shot," said Sergeant Vossoff. "Excellent work, sir."

"It certainly hadda hurt," agreed Sergeant Nimmitz.

"That was the point," Cyclops said. It was also fun, but he refrained from mentioning that. He spoke into his communicator. "All right, people. I want that sponkie handled, and I want all our procedures followed to the letter. No medical attention until *after* he's secured, understand? And even then I want him stashed at Pegasus until we can get a proper team assigned to his case. Move it!"

All over the lawn, cops began to converge on the fresh scar in the earth. Cyclops watched with deep satisfaction. Yes, from the reports he'd heard on his way here, their performance against the Air-Skater had been pathetic—but what they lacked in paranormal abilty they certainly possessed in numbers. They'd been able to engage the boy repeatedly, at several different points throughout the city, preventing him from finding a safe haven, wearing him down until they finally cornered him in the park. Even without Cyclops, they would have captured him in another hour or so. Spending another couple of million of the taxpayers' money, but still.

There was nothing like a well-oiled machine to make the day run smoothly.

One of the cops at the crash site gave a hand signal. Target secured. Cyclops relaxed, but not by much. He was already thinking of who to recommend for the Air-Skater investigation. Maybe Dr. DeCandido. She'd have a full dossier compiled by the end of the next working day . . .

"Sir?"

Cyclops turned. "What?"

Sergeant Vossoff was listening to a coded transmission on his ear-speaker. "The observation team's been inspecting their readouts . . . and they say the Cerebros picked up an anomaly during the operation."

There were times Cyclops wished he didn't wear a mask: a single raised eyebrow would have spoken a thousand words right about now. "What kind of an anomaly?"

"They say there's a better than seventy-five probability of more sponkies among the civilians we scared off. Not latents or inactives, either. Full Class A's, operating in the open. Kirby's hacking the data to make sure it wasn't doubling caused by the kid's flight speed, but says that if he's right, it looks like there may have been two." Vossoff hesitated, and listened to a clarification as it came in. "One standard-issue mutant, one situationally enhanced— who didn't seem to possess a reading. Moving in concert. Kirby—well, he sounds pretty sure."

"Are they still in range?"

"Not at the moment. Apparently they fled the scene with the rest of the civs."

Cyclops grimaced. This couldn't be good. Sponkies had once congregated in teams, but these days they rarely travelled together in public, since staying together only increased the chances of being picked up by Cerebro. Most of the ones still at large were individuals like the Air-Skater, who'd developed their powers only recently and had yet to forge any alliances with others of their kind. Sponkies travelling together, looking out for each other, usually avoided capture a lot longer. And tended to do considerably more damage before being run to ground . . .

It wasn't totally unexpected. Iceman, Wolverine,

and the Beast had encountered a pair of sponkies only two days ago. One was a muscular black man with an M tattooed on his face, the other an acrobat type in a gaudy red-and-blue bodysuit. They'd both proven surprisingly resourceful, and they'd both gotten away. If that was the same pair Kirby was talking about, then they were either reckless, crazy, stupid, suicidal— or so sure of their own abilities that they just didn't care.

And if one didn't possess a reading . . . maybe he was Registered. Which was bad news for everybody.

Vossoff spoke again. "I think we just got independent confirmation, sir. They just found Officer Frants knocked out, with his Cerebro inoperative on the ground beside him."

"Just unconscious?" Cyclops asked. "Not dead?"

"No, sir. Just unconscious."

"What a relief," Cyclops said. "That means when he wakes up, he'll be able to give us a description." He activated his own communicator, and sent out a broad-based signal to every police officer in range. "Attention! This is Cyclops! We have a Double Class-A situation here! Repeat, Double Class-A. Two sponkies of unknown abilities and unconfirmed description, believed to be fleeing the park. I want wide-angle scans from every chopper, full-intensity readings at every park exit. I don't want anybody leaving unless they've been checked. This is top priority, people. These are unknowns we're dealing with here, which means that they are to be considered dangerous and a threat to human life."

He didn't pause at all before he said the next part.

"If you find yourself in a survival situation, don't hesitate to kill . . ."

# SPIDER-MAN®

__SPIDER-MAN: CARNAGE IN NEW YORK by David
   Michelinie & Dean Wesley Smith   1-57297-019-7/$6.50

Spider-Man must go head-to-head with his most dangerous enemy, Carnage, a homicidal lunatic who revels in chaos. Carnage has been returned to New York in chains. But a bizarre accident sets Carnage loose upon the city once again! Now it's up to Spider-Man to stop his deadliest foe.

__THE ULTIMATE SPIDER-MAN   0-425-14610-3/$12.00

Beginning with a novella by Spider-Man cocreator Stan Lee and Peter David, this anthology includes all-new tales from established comics writers and popular authors of the fantastic, such as: Lawrence Watt-Evans, David Michelinie, Tom DeHaven, and Craig Shaw Gardner. An illustration by a well-known Marvel artist accompanies each story. *Trade*

__SPIDER-MAN: THE VENOM FACTOR by Diane Duane
1-57297-038-3/$6.50

In a Manhattan warehouse, the death of an innocent man points to the involvement of Venom—the alien symbiote who is obsessed with Spider-Man's destruction. Yet Venom has always safeguarded innocent lives. Either Venom has gone completely around the bend, or there is another, even more sinister suspect.

---